I0630261

The Russian Intrusion

A novel by

Tom Creary

ISBN: 978-0-9921520-6-2

To my boys, Ben and Simon

Other novels by Tom Creary

The Bohemian Connection (2013)

The Lady from Toledo (2014)

Survivor (2017)

Sisters (2018)

Preface

The story in this book is fiction. Although many readers will recognize that some of the characters in the novel are based on real people who operated in the political life of Canada, the principal characters are entirely fictional and the product of my imagination.

I wish to thank Michèle Thinel for her assistance in making this a readable story.

Tom Creary
April 2019

1

Northern Saskatchewan, March 1967

Nathan Hightower followed the wolves in the clearing across the lake. "Stay still, Nathan. They will be hungry. It has been a long winter and there is not much snow. The deer and elk will have fled and stayed out of their reach. I don't want them to see us or get to the trap line. Once they pass to the west, we will go back in the opposite direction. The wolves are dangerous, and we must beware of them, but they are essential to life here."

Nathan, thirteen years old, had been with his uncle Samuel since the first snows. He had escaped the school run by the priests 200 miles to the south. A few weeks before, a distant cousin there had told him of an uncle of theirs who lived on a lake shaped like an octopus far to the north. For months, Nathan had contemplated escaping the school he was forced to attend since he was six years old. He had not seen his family for years. One day after another night of abuse from a priest who had fancied him, he found a map of Saskatchewan in the library and saw what was surely the lake his cousin had told him about. It was mid-September. If he was to find his uncle before winter, he would soon have to make his escape.

One morning before dawn, Nathan walked out the normally locked back door of the dormitory and into the woods. With a coat on his back, a blanket under his arm, an extra sweater and some undershorts rolled up inside, he found his way out of the compound and began his journey to find his uncle. After an hour in the woods, he emerged on a road going north. He was picked up by the first truck that came along. The driver was going to a community fifty miles from the tip of the octopus-shaped lake that Nathan spoke about. He would be happy to take Nathan there. Soon after reaching the town, the boy met a Cree who knew the way to the lake, as well as the trapper named Sam. He welcomed Nathan into his home, then took the boy by canoe along the fifty miles of rivers and lakes to their destination. They found a trap line in the woods along the shore. Guessing it was Sam Hightower's line, they followed it by foot until they reached a cabin an hour later.

"Uncle Sam, it's me. Nathan."

"My God, what are you doing here? The last time I saw you, you were five years old."

"I escaped from the school run by the priests. I could not stay there any longer. I had to get away. I thought I could come here, where they would not find me. Boys who escape from the school are usually found and brought back. I could not bear that. Can I stay here with you, at least for a while?"

"Of course you can. You are my brother's son." The Cree returned the way he came the next day with a parting gift from Sam of a half-dozen beaver pelts for his troubles in helping the boy.

"How is my father? My mother as well? Have you seen them?"

"Your father died, Nathan. You did not know this?"

"No, nobody told me. My father is dead?"

"They didn't tell you? It has been over a year. He had a heart attack. I'm so sorry, my boy."

The boy looked at his uncle. Tears came to his eyes. He said nothing. He did not know what to say. After a moment, he asked, "And what about my mother? Is she alright?"

"I was told your mother left the reserve after that. No idea where she went, Nathan. I'm sorry. It was your cousin James Lightfoot, who came here last summer and told me this. Could not say where she is. She apparently took your little sister with her." Nathan rose, opened the door to the cabin, walked outside, looked off into the distance, and the tears came. The bitterness he had in his heart since his abduction to attend the school seven years before, culminating that day in his grief, would stay with Nathan Hightower the rest of his life.

The boy remained with his uncle for seven years. He had nowhere else to go. No other family. They were gone. Sam became his mentor and friend. It worked out well for both. Under Sam's tutelage, Nathan re-connected with his roots, became a good trapper and master hunter. With the boy around, Sam found a new mission - father to his brother's son - as well as a renewed zest for life.

There were no women in their lives. Nathan had asked his uncle soon after arriving why he did not have a woman, a wife. "I had a wife. She died. Many moons ago. She was good. I have good memory of her. I do not need another. Too old now. I am fine this way." Later in his teenage years, Nathan would fantasize about female company and wonder about it, but it would not be strong enough for him to leave the woods and his life there. He refrained from accompanying his uncle on trips to town for supplies for fear of being discovered and returned to the school, essentially cutting himself off from any socialization or contact with young women.

Despite the stirrings of interest in the opposite sex as he grew older, he avoided all opportunities to explore it. Overall, he had little interest in life in the south and what that could entail. He was a man of the woods.

Amongst all of the creatures Nathan came into contact with in those years on the lake, he observed the wolves the most, learned their habits, and became inspired by their cunning and intelligence, their sense of community and talent for survival. What he learned by observing them would greatly influence him as he travelled through life.

Nathan also became a voracious reader. He read every book in his uncle's possession. Half a wall of the cabin was filled from floor to ceiling with shelves packed with dog-eared paperback novels and books of history. Sam would come back from his trips to the town with dozens of used books and Nathan would read every one of them.

"Nathan, you must move on from here," Sam said one evening four years after his nephew's arrival. "There is so much to see, to do in the world, people to meet. It has been good that you are here, but you have a life to live and it should not be as a loner like your old uncle."

"I am happy here. All I know about the outside is hard times for us. The whites hate us. I don't care about them, and I am certain someone will come after me about leaving the school if I go back south."

"The school has forgotten about you. You are seventeen now. It is time you have friends, a girl. You have much going for you. For one, you have learned the history of the world, with everything you read."

"I don't want to leave here. There is nothing south that attracts me. I may be informed of some past history of the world, but I have lived part of the present, and I don't want to go anywhere near what that means for me and all the other natives in this country. If that means being a loner, yes, that is what I am. It means staying here, in the woods and on the water, with the creatures around us, and the way of life of generations and generations of our forefathers. I may want to leave some day, but not now."

"You can stay, although I don't have to tell you that."

One morning, almost seven years to the day after his nephew had come to live with him, Samuel Hightower rose from his bed, staggered across the one room of the cabin and collapsed. He was dead before his head hit the floor. Nathan was alone once again. After burying his uncle, he closed the cabin, left everything as it was, brought the last batch of pelts to town, and made his way to Regina. He thought he may return some day, but he doubted it. He didn't know what he would do, but despite his love for the north, the woods and the life he had on that lake, he realized that he didn't want to live alone. It was time to move on. He was twenty years old.

2

Chicago, January 1972.

Marc Dubé had come to Chicago two years before to study for a master's degree in political science at the University of Chicago. He had graduated in law from Laval University in Quebec City that year but had no interest in practicing law. His interests were political - political thought and action to affect change. He could not see himself pleading cases in a courtroom. Along with many members of his generation, Marc Dubé was an *indépendantiste*, committed to the separation of Quebec from the rest of Canada. A training in law would help him contribute to that outcome.

Born and raised in the quiet civil servant dominated bourgeoisie of Quebec City, his father worked for the government. A reserved man, he displayed little passion about anything, nurturing a self-imposed melancholy while descending into alcoholism in his son's teenage years. However, the Dionnes of east-end Montreal on his mother's side were a different story. Pro-union, anti-business, anti-English, nationalist, pro-independence of Quebec and loud in the expression of all that, with much of it rubbing off on the young Marc.

Many of Dubé's friends in law school went to work for Montreal and Quebec City law firms that did work for large companies, both home-grown and foreign owned. Marc could not see himself defending the interests of business owners. The working-class members of his family would have been aghast, but it was not in him to begin with. His idea was to work for the working man, to advance the cause of Quebec independence, to discover how to effect change towards what he saw as a fairer society. He had jumped at the opportunity to apply for the fellowship to study at the University of Chicago.

"Take a look at the article in the University of Chicago student newspaper, December 3 issue. Some guy from Quebec writing about Chicago companies exploiting Quebec workers. You should find out more about him. Remember our discussion about Canada. He could be a candidate. You know what we are looking for. Contact him. Report back to me through the usual procedure." The Russian who ran the Soviet Union spy network in the United States hung up the secure phone line with the agent in Chicago.

The Ugly Americans in Quebec, the title read. The article took up all of page 3. It described the activities of five Chicago based companies in Quebec and, in the view of the author, how these companies exploited their Quebec workers. The companies were all highly profitable according to publicly available financial information cited in the article. According to the article, all had resisted unionization, had employed strike breakers in the past, apparently employed no native French-speakers at any level of management, and had all internal company information and communications conducted in English, despite 95% of the workforce being French-speaking. Author: Marc Dubé, graduate student in political science with an undergraduate degree in law from Quebec City. Pretty much a diatribe, but well expressed and documented. The Russian agent with the pseudo name of Carl Unger, who looked, acted and spoke like any normal twenty-five year old American, took two weeks to find Dubé. With his picture from the article in hand, the Russian went to the student union every day, then the popular bars on State Street where he knew students hung out on Friday and Saturday nights. On the third Friday night of his search he saw the man he was looking for enter and take a place at the bar. It was him. Beard, shoulder length hair, wire-rim glasses. The agent who wore his hair long as well with a moustache but without the beard, went to a spot next to the Lennon look-alike and ordered a beer. "Hi, how are ya?" he said when Marc Dubé turned to look at the guy who had shown up next to him. "Fine, thank you," he replied.

"Bit of an accent. Where are you from?"

"Quebec. Heard of that? Snow. Hockey," replied the Quebecer.

"Heard of it. Cool place. Lots of classy women, I hear. What are you doing here? Playing hockey for the Blackhawks?" asked the agent with a smile.

"With this hair, et cetera, I don't think so. Here to study."

"Study what?"

"Political science. What about you? Where are you from?"

"Indiana. The big city of Indianapolis. Work for a company here in Chicago that makes computers."

Unger's real name was Dmitry Sinov, born in Leningrad, son of a Soviet diplomat. He was sent at an early age to a special school to make Americans out of smart Russian boys and have them shipped to America to spy for the motherland. Sinov had arrived in Chicago seven years before. He had taken a course in computer technology at Illinois State. He then had been hired by Cox Computers in the programming of the company's line of computers for schools and colleges. While at Illinois State, he had joined the SDS, the Students for a Democratic Society, to identify potential agents for the cause. He did his best to remain below the surface and out of sight of the police and FBI. He had managed to overcome several hurdles to hide his identity and past, not the least of which was avoiding the military draft. His papers included a false draft card with a classification of 4F, making him ineligible for military duty. If asked about his 4F, he was to say he was color-blind and flat-footed.

"I see you're drinking a Molson. Not many places around here sell Canadian beer."

"It's why I come here. I find American beer unbearable. *La pisse* they would say back home. Sorry."

"It is and you don't have to apologize," replied the Russian agent. "By the way, my name is Carl. Carl Unger," offering his hand.

"Mine is Marc. Marc Dubé. Nice to meet you," as they shook hands.

"Yes, nice to meet you as well," replied the Russian as he continued to size up the Canadian. "Some real funky chicks here tonight. Good place to pick someone up. You married or anything like that?"

"No. Not married. But I think you are right. Good place to meet girls," replied the Canadian.

"Well, I see someone over there I know," replied the Russian, "I will let you own this end of the bar and meet the brunette over there. By the way, we have a pickup hockey game on Monday nights. Bunch of Americans who are clueless about the game, but we have a good time. You're Canadian. You must play hockey. Eh? If so, would you like to join us?"

"Yes, that would be nice. I was looking forward to finding someone to play hockey with. I brought my equipment to Chicago and was wondering when I could use it."

"Great, Marc. What's your telephone number? I will call you tomorrow with the details. Where we play and at what time, although it is usually 9PM. We go for beers afterwards."

"They play hockey in Indianapolis?" asked Marc, while writing his telephone number on a piece of paper.

"Sure. And even more so in Chicago. Influence of the Blackhawks. Joined our group when I was in college and since then, we have expanded it into a little four team league. We have a great time. Good bunch of guys as well. You'll see. Talk to you tomorrow."

Dmitry Sinov had concluded step one in the checking out of Marc Dubé and had already set up step two. Over the next few months, around their weekly hockey games and beers afterward, the Russian agent explored the character, thoughts and motivations of the Quebecer.

After one of their Monday night hockey games, Sinov decided to get into it with him. "Marc, that incident with De Gaulle a few years ago in Montreal. Saying "Vive le Quebec libre" or something like that to a big crowd. You're from Quebec. What did you feel about that? Were you there?"

"I was there, and I was glad he did it. Most people my age felt the same way. You must understand that I am a supporter of the independence of Quebec. It is inevitable and it is right. All about justice, really. The Quebec people have been suppressed for close to two hundred years. Second class citizens in what is supposed to be their country as well. The only way to change things is to have our own."

"Wow. You come out pretty strong on that," replied the Russian.

"Yes, I truly believe in it. Americans also exploit Quebecers. It is not just the big companies from Toronto that do it. American companies, with many of them from Chicago, abuse us. They prevent us from forming unions, try to break the ones we already have, impose speaking English for work on everybody. We have factories in Montreal where 95% of the workers are French speaking but must converse with management in English. Are you not sympathetic to that sort of thing?"

"And then you had that stuff a couple of years ago. A government minister assassinated, some British guy kidnapped, army on the streets of Montreal, as I remember. Was all over the news here. What was that all about?" Sinov had to learn if Dubé was involved with the FLQ, the guys who had done what he was speaking about in October 1970. Canada's October Crisis. A no-no for his recruitment. He would be a target of Canadian police.

"Radicals. Very radical. I don't support killing people. I don't believe in that," responded Dubé. He thought about it. It had happened a month after he had arrived in Chicago. The abduction of the British commercial attaché in Montreal, then the abduction and murder of Laporte, the Minister of Labor of Quebec. The work of cells of the radical Front de Libération du Québec or FLQ. Hundreds of Quebec intellectuals, labor leaders, and militants known for their sympathy towards independence, were rounded up and incarcerated. A couple of his friends were jailed. Under an order of the Prime Minister of Canada, units of the Canadian Army patrolled the streets of Montreal. The perpetrators were caught; one cell negotiated its exile to Cuba; the other, the one that murdered the cabinet minister, met its fate in court and in prison. The effects of the crisis would be felt for years. A bad time.

Through the actions of the government, hundreds of moderates had been turned into committed indépéndantistes. Quebec society polarized. Hatred for the central government crystallized in many quarters of Quebec. It had a mobilizing effect upon Marc Dubé. Quebec must be free. Violence cannot work. His conclusion to the affair was that it would come to that, though, if Quebec could not be master of its own destiny. But he was not FLQ.

"No, I don't sympathize with that."

We'll see. Can't have anybody associated with that group now, thought the Russian. "Ok. Understand. That's bad stuff. But, we do certainly have some things in common, Marc. For one, I am no friend of corporate America. I belong to the SDS. Students for a Democratic Society. I do not advertise it. Not good to do so. Dangerous now. It did not use to be that way, but it is now. You surely have seen our activities against the war in Vietnam, but there is more to it than that," replied the Russian.

"I thought you worked for a big company. You are an activist. I had no idea. You surprise me with this."

"I work for a company to be able to pay the bills, Marc. Have to live. In reality, I spend a lot of time organizing student groups in Chicago against the war. We seem to be getting it done. Congress has called for an end to it."

"And against other things as well?" asked the Quebecer.

"Yes. Martin Luther King's and Bobby Kennedy's assassinations in '68. Symptomatic of America, Marc. Intolerance, people being used. The right-wing government of Richard Nixon. Society here is sick." He paused for a moment, then continued. "I saw the article you wrote in the school paper. I think we have some things in common."

"You must mean the article about Chicago companies exploiting workers in Quebec. When did you see it?"

"Last week. Came across it in the student union when I met with some people about a demonstration coming up. Bunch of issues of the newspaper on a coffee table. Recognized your name as the author." He lied. "We have just as many injustices here with corporate America as you have in Montreal. Maybe not the same, but similar. Environmental degradation, war profiteering, corruption, union-busting, suppression of blacks."

"Yes, Carl, we do have things in common......." replied the Quebecer. "Tell me more about the SDS. I want to know how you work. Maybe it could apply to us."

"OK. Why don't you join us at one of our meetings? There is a group at the U of C. You may want to learn about it. But in the meantime, I can invite you to one of the meetings."

"Yes. What do I do?"

Step two concluded. He will be with us. Coming, wrote Dmitry Sinov later that evening in the introduction to his report on the recruitment of the Canadian.

Marc went to the meeting. The group in front were talking about recruiting for demonstrations being planned.

"Hello, my friend. You made it," said Carl as he sat next to Marc.

"Yes. I showed them the SDS member card you gave me and got in. I told you I was interested. We could learn from what is being done here."

"You mean your stuff back in Quebec."

"In Quebec. Yes," replied Marc. "I want to see how you mobilize. We need to do it." He paused, looked around the room, then back at the Russian. "You are not worried about police infiltrating? This was easy to get into."

"They are paying more attention to us. We must be careful. But you saw the guys at the door. They would signal if they saw anything suspicious. And there are only fifteen people here. We have learned to keep our numbers at meetings down to minimize attention. We just have more groups and we keep them informed. In the meantime, we have fun at the same time as we organize disruption. Look at everyone here. They are all excited."

Marc Dubé and Dmitry Sinov met the following Friday evening for their Molson Exports. Sinov brought the discussion to a new track.

"Marc, the SDS is not just a network of campus demonstrators. There are many cells in the SDS. Some of them are involved in more serious stuff. I am part of one that could be of help to you in your struggles in Quebec. Can we talk about that? Are you interested? If not, we stop and say we never had this discussion."

"What are you talking about? What do you mean?"

"This goes further than what we have spoken about. If we go forward, we shall be honest with each other. And tell no one of our discussions. The SDS can help you in Montreal, but we must operate in secrecy. As I said, this is not just about waving placards on campuses."

"Again, Carl, what do you mean?"

"No, Marc. I must have your word. We keep this to ourselves and I have your word you tell no one else about this. Marc?..."

"I have no idea what you are going to tell me, so I can't say if I can keep it a secret," replied Dubé.

"My Quebec friend, I read what you wrote about companies exploiting people back home. You are anti-business, anti-corporations. It is written all over you. You sympathize with the working man. What I wish to propose goes right down that line. It is about changing this world. Listen, Marc, this is about proletarian revolution. Upsetting the order. It can be done. You can work with us for that, starting in Montreal when you go back. Do you want to hear more?"

"Yes. Tell me."

"OK. We trust each other, Marc. None of this gets shared with anyone else. Understand?"

"Understand."

"Here is what I propose. You go back to Quebec and supply us information on the major Canadian companies that operate in the United States and around the world, and on their leaders. We are looking to discredit corporations and expose their corrupt practices. Here are a few that are Canadian. There is Canadian Pacific, Power Corporation, Argus Corporation, Massey Ferguson, Dominion Engineering. There are more. Don't be surprised. We have done our homework on Canadian companies. We will pay you $500 per month, as long you want to continue and as long as our little program continues."

"That's it? Information on big companies for $500 a month? Where does the money come from? The SDS is all students, young people."

"I'm not a student anymore, but you have a valid question. There are people with money who do not like what is happening. There are donors. But we will not talk about who they are. You will have to accept that."

"OK. There is something more important than money that I want, although I will accept what you propose. It is help in organizing disruption, on organizing civil disobedience. Not revolt or killing people like what those guys had done in Montreal, but people are really upset at the police action last year. So many innocent people were put in jail. There are more than a few who want to do something to disrupt the order, work for the independence of Quebec. Can we work on that?"

"Yes. We can work on that."

"OK. When do we start?"

"When you get back to Quebec."

"No, let's start now. I want to learn how you operate. When can the money start coming?"

"All right. The money can start soon, but I need to organize it. We can meet next Monday. That should give me enough time. Let's see…How about meeting at the big gazebo at the northwest corner of Grant Park? Monday, 4 PM. Is that OK?"

"Why not the bar on Friday night?" replied Marc.

The Russian had to do it where the exchange could be photographed. "Can't do it Friday. Have something that evening. Let's do it Monday. Cannot be talking about this stuff in a bar anymore, by the way. And we will discuss a program for you here in Chicago before you go back. I have some ideas for that."

At 4 PM the following Monday afternoon, a camera with a long zoom took a series of pictures of Marc Dubé accepting a wad of bills from Dmitry Sinov, erstwhile Carl Unger. The KGB had their first evidence of the complicity of Marc Dubé. None of the photos taken showed the face of the man who handed him the money.

A month later, Dubé received confirmation that he had a job back in Quebec. He would be teaching political science at one of the colleges called CEGEP's (College d'enseignement général et professionnel).

3

Toronto April 1972.

"Father, I have something to tell you. I think you will be pleased."

"And what is that, Andrew?"

"I have been accepted at Cambridge. I received the letter today. I am quite pleased, and I hope you are as well." Andrew Brown was beaming as he produced the letter of his acceptance as he and his family convened for dinner at their home in Toronto's upscale Rosedale neighborhood.

"Well, well, I am happy for you. You will get a proper education there, not that the University of Toronto is all that bad, but Cambridge is Cambridge. It will be a bit more expensive than university here, but I think we can handle it. Good show!" replied Alistair Brown, scion of the 'old money' Brown family of Upper Canada.

"One of my friends has been accepted at Harvard, another at Princeton, father, and I thought I would be envious. But I am not," said Andrew. "I am quite happy about going to England."

"Yes, you should be. The dreadful Americans. Arrogant. I meet so many of them. I'm glad you won't be corrupted like I suppose your friends will be. Americans taking over more and more of our companies here. The government must do something about it. We can't have this. But, that is a subject for another day. Let us toast your good fortune!" Alistair Brown raised his glass of gin and tonic as his wife entered the room and asked what the celebrating was all about. "Andrew's off to Cambridge, my dear. Get yourself a glass!"

The Browns were direct descendants of United Empire Loyalists who came north in 1782 to escape the American War of Independence. The attitudes of the family toward Americans had not appreciably changed over the succeeding two hundred years. Alistair Brown and his two brothers, although wealthy and influential in the Canadian financial and publishing worlds, were unbendingly antagonistic to anything American. Alistair was a senior vice-president of a leading Bay Street stock brokerage. Brother George was an executive and major shareholder in a holding company with investments in several Canadian manufacturing concerns. His twin brother Jamieson was the principal shareholder of the company that owned the Toronto Herald. The Herald was Toronto's premier daily newspaper and reputed for its anti-American as well as left-of-centre bias, despite the Brown family's distinctive Upper Canada conservatism.

A few weeks later, the family congregated at the family cottage on Lake Muskoka north of Toronto for Andrew's farewell party. His uncles were there along with their families. Discussion would inevitably turn to politics at Brown family reunions and this one was no exception.

"Although I am not a great fan of that dilettante from Montreal, I admire Trudel for sticking up against this rat of a man, Nixon." Jamieson Brown, the newspaper man, rarely hid his views among family. He was reserved, neutral in his views in other settings, but not here. He went on. "This man will do anything to stay in power. Unfortunately, he will most likely whip McGovern,

25

that fumbling intellectual dunce. The Americans could not find anybody better to run up against Tricky Dick. Incredible."

"George, is it true that Illinois railway company has made a bid for Canadian Pacific?" asked Alistair. "Can you imagine.....Canadian Pacific falling into American hands?"

"Could be," said Jamieson Brown before his brother George could reply. "But we are on to it. Expect an editorial or two in the days to come. We have our friends in cabinet, as well. I am told the boys won't allow it. They are coming up with a new foreign investment review policy. Will be announced shortly. About time. If the Americans can't get around our tariffs, they try to buy everything they can up here, own as much as they can on both sides of the border. In the meantime, let's celebrate. The first of the Browns at Cambridge. Yes, very good, Andrew. We are proud of you."

The discussion forum was drawing to a close. "Mr. Brown, you have something to say. You have been quiet today, and I must say, we have not heard much from you since the beginning of the session. This is all about discussion, old boy. Where are you on this and, by the way, where have you been on the other issues we have been discussing? The study of current western civilization could use some Canadian input. Speak up. We are listening." Andrew Brown rose slowly from his chair behind the table.

"Sir, I have been trying to figure out where you are, and I must say everyone else in the class is as well, regarding American influence in the world. Many of you seem to welcome how American ways of doing things are shaking up the stodgy English ways and traditions. One of you said that it was high time that the upper classes on this island, the managerial class, got a spanking. It was said, "Let the Yanks show us the way. Maybe the old British Empire can regenerate itself with some American entrepreneurial energy." Well, I can give you a perspective of what it is like to let Americans and American ways, entrepreneurial energy as you say, take over a country. It is happening at home and it is not pretty. I dare say that Canada is losing the levers of its own destiny. The Americans are buying up our best companies, our resources, and corrupting our minds. Our television and radio are dominated by American content despite our equivalent of the BBC trying to balance it out. The almighty dollar. Free enterprise. Let the market rule. They say, "What is good for business, is good for America." They have managed to enlist our government's complicity in defense schemes, in common purchases of military hardware, all to make the continent one big American driven economic and military entity. If we demur or object to what they propose, we are browbeaten, subject to tirades of American presidents against our prime ministers, in public and in private. President Johnson berating our Prime Minister face to face in the Oval Office with "Don't piss on my rug" for the PM's public expression of doubt on the wisdom of the Vietnam War. Look out, my English friends. Beware of what you wish for." Andrew then sat down.

Everyone was looking at him. Nobody said a word. The professor broke the silence. "Well, well, it seems we have a disgruntled Canadian in our midst. I trust, Mr. Brown, that you will be able to expound further on your thoughts in the weeks to come as we explore what we believe to be the trends in this world that are shaping our future."

Beginning with that statement that day in Professor Milford's 1st year Western Civilization seminar, Andrew Brown became labeled at Cambridge as the anti-American Canadian. He did not object to it. It fit with the views and influences of his own family back in Toronto. What would not, however, fit with the views of his family would be Andrew's flirting with sympathy for Marxism.

In January of Andrew's first year at Cambridge, he was approached by a friend from his Western Civilization class to attend a private off-campus party. One of the people there that evening and the oldest person present was Edmund Shuttles, a tenured professor of ancient Greek Civilization and faculty advisor to the organizer of the party. Shuttles was more than a Cambridge professor of history. He was a Marxist and for years a clandestine recruiter for the KGB. The Soviets, through their embassy in London, relied on him to identify students who could become agents. Agents to work for proletarian revolution and the overthrow of capitalism. The network was nowhere near as extensive as the Cambridge one of the 1930's that spawned the spy cell of Kim Philby, Guy Burgess and Donald MacLean, but it existed, nonetheless. Surprisingly, given the history of communist sympathy and what it spawned coming out of Cambridge, Professor Shuttles had managed to avoid the scrutiny of MI5, Britain's counterintelligence service. MI5 kept an eye on Cambridge but Edmund Shuttles was not part of it. This had a lot to do with his lifestyle and he and his wife's social circles.

Shuttles was an articulate and engaging man, debonair, wore smart Savile Row suits rather than the usual tweeds and cardigans of his faculty colleagues. He wife was the managing editor of a popular London fashion magazine. He kept a low ideological profile, certainly one that avoided him being suspected of being a Soviet agent. He did not at all fit the portrait.

Over the fall and winter of Andrew Brown's first year at Cambridge, the professor had become aware of the articulate young man from Toronto who so easily spoke of the perils of American influence in the world as experienced in Canada.

Professor Shuttles' activities for the KGB over fifteen years had led to the successful recruitment of five agents. His technique was to befriend a student, advise him on his academic direction, and exchange views on life when appropriate in the intimate academic surroundings of Trinity College. While doing so, he would determine if the student was a candidate. He would build a psychological and motivational profile of the individual, then recommend his being approached by a real recruiter. He had done this on a dozen Cambridge students over the years, with five of them eventually becoming agents. Three Shuttles recruits worked for the British Government, one for the Government of Kenya and another for the central bank of Italy. He was confident that none of the ones contacted by the KGB ever realized that the source of it all was their friend Edmund Shuttles.

In addition to the recruiting, Shuttles reported to his handler on the views and activities of many members of the British upper and managerial classes. He and his wife were active in the course of his activities with Cambridge and his wife's business affairs. Madeleine, Maddy to everyone who knew her, had no idea her husband was a spy.

Edmund Shuttles had often asked himself why he did what he did. Every time, the answer was the same. The world was unfair. Capitalism was at the heart of it. Need to level the playing field. He was but a minor player, and no one was going to die because of what he did. Keep the fat cats on their toes. Besides, it was exhilarating. A lot more than Greek history.

In his contacts with Andrew Brown, Shuttles managed to maintain the professor to student relationship, giving no indication to Andrew of his true intent. They had regular exchanges of views on political and social philosophy, allowing Shuttles to observe and report on the thinking of this potential Canadian asset to his contact at the Embassy in London. The master spies in Moscow were aware of Andrew's pedigree, the position of his family in Canadian affairs, and could see the possibility of him having a role in their plans for Canada.

Within two years, Andrew Brown would become the professor's next recruit for the KGB. Over that time, Brown saw that his friend and mentor was certainly a socialist sympathizer, as many academics clearly were, but he never made the connection between Shuttles and the KGB recruitment process.

One day in the winter of his third year at Cambridge, as he sat alone in a booth in a pub, a man approached and asked Andrew if he could join him.

"Certainly. Have a seat. What can I do for you?" Andrew was always a self-assured person and rarely felt intimidated by strangers.

"You don't know me and I will not tell you my name. I just want to ask you a question." Andrew could not make out the man's accent. Could be German or Swiss or Belgian. He was dressed in a leather jacket with corduroy trousers and a long scarf draped around his neck.

"OK.... What is the question?"

"Are you interested in working to upset the American order of the world?" After a moment, without taking his gaze away from Andrew's eyes, with Andrew hesitating to answer, he asked the question again, "Are you interested in working to upset the American order of the world?"

Andrew realized immediately where this came from. His comments in discussion groups and the like where he would occasionally express his views. The anti-American.

"Who are you?"

"I told you I would not tell you that. You can call me Rudy, if you wish. Again, the question. Are you interested?"

"You will have to tell me more before I answer that," responded Andrew.

"All right. Let's go for a walk. Have no fear. We will stay on the street. There are many people around. I will tell you, but before I say much more, you will have to tell me if you are interested." The Russian realized that Andrew knew what he was talking about, at least in general terms.

"OK. You are asking me if I want to work against American interests. I am, but under certain conditions. Are you asking me to spy?"

"Listen, I would like to make a deal with you. You are part of a well-connected family in Canada. Your family controls the largest newspaper in the country. You are concerned about American control of your country. We can help you stop that. It is in our interests as well."

"Who are you? KGB? Stasi?"

"I said, I want to make a deal with you. Are you interested in talking about it?"

"Yes. OK. I am. But what next? What do you propose?"

"You say nothing to anyone about this. If you do, I will learn of it and you will never see me again. Meet me in London, Hyde Park, east bank of the duck pond nearest Speaker's Corner next Saturday at 3 PM. If you have anyone with you or you are being followed, we will see it. The meeting will be off and you will never see me again. If we manage to avoid all that, we will talk specifics then."

"OK. Hyde Park next Saturday."

The two met that Saturday at the park, then took the underground to a pub in North London.

"Are you in?" asked the agent as they sat down to a Guinness.

"Yes, I could be, but we need to talk about specifics." Not for you or your people, my friend, but for Canada, he thought.

"Well, Mr. Brown. You will have to be more definitive. Are you in?"

"OK, then. Yes. But the specifics. How do we work?"

Andrew's contact laid out specifically what they had in mind. The Russian pressed Andrew for a commitment to the cause, but without disclosing specifically what he wanted the young Canadian to do. They spent an hour discussing, sometimes testily, mutual expectations. Andrew came close to cutting off the discussion. Slowly, the arrangement came together. There would be no money. Andrew would decide what to provide. If the information was good, he would be given relevant information in return. Essentially, information from Washington. The basis for a deal. Maybe a way to turn the tide back home, thought Andrew. After an hour, he said yes.

"Someone will contact you in Toronto. Good luck," said the agent, who had a few thoughts of his own as they left the pub. They will need to test him quickly. Does not want money. Usually not a good sign.

Journal entry, June 15, 1975

If I am anything related to this business, I am a neo-Marxist, if a Marxist at all. I thought I was, but I am not. Can't stomach this stuff about bloody revolution, proletarian overthrow. Some people here are still into that. The world needs a new economic model, not blood and guts and warfare. An alternative to American corporate capitalism. A stop to the expansion of the American way, and the takeover of the world. If these guys can help me counter it in Canada, I'm with it. Collaboration - fine. But we will need to be smart about it. I will serve their anti-American interests as they serve me in mine. With what I can do through the newspaper, my value to them will be just as much as their value to me. Could be a good deal.

4

Regina, Saskatchewan, August 1974

"No alcohol. Not interested. You do what you want, but I'm not there." Nathan Hightower, sitting on the bench, pushed the wine bottle away. He got up, walked away from the men in the park, and made his way to the hostel where he had lived since the beginning of the summer.

"Hello, Woody. Working the night shift now?" asked the young man as he entered the place.

"Yes, Nathan. By the way, you will have to move out of here soon. Cheryl told me to tell you. Your three months are up. The rules. Temporary stays. Everybody has to move on."

"Yeah, I will." Nathan found the stairs and the room he shared with three other beds, sometimes occupied, sometimes not. He would have to move on. Since arriving in Regina two years before, he had lived in three hostels and an abandoned school bus before a friend set fire to it in a drunken stupor. He had lived with a native woman who disappeared with everything he had. He had shared an apartment with a girl he thought loved him but had taken up with another man, leaving him with a rent he could not pay. He had held four jobs, none of which lasted more than a few weeks. His last boss told him he was an angry man and had to change, that he could not continue with the company. He didn't drink and he didn't steal. He was simply a lone and angry Indian. Like so many others. He tried to survive in the seedy, decrepit urban world of displaced natives, far from their original homes and people.

"What are you, really, Nathan? Why don't you go back to your people?" asked the hostel clerk the following evening.

"What am I? I don't know. As to going back to my people, I have no people anymore. The system took them away from me. My parents are gone. Father died. I wasn't even aware he was dead until my uncle told me a year later, after I had escaped from the school. My mother left the reserve, took my little sister with her. For the past two years, I have tried to find them. Vancouver, Edmonton, Saskatoon. No trace of a Shirley or Emma Hightower. Disappeared. I don't know anybody on the reserve that I was taken from when I was five. I have no one to go back to, Woody. So, what am I, you ask? Good question."

"You read a lot. You're a smart guy. You don't drink. You don't mess around with any of the sleazy women around here. What is it?" asked Woody.

"I don't like what I see. I don't think you do either. You're Ojibway. I'm Cree. What's the difference? There is none. We're just fucking Indians. There is nothing for us in this world. I don't want to get into self-pity like a lot of our people. But our Indian world needs to be shaken up, my friend. Any ideas on that?"

"I wish I did, but I don't. We are our own worst enemies. Over six hundred bands in Canada that do not want to agree on anything. Yes. Something is needed to shake our world."

He spent the last three weeks of summer on the streets of Regina with a blanket and a change of clothes, panhandling for meal money and managing to steal some hours of sleep in places off

Main Street. One day in early September he came across a sidewalk work crew as he walked by where they were working. There was an argument. Somebody was being fired. The boss saw Nathan observing the incident and on impulse, asked the young man if he wanted to work. "I just fired the guy who lays the forms. Need to finish the job this week. Can you do this? Do you want to work? Pay four dollars an hour."

"Alright. I'm in. What do I do?" said Nathan.

"Here's a pair of gloves. It's simple. See how these are laid with the spikes on the perimeter? Just need to follow the plumb line and attach them together using the bolts. Make sure the line is even. Take this tool bib with the hammer and the pliers. But you will have to get some work boots. Those running shoes won't do. There's a Canadian Tire store down the street. If you can show me you can do this today, I'll advance you the money for some boots and you'll make some dough for the next few weeks, at least."

It was a job, but it would not last. By early October, the sidewalk season was over. He stayed a week at the rooming house to close out the month while looking for another job that never materialized, then went back to knocking on hostel doors.

The Russian had noticed the young Indian in the park with his blanket. He was the only one who did not seem to drink. Ran every morning. Not the usual pattern. Then he was no more. One day in late September, he saw him working with a construction crew. The Russian stuck around and followed the man at the end of the shift. Two blocks down the street, the Indian entered a café. The agent looked inside, saw that he was seated with another man, and decided to put off the first approach to a more appropriate setting.

Two weeks later..

"Hey, I used to see you in the park running in the morning. But I haven't seen you in a while. How are you? My name is Jeff Weller," said the Russian to the young man next to him at the lunch counter, taking a chance with a friendly approach. Nathan Hightower turned his head, looked at the man who had asked him the question, then said "What's it to you? You watching me in the park? What for? I don't know you and I don't want to." He then abruptly got up and moved to a booth, leaving the Russian alone at the counter. As the Indian glowered at him from the booth, Weller responded with a conciliatory "As you wish. Sorry I asked." The other people in the diner turned to see what was happening.

The Russian, whose real name was Yuri Grishin, ordered a cup of coffee, drank it slowly, then got up and left. He would try again.

White guy being nice. What the fuck? Police? RCMP? No regular white guys come on like that. Wonder what he wanted, thought Nathan as he took his order of toast and coffee before returning to the hostel for another day of inactivity. Maddening inactivity. I am going to explode. On the way to the shelter, he went into a used bookstore, found a paperback copy of John Steinbeck's The Grapes of Wrath, bought it for fifty cents, and took it to the basement dormitory.

"What got you here?" asked the young man facing Nathan across the table. It was the end of the dinner hour and the two were the last people in the dining room.

"A long walk from a lake a long way from here.".

"I see you reading a lot. You run. Nobody else here runs. You don't seem to be someone who grew up in the bush."

"Long story. Residential school. I left, went to live with an uncle on a lake way north. He had a lot of books and a trap line. I walked a lot, then in summer I ran in the woods. Something I always did."

"The school. Where was it?" asked the young man.

"Nowhere. Somewhere. Doesn't make any difference. Just a place I hated."

"I never lived any of that stuff. I grew up in Saskatoon. They left us kids alone. I know of others, though, who were forced into some of those places. Bad stories."

"Yep. That school wasted my youth, wasted my family."

"Wasted your family. They all gone?"

"Yeah. Gone for over a year when I was at the school and I was never told. Learned of it when I escaped and found my uncle in the woods."

"Makes you want to hate the white man," said the young native across the table.

"It has. You don't forget it. I don't, even after trying all the years since. I never got to know my father. Or my mother. Thought I would find a way to move on here in the city. It's only made it worse. This is not our world. We exist. We drink, we smoke, although I don't on that score. I say we. I mean our people. We go from day to day, far away from our real world. But I have no one to go back to there. Nobody knows me on that reserve...... Someday this is all going to explode. Not sure that I won't be part of it. What's your name, by the way?"

"Jimmy."

"OK, Jimmy. Nice talking to you. Maybe see you tomorrow. Stay away from the hard stuff and the dope. Doesn't help."

A week later, the agent who went by the name of Jeff saw Nathan at the café reading a copy of The Globe and Mail. He decided to re-engage.

"Hey, I'm sorry about our exchange a few days ago. I was being nosy. Can I apologize?"

"What do you want from me?" replied Nathan. He said it loud enough for people at the counter to turn and notice.

"Hey, take it easy. Can I join you?"

"No, you can't. What do you want?" replied Nathan.

"OK." The Russian walked closer to Nathan, bent over and lowered his voice. "Listen, I'm doing a documentary on residential schools. The ones that many of your people had to endure, still do in some cases. The ones that many of you were put in. You could have perspectives on that. I used to see you in the park reading and now I see you with The Globe and Mail. Seems like you are a well-read guy."

"Anyway, that's what I am talking about," continued the Russian. "The special schools run by the priests and the nuns. I have been trying to engage people here and in Saskatoon and elsewhere, guys like you, to talk about it. Some people want to, most don't. I don't know if you ever were in a residential school. If you were, you could perhaps tell me about the experience. Anything to share with me on that?"

"Yeah, I do. I was at one of them. I'm just not interested in sharing it with you or anyone for that matter. Who are you?" replied Nathan.

"Like I said the first time we met my name is Jeff Weller. I'm from Vancouver. Here's my card. Can we talk about this sometime?"

"Let me think about it. If I did, it would not be here."

"Can we meet again? Just say yes or no. Let's start with that," said the Russian.

"If I decide to do this, I will be in the park tomorrow at 10AM on one of the benches at the northeast corner. If it's raining, you will find me in the café across the street. There is only one. If you can't find me, the answer's no."

Who is this guy, really? Nathan Hightower asked himself as he returned to the hostel. Do I do this? A documentary. TV. Exposure. Maybe a good thing. Hardly any whites know what it was like. I'll talk to him. In any case, I'm going slowly crazy. Have to do something. Find a job or back to the bush. The cabin on the lake. Not too late before the snows.

It was a cold day, snowing, with the wind blowing. The first snows of the year. The undercover Russian had spent six months in Saskatchewan, alternating between Regina and Saskatoon. The plan was going nowhere. Of the six young native men he had identified as possible recruits, there was only one he thought would be suitable.

"Five of the six unsuitable. Common trait: lack of personal discipline. Although all have the prerequisite motivation, only one – the Cree – seems to keep himself in good physical condition, avoids alcohol and womanizing. An angry young man, but a smart and learned one. Three meetings with him so far. Have ascertained his anger and a possible motivation for him to work with us. Being elusive, however. Not sure at all if he will bite. Will propose Cuba and long-term engagement to help him organize in Canada. Am abandoning the others. If recruitment of the Cree fails, I will have to disappear. Efforts will have to be organized elsewhere." He put the coded dispatch under the steps of the back porch of the abandoned house for the regular pickup.

Three months later, Nathan Hightower arrived in Montreal and made contact. In the middle of the night the day he arrived, he was brought to a gate at the port, was met there by another contact and led to the freighter and a hidden compartment in the hold of the ship. A day later, in the late winter of 1976, the freighter left port with a load of grain and canola oil bound for Riga, Latvia.

5

Montreal, September 1974

"*Monsieur Dubé, est ce que je pourrais vous voir?*" The voice at the other end of the line was French....from France.

"Who is calling? I don't recognize your voice," replied Dubé.

"My name is Serge. I need to see you. I am a friend of Carl Unger."

Unger had disappeared. In June of '73 Marc had received a call from Carl saying he would be going underground. Nothing since then. The money had kept coming, but he had had no contact from anyone with the SDS other than occasionally in relation to the information submitted to the address in New York. "Carl Unger. I have not heard from him for over a year. We were friends in Chicago. What can I do for you? How did you get my number, by the way?"

"Carl asked me to call you. He has something for you. You teach at the College of Vieux Montréal. You told Carl that. Simple to find you. I just called the college number. Where can we meet, Monsieur Dubé? And when? Could we do it this week?" asked the Frenchman.

"Very good. Tomorrow at 3. Carré Saint-Louis, rue St-Denis. I will have a Montreal Expos baseball cap on."

"Excellent. See you then," replied the man.

Is this guy just a friend of Carl or is he involved? I will soon find out, thought Marc as he hung up the phone.

Dubé was in the park. He did not see the man approaching. Suddenly, someone from behind called his name. "M. Dubé."

Marc turned and observed a guy with curly sandy hair wearing a baggy burgundy colored sweater, tight jeans that went down to mid ankle and sandals with red socks. "You must be Serge."

"Yes. Good to meet you." The erstwhile Frenchman, whose real name was Pavel Tedorenko, offered his hand. They shook hands while observing each other. "Can we talk here, Marc, if I may call you that? Our American friends do that easily. We are not so inclined, are we?"

"No, we are more formal. Quebec is changing, though. What do you have to tell me about Carl?" asked Marc.

"Can we sit somewhere? There are benches over there."

"We can go across the street, to the Café Cherrier. We can talk there".

"No, not in a café. It must be private. The bench over there would be good," replied the Frenchman.

Serge wasted no time. "M. Dubé, I am French. You can see that. I am with an organization that works closely with the SDS and the organizations that have evolved from it. We have many objectives that are in common, although I am sure you are aware the SDS has become more discreet, much less in the public eye. I am your new contact."

"But you are not SDS. Who are you with?"

"I am with the wing of the Union Nationale des Étudiants de France that is the most active of all the cells of the Union that came out of the Événements de mai of 1968. We seek to disrupt the existing order, the American capitalist order, if you wish. Many SDS units have become our allies in this. They have no working cells in Canada, apart from a few individuals like you, but we do. So we work together. The SDS pays you every month to provide information on companies here. We want to go further, with payments to continue. You are an indépendantiste. We would like to help you in that. I understand you are actively involved in the Quebec independence movement."

"So this is about something else."

"Quebecers deserve their own country. They are being exploited. We can help," replied the Frenchman.

"The deal with Carl is that I would receive $500 a month in exchange for information on big Canadian and American companies operating in Quebec and elsewhere in Canada. We are talking about something else now, although I did tell Carl I was interested in that."

"Yes, this is something different. We still want the intelligence on corporations here. That is what the SDS was willing to pay for and that will continue. The money will still come from the Americans, not from France. But, M. Dubé, anything that weakens Canada, weakens America and its hold on the world. Our interests complement each other."

"What do you want from me? You said you had something for me from Carl. What has happened to him?"

"Carl has gone underground. He is being sought by the police. He simply asked us to contact you to say he was all right and that he wanted you to continue to work with for the cause."

"All right, then. How do we work? What will you want from me? I follow the activities of thirty or so U.S. and Canadian companies and send the information to a mailbox in New York City. I have received nothing in return for over a year now, except for the monthly payment in cash in an envelope at a drop point we have. Will this continue that way?"

"Yes, but you will provide the information to me now. We also want more from you. We want information on politicians here. People in the government. What policies are being considered, who the influencers are, who they deal with. Government works closely with companies here," said the Frenchman.

"I have little exposure to how the government in Ottawa works. I do know more about what happens inside our government in Quebec. I have many friends who work there. Teaching political science, it is part of my job to follow government affairs here. I have little interest in Ottawa, other than what they do to suppress Quebec. They are oppressors in my view. I work with the Parti National. The party still has a few members in the provincial assembly. I have worked with them."

"Very good. We can start with that."

"What do you mean, start with that? You are asking me to spy on my friends, on my associates devoted to making Quebec a country?"

"Non, non, M. Dubé. What I mean is providing information on matters that continue to maintain the status quo, that perpetuate the capitalist hold on Quebec, on Canada, on the world. We will help you in your efforts to make Quebec a country. Spy on the enemies, not the friends. Our interests complement each other."

"All right. There is one other thing, though. I need more money. What you are asking me to do involves more work and more risk."

"I see. What do you wish now, in terms of payment?"

"One thousand dollars a month."

"It is a lot of money, M. Dubé. We are students."

"You are more than students. The SDS receives money from many sources. I am not sure about your organization in France, but I do know the Americans can pay. You said they would continue to pay me. For me to do what you ask, I must have what I am requesting."

"I will get back to you. Where do I reach you from now on?"

"Here is my number at my apartment. I have no answering machine. For the moment, I live alone. That may change, but for the moment, no one else will be there to answer the phone. If I do not answer, try again. Do not call the college."

"One last thing, M. Dubé. Do any of the people in the Parti National or anybody else here you work with know you are with the SDS?"

"No, of course not. They know nothing of that. It is my secret here. "

"Very good. I suggest it stay that way. I will check about the money. *Au revoir, M. Dubé.*"

"*Au revoir, M. Serge.* By the way, do you have a last name?"

"Of course, but you do not need it. It is best that way. Goodbye."

At one of their meetings, Dubé asked Serge a question. Something he could not overlook. "Were you guys involved with the FLQ? Back in '70, anytime since?

"No, we have not been involved with the FLQ. I can perhaps sympathize with some of what they said in their manifestos, but operations and kidnappings of the sort of October 1970 are not part of our activities, and never were." He was only being partly truthful. The KGB along with Cuban agents had had contacts over the years with various elements of what had become the FLQ. And there had been the raid on the farm a few months before.

Earlier that summer, the LaPresse daily newspaper broke the story of a raid of the Royal Canadian Mounted Police on a farm in the Quebec countryside. A barn was burned down along with some motorcycles and pickup trucks, with many people scattering and avoiding capture. It was unclear in the report why the RCMP had targeted the place for a raid that apparently involved ten agents but had produced no arrests. According to the reporter, sources were of the opinion that the RCMP believed the farm was the setting for meetings between rogue elements of the Parti National, the Front de Liberation du Québec and representatives of the Black Panthers and the Weatherman branch of the SDS. The sources also said they believed the KGB was somehow involved.

"The farm that the RCMP raided. What was all over the newspapers. Were you or any of your people involved in that?" asked Dubé.

"No." The Russian was lying. One of his agents, a Russian disguised as a member of the Weathermen, was there, had assisted in the organization of the meeting and had barely escaped the police. "No. Not involved. Pretty clumsy police operation, I gather. No one was brought in. Very strange."

The Russian, along with his boss in Ottawa, did not want Marc Dubé to be aware they had decided a year earlier to work with the radical side of the Quebec independence movement. Dubé, their key contact with the Parti National now, would object and perhaps end his cooperation. They could not afford that. In addition, they learned from a source in Ottawa that the RCMP believed one of the participants they observed leaving the scene was a Russian attached to the embassy and that they had a picture of him. The agent who was at the farm had to be disengaged. He was already back in Moscow.

At that time, Marc was not certain Serge was a KGB agent. It would be confirmed to him soon enough. The cover of the SDS and the Union des Étudiants de France could not last long. It didn't add up. By the end of 1974, Marc realized he was working with Soviet intelligence. He also realized that Carl Unger was a Russian and that he had been recruited not by the SDS but by the KGB. And he concluded that Serge was also Russian. Perfect impersonations. Very clever. So what, he thought. They can help us.

It will be worth it. I tell them what is going on in Quebec, they tell me useful things about what is going on in Ottawa and elsewhere that is relevant. And the money. So useful. Just need to be careful. Nobody knows.

"You are not French, are you? You are Russian. Let's be honest about it." The two were at one of their meetings two weeks later on a park bench on a secluded stretch of the Lachine Canal.

"Yes, I am Russian, but I am also French. My mother is French. That is all I will say. Let's move on. We have similar objectives and we can work with each other. I have something else I want to talk to you about."

"Alright. So at least now I know I'm dealing with the KGB and not something else. I have suspected that for a while," responded Marc.

"OK. Fair enough. Now, what I wanted to discuss with you.....The colleges and universities here have many Marxist-Lenin sympathizers. It is clear. You teach in a faculty that would probably have a few of them right under your nose." The Russian paused a second or two, then continued, looking intently at Dubé. "Can we work on making these movements more effective? Can we work on that?"

"What do you have in my mind? I have similar sympathies myself, but I am constrained."

"Alright, constrained. But I need to identify leaders in the Marxist movement and organize to influence them, support their activities, if you like, without it coming back to me and the people I work with. As a first step, could you identify some of the students in your college who could become collaborators?"

"I could. What would be your plan for them?"

"Feed them with materiel from movements elsewhere. Enlist a few of the leaders to organize demonstrations. We have experience with this. The SDS, the Weathermen and the Black Panthers are examples of it. That should be no surprise to you."

"Alright. I need to think about it. The Marxists can be disruptive but have not had much success. You must be aware of the Groupe Marxiste Révolutionnaire, on our university campuses. Started a few years ago. They are active, but not efficient. They write and publish manifestos but are otherwise ineffective in arousing anyone to disrupt anything. They organize class boycotts, demonstrate against capitalist speakers at university forums, and are not trusted by the Parti National leadership. The PN people stay away from the most radical elements."

"We would like to get inside that group. Can you help with that?"

"I could, but I can't be identified as a collaborator of Marxist groups. It would jeopardize my influence in the Party. I could identify some people at the college who are involved and pass you the names. That's the best I can do. I must say, though, that there is another group of Marxists that is somewhat organized. It comes out of the labor movement. It is called the Groupe Socialiste des Travailleurs du Québec."

"I have heard of it but am not acquainted with anyone involved. When was it formed?"

"A couple of years ago. A cousin of mine could be part of it. It is something he would be sympathetic to." Dubé thought of his mother's side of the family that was so anti-business.

"A cousin. What does he do?"

"Works in an east-end factory that turns out axles and wheel assemblies for locomotives. Has been an angry union man for years, just like his father, who is now disabled from a job accident years ago. I could try to find out if he would be interested, but I won't. It would expose me. I cannot afford that, and you can't either. I will give you his name and how you can reach him. You must avoid any possible link back to me."

"Agreed. But why does the PN so publicly shun these groups to the extent that it appears? The party is as much socialist as independence driven."

"Serge, the PN wants to win elections; take power democratically. It needs to attract the mainstream. It may be social-democratic in its policy orientations, but it will never accept being labeled publicly as socialist. It will avoid that. Sympathizing with Marxist-Leninists will not move the party towards being elected. You must always keep this in mind. The leader is not a socialist. He is not driven by ideology. He is a pragmatist who simply wants a better deal for Quebec with the rest of Canada. Drives us mad. But that's the way he is, and we have to work with that."

Marc Dubé continued to supply Serge information on Quebec political matters and politicians and what he managed to learn of the activities of large Canadian companies. The KGB agent, in turn, every month put an envelope with ten one hundred-dollar bills in a battered tin box under the stairs behind Dubé's walk-up apartment. Dubé gave Serge the names of the leadership of his college's Marxist-Leninist sympathizers. Ever since the late 1960's, demonstrations, university sit-ins, worker protests and labor conflicts across Quebec had Marxist-Leninist twists to them. The movement was active. Support was coming from somewhere, and it was not just from the labor movement.

The Royal Canadian Mounted Police were not ignorant of all of this. The Mounties were aware there was Russian activity in the movement and had infiltrated it but never succeeded in identifying the links involved.

The organizer for the Parti National had invited Marc to meet him at the Bistro St. Denis. It was late March 1975. At that time, the café was a popular meeting place of Quebec intellectuals not far from the college where Dubé taught.

"Marc, we want you come work with us. We need your brains."

"What do you mean? Work for the Party?"

"Yes, for the Party."

"To do what? I am not a political organizer. I am a college professor. What could I possibly do to be productive for the party?" Marc replied.

"You have a disciplined mind, mon ami. Our leader needs help on our *projet de société*. He is sometimes all over the place. He is a former journalist and works on twenty ideas at once. He needs, we need, discipline in our thinking and in our actions. We lost badly in the last election. There is anger in the party, a lot of people are upset. Things must change. We need to be more professional, more focused. Be far more ready next time. There will be another election before long. The Liberal Premier may have won the last election, but he is not popular. We could win next time, but we need to be better organized."

"You are sure about me doing this? I write about the need for Quebec as a country. I give a historical perspective to it to students. I am careful about it. Now you want me to operate for it from the inside."

"Yes. It is time for you to engage yourself in this. The academic view is fine, but action is more important. We need strategy, organization and discipline and we need to better explain the advantages of independence to the people."

The man continued. "Right now, we are little more than a nationalist rump headed by a popular leader who is not elected and spends his time writing articles for newspapers. We have a bunch of dreamers at party headquarters. We are going nowhere. We must do something else. Are you with us, Marc?"

Behind his professed reluctance, Marc Dubé was incredulous at his good fortune. He was being asked to be one of the key thinkers and strategists behind the project of sovereignty for Quebec. This was almost too good to be true. He hid his enthusiasm from the man in front of him. The implications of this would be many. Although working for the Russians as part of the new job he was being offered was not top of mind, it was there. It was part of the mix. The whole independence thing could be leveraged by his Russian connection. They learned of stuff happening in Ottawa that he could never know. He needed to speak with Serge.

"Let me think about it. We should speak in a couple of days. I will call you," said Marc. As he walked away from that meeting, he thought of what this would mean. He was conflicted, but also excited. He would be on the inside. But do I need the Russians?

"Very good, Marc. This is excellent." Pavel Tedorenko immediately realized the importance of what he was being told. Marc Dubé was to be on the inside of the core of the Parti National, an advisor on strategy, which meant strategy for reaching independence. "You should accept it. It helps you fulfill your plan, your dream, my friend. You have come a long way already. This will be very good for our relationship, as well. And you will know so much. It really ties us together." Marc Dubé immediately recognized the implication. He had come to the meeting to tell the Frenchman that he was not going to go any further. But he couldn't do it. The man was letting him know that he could not. He buckled.

"I will, Serge, however, I need assurances from you," replied Marc.

"What? You mean the money? It will continue, of course."

"No. More than that. I will need an augmentation as they say here. More risk involved….very much higher profile. But I will need more. For me to continue, I will need more than just the money. You will have to give me information on what Ottawa is doing. What they are doing concerning Quebec. Whatever you have. You are of course organized for that. Policies about economic development and relations with the provinces, support for cultural activities, but mostly about their plans for dealing with us, with Quebec. The prime minister's push for a new constitution. These things are the most important for us. We have people looking into these things of course, but I am sure you do as well. You have your sources in Ottawa. We have spoken about that. With that, we will continue. I will work with you." Dubé paused a moment and looked at his contact. *If I am going to do this, I need to know who these guys are.* "Listen, Serge, you are not French. We have spoken about this. I understand your motives in supporting me. You are Russian and it is the KGB who is paying me. So let us not kid ourselves or play the charade any more. You want the breakup of Canada. So do I. We have a complementarity of objectives. I need your intelligence from Ottawa. Can we work with that principle?"

"Of course. A two-way street, M. Dubé. I trust you will keep us informed of your own strategies for Quebec. Yes?"

"Yes, but about the money. We need to agree on that."

"How much do you want now? I must ask my superiors about it," replied the Russian.

"Two thousand dollars a month. It is what I need to continue to work with you. The risk is much greater now. "

"I will ask. I will see what they say," replied Serge. The Russian spy rose from the bench, threw his long scarf around his neck and walked away without saying a word.

What have I done? thought Marc as he walked away. Do I really need to do this?

The meeting of the two KGB agents was at the secret apartment used for special meetings. It was outside the surveillance net of the Canadian police. Meetings of this sort were out of the question at the Embassy. The Royal Canadian Mounted Police owned the large house across the street, had cameras trained on all entrances to the Embassy, and filmed all comings and goings. To counter this inconvenience, the Soviet Embassy had a half-dozen apartments in Ottawa leased under false names, using them for special encounters under tight security and cover.

"He is hesitant. I think he came to the meeting to tell me he was not going to continue. I implied that would be difficult for him to do that. He is conflicted, and we will have to be careful. But we have never had someone inside that party. Radicals, revolutionaries, dreamers who we could never trust or control. He is different. We need to make it easy for him to work with us - give him what he wants, the money and the information from Ottawa. Let's not bully him. He is our jewel in Quebec. His party will come back. They will take power someday. Their leader is loved, and trusted."

"Excellent work, Pavel Andreivitch. We now have a mole inside the inner sanctum of the independence movement. Tell your friend he will receive what he requests. This is very good. Very promising for our plan." The cultural attaché of the Soviet Union in Canada raised his glass for a toast. Serge, without his wig of long brown hair, moustache and baggy clothes, raised his glass of vodka. *"Boo-deem zda-ro-vye!* To our health."

"We believe there is a KGB mole inside the Parti National. We have picked up something on this through a source in the Middle East." The head of the CIA for Canada, attached to the U.S. Embassy, was meeting with his contact, Frank Russo, responsible for counterintelligence at the Royal Canadian Mounted Police.

"Mole in the Parti National. Why am I not surprised? Best way for them to upset things. Fortunately, the Parti National is not very successful these days. They lost badly in the last election. They are a long way from being in government, but they are stirring things up. Their leader has managed to control the radicals so far, but I'm not sure he can continue. We should have known they have somebody involved with the Russians. Do you guys know who it could be?" Russo managed to hide his irritation at learning something from the CIA that the RCMP should have been aware of.

"Not really. The word was it was somebody in the party. That could be a lot of people. But a few years ago, we heard the SDS wanted to stir things up here."

"I remember we looked into that. Your predecessor here was pretty sure of it."

"The SDS turned radical in '69 if not before, and works with the Black Panthers, people in France, Germany and Italy. Makes sense they would try to contact radicals here."

"Jim, the FLQ is pretty dead. Pageau doesn't tolerate anybody with that crowd being anywhere near the inner circle of the party. A lot of internal friction about that. But we will look into it. Thanks."

The botched raid on the farm in the summer of '74 had become a *cause célèbre* in Quebec. It led to the withdrawal of authority for security intelligence from the RCMP. The Mounties had overstepped, and it was determined later they had conducted an illegal operation. That action, as well as other dubious ones on their part, led the government of the day to order a public inquiry into their activities. Within a few years, all security intelligence operations had been taken from the RCMP and transferred to a new entity, the Canadian Security Intelligence Service, or CSIS, in 1984. But it was never determined that the Soviet KGB had had anything to do with the meeting at the farm.

6

Toronto, August 1975

"Welcome to the Herald, Andrew."

"Glad to be here, sir. Thank you for the opportunity," answered Andrew Brown as he was introduced to the managing editor of The Toronto Herald.

"Your uncle has a high regard for you. I told Jamison that if his nephew made it through four years at Trinity College, he could probably write." Gordon McNeil had little option but to accept Andrew Brown into the organization. Jamison Brown all but owned the paper. Nevertheless, he believed there would be little downside to the hiring of this young man, nephew of the owner or not.

"I think I can do that. I look forward to it," replied Andrew.

"Very good, then. You will be working on the City Desk. Your boss, Ed Kline, will be here in a moment. I think you will get along. Here he is, coming down the hall."

The portly crew cut man entered the room. "Ed, this is Andrew Brown. He will be working with you. He is in your hands. Turn him into a journalist."

"Very good, Gord. We'll get Mr. Brown involved in short order." Ed Kline was aware that the young man before him was the nephew of the owner. He would be careful.

"Well, Andrew. Follow me. We will get right into it."

Andrew was sure that in time he would be in charge. It was just a matter of time. Not because anybody else knew it, although he suspected it was his uncle's intent. He would work towards that, gain the confidence of key people, and move up to greater responsibility and influence. He had always had a special relationship with his father's twin brother. Jamison Brown had three children, all girls, and none of them were interested in the newspaper world. Jamison had always planned to get his nephew into the business. The Brown Herald legacy. Andrew would carry it further.

These clumsy Russians. Andrew's London contact had given him a number to call. He called it three weeks after arriving. It was the number for a dry-cleaning shop on Spadina Avenue, in the area of Toronto largely inhabited by immigrants. The man who answered had an Indian accent. This can't be it, he thought. He hung up the phone.

Six weeks later, he received a call at the office. It was a man who said he had some information on a situation of graft in the city's public works department. He asked Andrew to meet him that evening at a boathouse at the west end of The Beaches, a neighborhood in Toronto's east end.

"Mr. Brown, you have avoided us. You were supposed to call the number given to you in London."

Ahah. Here he is. My contact. Nothing to do with Public Works, obviously. "I called that number. Some guy with an Indian or Pakistani accent answered. I thought it was a wrong number. Pakistani dry-cleaning shop? Really."

"It was the right number. You should trust us more. Are you still with us, Mr. Brown? I need to have that from you. If you are not, we end it here. You cannot afford to disclose any of this, but that should be no surprise to you. Are you still with us?"

"I'm still with you. But we must be even more clandestine than I was with you guys back in England. I am part of an influential family. You are aware of that. I work now for the largest circulation daily newspaper in Canada. My motivation for doing this is known. London did and I suppose you do too. If you help me with discrediting the Americans, I will help you with what you want. I ask for no money. I have been clear. It will be a two-way street, but I can't have you or anyone else calling me at the newspaper."

The Russian looked at Andrew. What an arrogant little prick, he thought. "How do you propose we communicate then? We have much inside information on American activities I am sure you would like to have, but what do you propose?"

"I call you. Not at the cleaning shop. Please. Do you have a number where you will be the one answering? Nobody else. If so, I will call you every three or four weeks. I will ask you if you have anything for me. You will ask me I have anything for you. If either answer is yes, we meet. We set up three or four places for the meetings. We choose which one to go to when we speak. Can we do that?"

"Alright. We will do as you wish. As you say, though, it must be a two-way street," replied the Russian who could see that this young man was wiser than his age.

"What is your name by the way?" asked Andrew.

"Call me Robert. What do you want to know about the Americans here that could interest you?" asked the Russian whose real name was Andrei Timlikov.

"OK." responded Andrew. "Big changes have been happening here. There are rumblings in Quebec. The separatist party is gaining ground. The Americans up to something about that? I'm sure they would be, but it may be too early to determine. Would be interesting to have insight about what the Ford administration thinks of this from your sources in Washington. Furthermore, the military wants greater defense cooperation with Canada. Usually means drawing Canada deeper into the American orbit. American designs on Canadian energy. Accelerating. I will have other subjects that would be of interest to me and to Canadian readers in time. As to what you want from me, at our next meeting you will tell me what that is and I will be frank on what I can provide or not."

Arrogant. Presumptuous. Quick-tongued. Smart. Shows little fear. Will be difficult to deal with. Timlikov sent his impressions to Ottawa about Andrew Brown along with a description of what the man was looking to receive. Could very well be worth the trouble, thought the KGB coordinator in Ottawa. Insider at the Toronto Herald. He could be a productive mouthpiece for us. We will go along with what he wants, but we will have to find a way to lock him in. Should be easy enough....

Trying to blackmail me. What do they have? That I write on Canadian-American affairs with an anti-American bias. So what. They provide me with inside stuff from their activities in Washington, that I use to serve their interests as well as mine. Now they are asking me for inside stuff about the Canadian government. To compromise me. I do not have anything secret to give. I do not have access to any. I don't betray anyone. They have nothing on me. All we have is a common objective - the weakening of the Canadian-American relationship and particularly for me the American control of Canada. They give me stuff. I use it. What have I betrayed? Canada? No. I am actually doing Canada a service.

If they pull the trigger on their threat, I will expose their stuff in Washington. They can stop feeding me, but what will that do? Just stop the flow of stuff for me to use, which is not in their interest. They can expose me to the Americans as using inside information. I will merely expose them as the conduit. I am not the spy who got the information. In any case, I don't use any of the military stuff they want to give me. I tell them to keep it. That would cause trouble. The political and economic stuff I can use. It is not in their interest to stop this arrangement. And... if they go too far, they know I can expose some of their people back in England. Professor Ed is probably a Soviet agent. Quid pro quo.

Why am I keeping this? Somebody finds it, it's trouble...but they won't. Need to be able to keep track.

Andrew closed the notebook, put it back in the drawer and withdrew the key.

The KGB agents met at their usual place.

"We can't control him. He does what he wants."

"He serves our interests. The newspaper is the most influential in Canada. Stop trying to blackmail him. Just keep feeding him, but be careful. Whatever you give him must not expose our operation in Washington."

"We could threaten to expose him as a Marxist. It would not look good for him with his family."

"What good would that do? It would just take him out of an influential position at the newspaper. We need to have him where he is. In any case, he has never written anything that can be said to be Marxist. He was a sympathizer at Cambridge, but I doubt if he really is one. Spoke out against America in lectures. So what? Young people at university do that everywhere, then go out into the world and their views change. Let's keep on. The arrangement is not ideal, but it serves us. It serves our plan. Maybe we can use him the way we are using our agents in Cuba.

"Look what we did with Trudel and Castro. Something that will certainly cause trouble between Washington and Ottawa. Trudel's in Cuba. Bit of a love affair between he and Fidel, just as we wanted, but beyond expectations. Numerous meetings between the two. They have gone scuba diving together, spent time in a beach hacienda, have given rising speeches together. Appears the Canadian has even softened his views on Cuban intervention in Angola. The work we did with Fidel's people on preparing for Trudel's visit has paid off. The information from Ottawa on his ideas, his likes, dislikes, tastes in food, music and literature has provided Castro with strings for influencing the man. And, the information we provided to Trudel's people about Cuba and it's noble activities and intentions through our contacts has paid off as well. Our people in Washington say the Americans are quite upset and are saying this will put back several initiatives on easing trade between the countries. The Canadian opposition leader believes Trudel is deliberately weakening the Canadian-American alliance through his dalliance with Castro. Our strategy is working. Tell our people in Havana they have done excellent work. Let's stay the course with Brown here."

7

April 1976, Havana, Cuba

The ship from Riga was docked and unloading had begun. Farm machinery from East Germany, plastic piping for irrigation and wastewater treatment from Latvia. Cuba depended upon the Soviet Union for just about everything that was manufactured. Nathan observed the operation from a railing on the top deck, while he waited for the contact who would introduce him to Havana and bring him to the training camp.

Training, he thought. Revolutionizing. The guy in Moscow said three years. A long time. Trust them? No. Learn something? Surely. Spy for them? Not really interested. Learn how to organize disruption with the people back home? Yes. That's something else. Why I'm doing iti. Bring it on...

"El companero Cannon (the name he would have in Cuba – there was to be no reference to a Hightower - the CIA operated in Cuba. Nathan Hightower had disappeared from the streets of Saskatchewan and the Russians did not want to make it easy for him to be traced to them or to Cuba) – you will start off with language training, in Spanish, of course. You will be here for three years at a minimum, so you must learn the language. You will also be working with our revolutionary forces... as required. In the meantime, you will receive military training – weapons, tactics, leadership. We start tomorrow." El companero (comrade) Felipe, who was speaking, would be Nathan's control during his indoctrination in terrorist technique and organization.

Companero Cannon was in a little town down the coast from the capital. There was no one else in his class. Just the instructor and him. He was lodged in a hacienda-style house that had seen better days along with four other non-Cubans, one of whom was probably from somewhere in South America. Big, burly man who looked to be in his early thirties by the name of Roberto. They had exchanged pleasantries at dinner a couple of times. On this evening with the sun setting behind the ridge of mountains after dinner, no one else, including the Cubans who were tasked with tracking and reporting on whatever the residents did, was around. Just the burly Roberto and him. *Annoying*, thought Nathan about the usual surveillance. *Not sure I can put up with this stuff.*

"Where are you from, senor Roberto?" asked the Canadian.

"You are using the wrong name. Companero is what we should be using. You have my real name, though," replied the Chilean, suddenly jovial. "Valparaiso Chile, by way of Quito, Ecuador. And you? American Indian....yes....no?"

"Indian, yes. American, no. I am a Canadian Cree."

"Why are you here? Not just to learn Spanish, I am sure."

"World revolution, my friend. That's why we are all here, is it not?" said Nathan in a teasing, cynical tone.

"Ah, yes. But I must tell you that I have already lived what they talk about here. But back in Chile we did our revolution another way."

"What do you mean?"

"The democratic way. We got our man elected. Salvador Allende. Then the generals decided to end it. Our beautiful revolution. By the people for the people. It was the right way, the bloodless way. They say here it cannot work. They may be right."

"What happened? I don't know anything about your revolution. When did it happen?"

"Began in 1970 when Allende, a gentle, intelligent man who cared for his people, was elected President. Then, in 1973, he was assassinated, and the military took over. Killed many people. I had to leave. I was working in the President's office, involved in bringing in and applying new methods of management. Cybernetics, operations research, all about improving the effectiveness of government services for the people. It was my specialty."

"Where did you go? It's now 1976."

"Quito, Ecuador. Found a job with the national petroleum corporation. Said I was Argentine. Told them what I knew about getting large organizations to work better. That I had worked with a British managerial guru and cybernetician who worked on reorganizations of state-run enterprises in Argentina. I had a forged Argentine passport. Former associates of Allende and the socialist government in my country were viewed with suspicion everywhere in South America, so I had to change my identity."

"Humm....managerial science in the service of revolution. Doesn't sound like the model they talk about here," said Nathan.

"No. It is not their way, it seems."

"So, what brought you here? Sounds like you had a good set-up in Ecuador."

"They found out about me. I suspect someone at the Chilean Embassy, somebody loyal to the junta, the Pinochet people, recognized me somewhere in Quito, found out where I worked and betrayed my identity to the company. I was told by a colleague to disappear. Found my way here through Colombia and Nicaragua. I have been here for five months."

"What's next for you?" asked Nathan.

"Going back to somewhere in South America. There is work to be done. The time is ripe. Military regimes everywhere. Argentina, for one. Young people disappearing everywhere. Has to change....."

"Take up arms?"

"Yes, probably, but in the meantime, they may have me work on organization, work with the East Germans here, organize revolutionary activities in Latin America. There is the stuff in Angola. I may end up there, with a gun or not. What do they propose for you?"

"Upset the order of things back where I come from. We'll see." Nathan had the thought he had maybe gone too far. But he was cognizant he had to be careful about expressing any lack of resolve to anyone here. Anyone. Oversight was everywhere. "By the way, Roberto, will we keep these discussions to ourselves? Can we trust each other?"

"Yes, you can trust me, and I will trust you."

Six months later, Nathan Hightower, Comrade Cannon, was in Angola, part of the 25,000 Cuban troops supporting the People's

Movement for the Liberation of Angola or MPLA, in its fight in the Angolan civil war against forces backed by South Africa and the United States. So was Roberto, and the two managed, when they had the opportunity to meet, to have long discussions on managing popular dissent, mobilizing for action and getting people to act. Nathan was in the field with the troops. Roberto was embedded within the MPLA, helping the Angolans organize the government of the territories they held. The two managed, nevertheless, to spend time together whenever they could.

Nathan spent a year there, in the bush and the jungle, in firefights, in hand to hand combat. He saw men die, villages pillaged, women and children killed by both sides. The Cubans tried to minimize that, but it was a nasty and brutal war by any measure. Much of what Nathan saw turned his stomach, but by the end of his time there, he had become a well-versed observer of actions that he would be able to use upon his return to Canada.

8

Montreal, March 1976

"M. Dubé, I need you. Close by my side." Adrien Pageau, leader and founder of the Parti National, had invited Marc Dubé to his office and had a proposition for him. "I want you to be my principal advisor on strategy vis-a-vis the rest of Canada, meaning Ottawa, before and during the election campaign that is surely coming. We will have it within a year, maybe sooner. We must prepare. You understand all this. You teach it and have done so for years. Your views are well respected."

"I am honored by this, sir. Truly honored. Before I say yes, which I can tell you I most probably will, you must tell me some things. It is important for how we go forward," said Dubé. He had been told this was coming.

"And what could that be?"

"Timing, Monsieur. Your view on timing of the election. It has only been two and a half years. What do you believe to be the intention of the current government?"

"M. Barbeau could surprise us at any time. He is having troubles with the unions, language, all the jobs he promised are not there. He is looking for a fight he thinks he can win. I know him." The man paused, took a puff on his cigarette, then continued. "I need you with me here, M. Dubé. The election will come. The precise timing is not important. The job will be full time, you must realize. You will have to take a leave of absence from your teaching, from the college. Can I count on you? Constitutional advisor to the leader. What do you say to that?"

"I accept. I am honored, sir." Marc was already the key advisor to the party on constitutional affairs to begin with. It was just that the leader did not know it. He thought HE was the expert on this. The shoe would now be on the other foot, although he was aware that managing this man in the constitutional file with the future of Quebec independence at stake would be a chore. But everything would be up front for him now in these matters. No more behind the scenes. He would work directly with the man who dominated everything in the Parti National.

"Très bien. We have much preparation to do. My old friends Barbeau and Trudel have much up their sleeves. But I intend to make this coming election about pride in being Quebecers. And about confidence that we can run our own country. We have many competent people who will be running for us. An excellent team. We will do it."

"I look forward to it, Monsieur. I will advise the college, however, I must continue to the end of term in April. I could not leave the college with them having to hire a replacement for six weeks. I will be with you starting May 1. In the meantime, I will not be far. Is that acceptable?"

"Yes, that will be fine. I will tell the other key people, but not the public yet, although these jobs are not normally announced. In any case, nothing for the journalists on or off the record before May 1," said the leader of the party that would win the Quebec election eight months later and throw Canada into crisis for the following four years and more. The Soviet Union had their mole at centre-stage of the machinations to disrupt the future of Canada.

9

Ottawa, April 1979

"You say you have a proposition for me? What are you talking about? Who are you?" Adela Cerny felt it immediately. Fear. The man had an accent. She had never seen him before. He had approached her as she was finishing her run on the pathway next to the Rideau Canal.

"Can we talk? Somewhere private. I will explain," replied the tall fit man.

"Right here. What is this about?" The young woman looked around. "There is no one close by. Tell me what this is about. Right here. I will not go anywhere with you."

"Very well. Your father. He is in danger. I can tell you more, but it cannot be here. You will have to agree to meet me somewhere to learn what this is about. If you refuse, something may happen to your father."

"My father? Who are you?"

"Miss Cerny, I am telling you. Your father is in danger. If we can talk, I will explain. We can discuss as well how the danger can be avoided. As I said, if you refuse, things could go badly. And if you speak to anyone about this, things will very much go badly. So, can we meet somewhere private?"

"Yes, alright then." Adela at that moment was fearful for her own safety. "You scare me, whoever you are."

"You have nothing to fear concerning your own safety, Miss. But you must not tell anyone about this. This is about the safety of your father. I propose the pathway beneath the Rockcliffe Parkway, the Boat Club clubhouse on the river down from the pathway. There are stairs to get to the boathouse. 7 AM Sunday morning. Many people run there but no one goes down to the boathouse at this time of year. You wear your running gear. I will be wearing mine. I will see you there, Miss Cerny?"

"OK. I don't like this, but I will be there," said Adela.

Adela Cerny stood there on the pathway along the canal, stupefied, fearful as she contemplated what the encounter she just had could be about. She had to return to the office – the noon break she used every day for a run was almost up - but was immobilized. What was it? Daddy's business interests? Stuff with the Czech community? The time of the war? she asked herself.

Alexandr Cerny had escaped. He thought himself lucky. He had succeeded in bringing his family across the Czech-German border, avoiding the patrols and the secret police. He took the family to Munich, then travelled to the French coast to find passage on a freighter to Canada, landing in Quebec City in July of 1950. Upon arriving, he told immigration authorities he wished to go with his young family to Toronto and travelled there by train, with all of fifty American dollars in his pocket. Within a few days, while being housed in a hostel for immigrants, he found work in a bottle factory on Richmond Street. His children were seven, four and one year old with his little girl Adela being the youngest.

Cerny was born in 1919 in the Sudetenland, the German-speaking part of Czechoslovakia that was annexed to the Third Reich by Hitler in 1938 and occupied during the war. As an educated Czech amid ethnic Germans who sought out all forms of Czech opposition to the Nazi regime, the outspoken young man was an easy target. He was caught and imprisoned in 1943 and nearly died in captivity

Before being rounded up, he became a committed socialist and joined the underground Socialist Party of Czechoslovakia. At war's end, Cerny was recruited by a group of men working to democratically defeat the postwar government that had little credibility among the common Czech people. The intent of the group was to create a socialist state for the benefit of all Czechs. In reality, as Alexandr Cerny and many others were to learn in time, the true objective of the group was to institute, in close cooperation with the occupying Russians, a Communist state along the lines of the Soviet Union.

In 1950, as he built his new life in Canada, Cerny had a secret that he had to avoid becoming known at all costs. He had been an unwitting accomplice in 1948 in the murder of one of Czechoslovakia's national heroes. Jan Masaryk was the country's foreign minister at the time and the son of Tomas Masaryk, the founder of modern Czechoslovakia in 1919. In 1948, Cerny was an aide to Masaryk. One day he had called his boss to an evening meeting at the Cernin Palace, which housed the Foreign Ministry, upon the request of an official in the Prime Minister's office. The official was unknown to Cerny, but had announced his credentials in convincing fashion. Waiting for Masaryk, however, who had insisted on going alone to the meeting, were not the people who had been announced in the request to Cerny, but four agents of Soviet army intelligence. The men overpowered the minister upon his arrival, interrogated him, then threw him out the window on to the plaza five floors below. Jan Masaryk's murder, the last of a long line of political defenestrations in the history of the Czech people, was made to appear as a suicide. However, there were people who knew that Alexandr Cerny had been involved in the arrangement of the meeting that night. No one believed Masaryk had committed suicide. No one believed he had declined to have an aide with him. Cerny was fingered. He had to disappear. Within days of Masaryk's death, he had succeeded in taking his family into hiding in a small hamlet in Western Bohemia under an assumed name. He soon found work on a farm. With so many displacements after the war, hardly anyone cared if there were new people around, as long as they were Czech. No one asked questions. Everybody had their own story, their own secrets from the war. But Alexandr Cerny knew he had to move on and leave the country. Someone would eventually find out who he was. He waited for the right moment.

By 1952, Cerny had managed to save enough money to open a small Bohemian restaurant on Toronto's Spadina Avenue, tending to the restaurant in the evenings while working at the bottle factory during the day. Within a few years the restaurant was sufficiently prosperous that he could quit the factory job and devote all his time to the business. Twenty years later, Cerny had a small chain of three restaurants in the Toronto area as well as a food supply business. He had remade his life and believed the menace related to the Masaryk affair behind him. No one had ever contacted him about it in Canada. For him, it was another part of his life, long since passed. By 1979, his children, very much Canadian by that time, were 36, 33 and 30 years old. The oldest of the boys was a lawyer with a large Toronto firm and on his way to a promising legal career. His second son, destined to take over the family business eventually, ran one of the Cerny restaurants. His daughter Adela had graduated from Queen's University and was working for the Government of Canada's Department of Secretary of State. He was proud she had become an important person, part of the group responsible for the management of intergovernmental affairs, the unit of government that oversaw relations with the provinces, including constitutional affairs.

Adela's time in Ottawa was part of the highly visible and controversial period of Canada's public life of the 1970's, with considerable attention given to constitutional affairs and relations with the provinces. The government was focused on developing a new constitution for Canada, one that would be independent of the act of the British parliament that had governed Canada since 1867. It was a period of discord between Ottawa and Quebec. English-speaking Canada was increasingly unsympathetic to Quebec's demands for special considerations related to its language, culture and institutions. The province had erupted in the '60's with a cultural and political impetus for change and affirmation as a people. It pressured Ottawa for a new deal to recognize Quebec's differences and special needs for language and cultural protection. Many circles demanded outright sovereignty. Adela Cerny worked for the department of the Government of Canada that was tasked for dealing with these matters. She was in the thick of it.

Adela was at the rendezvous. "Come with me. To the deck down there. Have no fear. I'm not here to harm you."

"What is this about, whoever you are?" Adela asked abruptly as she reached the deck at the bottom of the stairs.

"Your father was involved in the murder of the foreign minister of Czechoslovakia in Prague in 1948."

"What? My father? Murder?" Adela was incredulous. And scared. The tension she had been feeling the past four days was deepening.

"Unfortunately, yes. Jan Masaryk was apparently thrown out the window of his office in the middle of the night. It was never determined who did it, but your father, who worked for him, arranged the meeting where the minister met his killers and his fate. Your father was not there. No one was there, apparently, other than Masaryk and his assassins. Many people believed your father had set it up. He had joined the Socialist party during the war and was associated with the men who took the country to a full Marxist state later in 1948. Your father fled Prague. He went into hiding, then came to Canada a short time later. It would be very damaging to him if the details of his involvement with the death of Jan Masaryk, however speculative, were exposed and that he was living in Canada and precisely where. The émigré Czech community in London and elsewhere in Europe would most surely appreciate learning of this. Who knows what they would do. We are aware of all this and prepared to expose the facts of Masaryk's demise and your father's involvement.......or, we will say nothing to anyone if you cooperate with us."

"Who are you? Who do you work for?" asked a stunned Adela Cerny.

"I won't tell you who I am, but I can say I work for the Czech secret service." The man was really an agent of the Soviet KGB but the young lady in front of him did not have to know that. If we learn of you speaking to anyone about this, we will expose your father. You can avoid all that by cooperating."

"What do you mean by cooperating? What is it you want from me?" asked Adela.

"We want information on the workings of your government. You are Czech by birth. You will be doing service to the country of your birth."

"You mean spy, I gather. What? How?" asked an alarmed Adela Cerny. *This can't be. They can't be asking me to do this.*

"You are involved in government negotiations and many other affairs here affecting national unity that we are interested in. In the sensitive dealings with all the provinces about a new constitution for the country. You also accompany your minister to cabinet briefings. You review all the cabinet documents your minister is provided with. He is a member of what you people call P&P - the Priorities and Planning Committee of Cabinet - where everything of importance is apparently debated and decided. You are the principal regular contact at your department for supplying the Minister's office with whatever information they need to have. There are things we would like to know."

"Oh, my God." Adela put her face in her hands. She slowly raised her head and looked at the man. "You can't ask me to do this. I won't. Get away. Leave me alone. I won't do it."

"I'm sorry, then. We will have to carry out the plan about your father. Only you can stop it," replied the Russian. "This is how our world operates." He moved to regain the steps up the stairs to the path.

"Wait…. This is difficult for me. You can't really be asking me to do this. You can't."

"Yes, I can. You think about it. We meet here tomorrow morning, same time, or we expose your father. His life will be in danger once we do. I hope you realize that." The man walked up the stairs and was gone.

"What's wrong, Adela? You're not here. Where are you?" Brian Carlson was Adela's boyfriend. They had known each other since Queen's, hooked up later in Ottawa, became lovers and decided to live together.

"Stuff at work. Can't talk about it. As usual," replied Adela as she finished the dishes after a silent dinner.

"Work? It's Sunday. You have been a bit silent the past few days, but nothing like today. Never seen you this way. You look a mess, baby."

"It's work, Brian. Things happening. I can't talk about it. Please don't press."

The next morning, she was on the path, waiting.

"I can't do this. You need to find somebody else."

"There is nobody else, Miss Cerny."

"What do you want from me? Tell me. Specifically. Information? Files? One time? Two times? Three times? Forever, damn you!!? I can't do this!"

"Calm down. Should you decide to cooperate, I will inform you regularly of what we are looking for. You will tell me if you can provide it. If you cannot because you have no access to it, you will tell me. I will be reasonable. We don't want you detected. I can tell you, however, that what we will be asking you for will not lead to the loss of life for anyone. Does that soften your resentment at this?" asked the Russian.

"Not really. You have me blackmailed. This is terrible."

"OK, but do you accept to cooperate with us? Yes or no?"

Adela needed to go to Toronto. See her father. Find out if it was true. "I will have to think about it some more. What you are asking me to do it very difficult. I need a few days."

"No few days, Miss Cerny. It is now. You agree to work with us or we expose your father. What will it be?"

Adela hesitated. She was trapped and was seeing no way out. She needed time, advice, but from whom? Who could she go to?

"Miss Cerny, what will it be?" pressed the Russian.

"You are leaving me no choice, damn you."

"Then it is yes. Yes, Miss Cerny?"

"No, not yet." Adela's mind was racing. She had to speak with someone, but who.

"We will have to expose your father. We will do it. I am sorry. It does not have to be this way. I will give you until Sunday. After that, you will have to live with the consequences if you refuse. See you at the boathouse Sunday morning 7 AM." He turned and walked away.

10

September 1981, Winnipeg, Manitoba

The KGB had objectives for Nathan and he had his own. His were revenge and a better life for his people. Theirs were disruption and the weakening of Canada. He knew their explanation about better lives for natives was bogus, but recognized the value of their support.

There was to be regular contact, but Nathan was given free rein to act according to opportunities as they arose. Activity was to start when he got back to Canada, got a job, made some connections, and inserted himself into the circles of people relevant to the execution of the plan.

By the end of July of 1981, Nathan had found a job, assisted by a fake resumé, as a substitute teacher in the high school of a small town four hundred kilometers north of Winnipeg. He was now Nathan Cromwell, equipped with a Bachelor of Arts degree from Grand Valley State College in Arizona. There actually had been a real Nathan Cromwell at Grand Valley State, but who had died six years before in Australia, leaving little trace of anything other than his attendance and graduation from the college. The real Nathan Cromwell had dual citizenship - American and Canadian. His father had been born in Canada as an Ojibway and his mother was Navajo from Arizona. Both were deceased and there were no other siblings. The Canadian citizenship of the real Nathan

Cromwell allowed him to live and work in Canada, but he never did. His imposter would be able to do that, however. The papers were in order and there was little trace of the real Cromwell and his death in Australia. The KGB was resourceful.

Nathan got the teaching job based on his own capabilities. He was smart, well read, conversant and organized in his thoughts when interviewed, and had an undergraduate degree to show. He came across as a smart guy. It was not easy to find part-time teachers in remote areas, so he was hired. He would teach History and English literature to 2nd and 3rd year high school students. The subjects were right up his alley with all the reading he had done.

He had used his time in Cuba productively. The Russians and Cubans took him through the same program they used to train Bolivians, Nicaraguans, Venezuelans, Angolans, South Africans and others who they recruited and brought to Cuba for indoctrination. Despite all the attention spent on what the Russians wanted him to spend his time on, Nathan managed to read whatever he could get his hands on. English or Spanish. Didn't make any difference in the end. All the reading he had done in his teenage years had made him a well-read person to begin with. He knew a lot about history and civilization, both his own and others. He knew something about organization as well. He had learned a lot from Roberto, the Chilean.

Nathan would not remain a substitute teacher for very long, however. It would be a means to an end, a step along the way to allow the Cuba-trained revolutionary to scout the possibilities for what he had the intention of doing.

An opportunity to set the stage would soon present itself. He crossed paths by chance with someone who would turn out to be a facilitator, albeit an unwitting one. It was at a fundraiser for the local member of the Manitoba Legislature. One of the member's colleagues from the Legislature was there. Nathan and he struck up a conversation. The member in question said in passing that he was looking for an assistant who could help with connecting with the natives in his constituency who were living off-reserve. Nathan mentioned he could be interested in doing that. Substitute teaching was OK, but he was looking for something more substantive. Within a few minutes, Nathan was offered the job and he readily accepted. He would move to the member's constituency and would start four weeks from then, allowing him to give notice to the high school to find a replacement.

Nathan Hightower, now Cromwell, was completely under the radar of the RCMP and the CIA and would remain that way for a long time. The CIA had knowledge of a Saskatchewan Indian recruited to Cuba years before, but they had never learned his identity and over time the faint, unsubstantiated trail had gone cold.

The job was the ideal one for Nathan to begin executing his plan for change and disruption. He had his own revenge to act on. Payback for the loss of his heritage, his family, his lost youth. But that was not all of it. Things had to change for his people. It could not go on. Destitution, drunkenness, family violence, vast numbers of unemployed and angry young people, elders often corrupt and complicit. Somebody had to shake the system. He accepted the assistance of the Russians, who were glad to see him working in politics. It was a means to an end. But he needed to get it going. Organization, organization, organization. Roberto, old boy, your theories will be put to use.

He worked hard to ingratiate himself with the local native leaders who appreciated his pragmatic approach to problems and his way with people. He was a native himself, which the local leaders could readily see and appreciate. He became a friend as well as a trusted ally of the member of the legislature who had hired him. In the fall of 1983, a year and a half after joining the member's team, Nathan's boss was asked to join the provincial cabinet. Nathan found himself in Winnipeg as Policy Advisor to the Minister of Labor of Manitoba. His job was to develop lines of communications and working relationships with the off-reserve aboriginal communities of the Province. Those communities formed a growing portion of the population and the government was intent on finding ways for them to become part of the active workforce more easily. Get them off the streets and into jobs, something that Nathan knew a lot about, but never spoke of just how much he did.

The job would not last, however, as the government had to call an election in 1984 and was defeated at the polls. Nathan's boss won re-election but was no longer a minister. Nathan left his employ after the defeat. Through contacts gained during his time in Winnipeg, he went to work for a non-governmental organization that assisted in the education of on-reserve aboriginal children. The new job with the NGO brought him to native communities across Canada where he forged contacts and relationships that would prove useful in the years to come.

During this time, Nathan had regular contact with his KGB handlers and received $3000 a month as part of the agreement forged in Moscow before his return to Canada in 1981. He had not asked for money. He had his own ideas on disruption. Money was not part of it, but the Russians were insistent. He had been trained. There was an investment in him. His activities had to lead to something. He would need funds to move around, independently of his work and travels with the NGO. $3000 a month would be a start. Later, more funds would flow as Nathan recruited key individuals in his master plan for disruption.

His work took him from the Yukon to Labrador, allowing him to build relationships with leaders in dozens of communities. These included the Mohawk nation communities of southwestern and eastern Ontario and those around Montreal, of the Algonquins in western Quebec, those of the MicMac in New Brunswick and Nova Scotia and the Innu of Labrador. Through it all, he spotted young radicals and malcontents who could be counted on to act when the time was right - the Warriors of the native uprising that would force change …..and payback for the humiliations, the deprivation, and the poverty of the original peoples of Canada.

11

Adela walked down the steps from the pathway. The agent came around the corner from the river side. She looked at him. "You have me. I will do it." Tears were in her eyes. She turned away, then continued to speak in a low voice while looking out over the river. "If I cannot provide you with something, I will tell you. You will have to accept that. I will be able to provide you only so much." She felt terrible. As if a stone had dropped into her interior, bringing her down.

"Very good, Miss Cerny. Here is what we will begin with." The agent noticed Adela was transfixed, looking out over the water. "Miss Cerny. Miss Cerny. Are you listening?"

"Yes. Tell me. I'm here." She continued to look out over the water.

"There is a cabinet submission coming forward for ministers outlining the Prime Minister's proposal to force Quebec to show its true intentions in the current constitutional negotiations. You have worked on that proposal. The Parti National government in Quebec has its own plans after the defeat of the referendum last year. We would like to know what the Prime Minister's strategy for preserving national unity is. We want a copy of the submission."

This is crazy, she thought. "Damn you, why would you people want to be aware of what is going on between the Prime

Minister of Canada and Quebec?" She was angry and facing the man.

"Calm down. That is for us to determine. Suffice to say we have a deep curiosity in the health of the governments of this world that do not view the world as we do," responded the Russian.

"This is so much bullshit. You can get just about any of this from any decent journalist covering the hill here. Why me?"

"Because you are on the inside. You have direct access to all of it. Journalists can only get so far. Sorry, Miss Cerny."

"What you are talking about is not military or defense related. I hope you don't expect me to go there. I have little or no exposure to that. Anyway, I cannot give you copies of cabinet submissions. They are coded and if photocopied can be detected as having been photocopied."

"What can you provide us then? Certainly there are other documents, files, briefing notes going through the system dealing with the same matters that can be accessed. You need to give us something."

What can I do? I must keep them away from Daddy. "There is something. Maybe briefing notes from within the department that are not included with the cabinet submissions." Adela was aware, however, that those notes would be just as incriminating. They would contain information classified as Secret.

"These would be notes for ministers, would they not?" asked the agent.

"Yes, many of them would."

"Ok, then. That could be enough. We will see when we get them," responded the Russian. "We will meet here next Monday morning. Same time. We will both be in our running outfits. Bring whatever you have in this gym bag. I will have an identical one to switch with you. I will tell you what we will require next. There will be nothing in writing between us. Do not do anything foolish in the meantime. Miss Cerny, I look forward to this relationship."

"I don't. I have no idea you are who you say you are."

"You will have to take the chance on that, I'm afraid," replied the agent.

"What is your name? What should I call you?" asked Adela.

"No name. It is not relevant."

"Bastards."

"Now, now, Miss Cerny. This is no way to start a relationship."

"I don't want a relationship. Certainly not this one."

"So be it, but we will meet here next Monday, and you will have something meaningful with you."

"You promise me nothing will happen to my father. Right?"

"Right."

She turned, went around the corner of the balcony and up the stairs to the bicycle path.

Adela drove to Toronto the following Friday after work. She had been careful to hide her emotions from Brian since the last meeting with the agent. She didn't need the inquisition every day. He played in a jazz combo and the group had a gig for Saturday night at a club in Kingston. She could go to Toronto on her own and spend some time with her father without Brian being around. She loved Brian, had been increasingly accepting of marrying him eventually, but she had to find a way to shield him from her secret and her fears.

Alexandr Cerny lived with his wife in the modest Toronto suburb of Scarborough. Their children had long since moved on, leaving the home to the couple who had finally started to enjoy the better things of life. At 59, Cerny was prosperous, in reasonably good health, and could look forward to his businesses being in good hands. He was proud of his children and content with what he had accomplished since coming to Canada. It was Saturday and his lovely daughter was home for the weekend. Life was good. They sat down to dinner.

After Adela and her parents had finished their meal of roast pork and potato dumplings, a favorite of Czechs wherever they were, she got right into the discussion she wanted to have with her father. "Daddy, you never talk much about the war. You were there, back in Czechoslovakia at that time. What did you do during the war? You never said you fought." She was looking at her father, who had a sudden frown on his face. "What did you do? And what did you do between then and when you brought us to Canada? We have never talked about that."

Her father looked at his daughter, paused a moment, lowered his head, kept it there for a moment, then said, "Adela, you are asking me about things I have spent my life here trying to forget. I do not want to talk about them. It has been a long time. They are no longer important to me nor should they be to you. No one who went through the war wants to talk about it."

"Daddy, I understand about the war. But afterwards, what did you do? Work for the government? How did we live?"

"I never worked for the government, Adela." He was lying, but he could not afford to go there. "I worked for a farmer and saved enough money to eventually leave Czechoslovakia."

"It must have been difficult. The Communists took over and I understand abolished private ownership of farms."

"That is why we had to leave. I would have had to work for the state that was taking away all our freedoms we had fought for under the Nazis. I did not want to do that."

Adela looked intently at her father. "There were assassinations during that time. I got curious recently about our past. I went to the library in Ottawa and did some research on Czechoslovakia after the war. That is why I am asking you these questions, Daddy. You were there. The Communist takeover, the assassination of the Foreign Minister, the expulsion of all the Germans. I just thought you could share your memories of that, but I can understand why you would prefer to leave it be."

Alexandr froze.

"Adela, I know little of what you are asking. We were in the countryside. I saw Germans leaving. It was bad. They deserved it, but the rest, I knew little about. We came here as soon as we could. Don't ask me about the war and the time there afterward. It was difficult."

"Well, anyway, I read about our heroes. The ones from medieval times down to Tomas Masaryk and to Jan, his son. Assassinated. Thrown out of a window. Defenestration. One of many in Czech history." She saw the alarm in her father's eyes. His hand was shaking. It was true. She did not have to go any further. She would have to cooperate.

"God damn it!!! How do I deserve this?" Adela yelled out loud to herself as she drove the 401 back to Ottawa that Sunday afternoon. A few kilometers out of Toronto, she decided she would have to see the police, whoever is responsible for intelligence, spies and all of that. She needed help. There was no one else. How would she do that without putting her father at risk? What was worse, betraying your country or betraying your family? Family. She needed to find a way out.

The note from Berezov to the station chief at the Embassy outlined the discussions with Adela Cerny. It ended with the observation that the agent could not be certain she would be a productive source of information, nor could he be certain she would not go to the authorities, however dangerous that could be for her father. The agent noted that Cerny had driven to Toronto that weekend and had spent it at the family home. Was her intent to ask her father about his past? Was it triggered by his proposal to her? He was certain that it was, reported Sergei Berezov to his superior.

They met at the boathouse the Monday morning. "You went to Toronto. Saw your family. You didn't speak of our affair with your father, did you?"

They know everything I do. This is a nightmare. What do I do? "Yes, I went to Toronto. I drive there for weekends four or five times a year. This was one of them. Neither my father nor anyone else is aware of our discussions. Here is what I said I would provide to you. Is there anything else?"

The Russian browsed the document quickly. "This is fine. I will be in touch with you. Do not do anything foolish, Adela. In case you are thinking of it, it would not be a good idea to go to the RCMP, the police, or anybody else with this. We will learn of it if you do. It would guarantee the exposure of your father and the end of your career, if not worse. Believe me."

Adela felt a chill throughout her body as the man disappeared. She knew at that moment that she could not go to the RCMP. Not then, anyway. Maybe never. She was caught.

She's stuck now, thought the Russian as he found his car at the far end of the parkway. With what she has given me, she has betrayed the Official Secrets Act of the Government of Canada. She will have difficulty getting out of this. We have her.

12

Four months later, Vancouver, British Columbia

The conference involving federal and provincial government representatives on intergovernmental affairs had broken up that afternoon. Adela and a colleague were at the little restaurant at the edge of English Bay. She had excused herself to go to the ladies' room. As she was returning to the table, she heard someone speaking Russian. She turned and observed Marc Dubé of the Quebec delegation speaking with a waiter. It was clearly in Russian. They were behind a partition, only partly visible to her. But it was unmistakable. Marc Dubé. No one else appeared to be in earshot and she felt certain she had not been noticed. The fear returned.

Two days later in the park, Dubé was with his control. "People from the Ottawa delegation were at the restaurant in Vancouver. One of them could have heard me speaking Russian with my contact. I am not certain of it, but it could have been. I cannot be taking chances any more with contacts, Serge. Cover must be better. Canada is a village."

"Who was it? Do you know the person?" asked the Russian.

"Adela Cerny. Works at Secretary of State. Do you know her? I understand she is of Czech ancestry."

"No, I don't." He was not being truthful. A fellow agent was her control. "We will have to watch her now, though. No more Russian spoken anywhere for you, Marc. Only English or French. Our people will have to accept that. Do you have direct dealings with this lady?" The Russian was aware that he did, but could not let that be known.

"Yes, I do. It will be sticky if she actually heard or saw me."

"What will you tell her if she brings it up?" asked the Russian. This was getting close to exposing the Quebec and Ottawa intrusions to each other.

"I will tell her I learned the language when I was studying international political affairs in graduate school. The best answer I can think of."

"What about the waiter?"

"I will say I overheard him speaking Russian and I just wanted to be friendly. Practice my Russian."

"Weak, but there should be no reason the woman would doubt that," replied the Russian who was aware that if the discussion was overheard, it could set Adela Cerny on to a path they were not ready to take. Not yet, anyway. Dubé was not to learn the identity of the source they had in the office of the minister looking after Canada's management of its separatist threat.

October 1981

It had been a few weeks since Adela had had contact with the agent. She had spoken to no one about the blackmail. Maybe this nightmare is over, she thought as she prepared to meet with the team preparing for the upcoming meeting of the Prime Minister with the premiers of the provinces. The conference was to discuss provisions for a new constitution, to deliver on what the Prime Minister had promised during the Quebec referendum crisis the previous year. She looked at the roster of officials who would be part of each province's delegation to the meeting to be held in two weeks' time.

Marc Dubé, chief advisor on constitutional affairs to the Premier of Quebec. Of course. Always front and center on these things. But....speaking Russian at that restaurant. She thought of her Czech-Russian contact - the requests for information on the constitutional file. Could he be part of this whole thing? Working with the Russians? No, can't be. If it is, it is much bigger than me and my little problem of protecting my father. I will watch him at the conference. I may, after all, have to go to the RCMP and talk about all this. I cannot go on with it forever.

A month later, in Ottawa

Marc Dubé understood what was going on. From information gleaned by the Russians, he surmised that the Prime Minister was determined to arrive at an agreement on the Constitution, no matter what. The process had taken years. Trudel had had enough. November 1981 would be the end of it. The Premiers were leaving in the morning. The occasion would be lost. The PM was determined to do it. It would have to be tonight.

Trudel wanted to replace the Act of the British Parliament that had governed the workings of Canada since 1867. He and the premiers had been discussing for the past two days. Marc had fears of his Premier giving in somewhere along the line. He had to make sure the agreement would not work for Quebec. Quebecers had to be angry so the Party could promote independence.

Adela Cerny knew that the Prime Minister had a compromise to present to the Premiers that evening. He was determined to get an agreement. She had already, that afternoon, informed the Quebec delegation that the Premiers and the PM would have an after-dinner drink and that their Premier was invited. The Quebec official had expressed his regrets. Their delegates were having their own party across the river in Hull. In the early evening, seeing that Quebec was not present, Adela sent an anonymous note to the delegation warning them of Trudel's intention and suggesting they get their Premier to the meeting. If there were to be an agreement tonight and Quebec was not there, it could turn out to be a big problem.

Her message never reached its destination. Marc Dubé intercepted it. The handwriting was familiar. He took a note from his briefcase that had been annotated by Cerny in a working meeting the day before. Same handwriting. She's doing this. Guys, she is betraying you (he had been told the week before that she was the mole). He contacted his KGB control and told him of her action. But the crisis Adela wanted to avert would serve their purpose. Let it happen!

The Premiers did arrive at a consensus. The Quebec Premier was advised the next day of the fait accompli by the press. The spokesperson for the PM informed the media that the Quebec Premier had been invited to the get-together but had begged off through the word of one of his officials. "They had a chance to participate but declined" he concluded. The media and political class in Quebec exploded in indignation. Betrayal by English Canada! The deal in the backroom of the hotel did it, thought Marc Dubé. He kept secret his own part in the disaster and let the official who received the initial invitation to the after-dinner drink take the blame.

The Quebec delegation left Ottawa later that day, with ministers saying the province and its people had been stabbed in the back in what became known as the night of the long knives. The simmering distrust and animosity between the Parti National and the federal government was given new life.

"She knows about Dubé," said the Russian to his boss. "I'm sure of it. She will expose him sooner or later. We have to take care of this."

Adela Cerny received the order to meet her handler at a small restaurant in Ottawa's west end. When she got there, the agent caught her elbow before she entered, directing her to the car parked down the street. They got into the back seat and the driver pulled away from the curb.

"You are betraying our arrangement. What were you trying to do, warning Quebec about something that was developing? Are you telling people about what we have been doing? Be careful, Miss Cerny. You were not supposed to do this," said the Russian.

So, there is someone working for them on the Quebec side - Marc Dubé. Of course, thought Adela.

"You have been using me to help arrange the breakup of Canada. It has always been that. What more do you want from me? What else must I do to betray my country?" she said in anger.

"We don't ask you for very much, Miss Cerny. But what we do ask of you is to be discreet. If you are not, we will expose your father."

"I have given you enough. Enough, damn it, whoever you really are! I am getting out of this. I have cooperated enough with you. It is ending. Now."

"Miss Cerny, you don't resign from something like this. It just does not work that way. This is not something you can walk away from. Be careful. I will be in touch with you for our next meeting." The car stopped at the next corner. It was clear the discussion was over. Adela got out and watched the car continue down the street.

13

Toronto Herald, December 21 1981

Andrew Brown Named to Editorial Board

Andrew Brown, journalist and nephew of Jamieson Brown, Chairman of The Herald Corporation, owner of the Toronto Herald and other leading Canadian publications, has been appointed to the Editorial Board of the paper. Mr. Brown, 30, is a graduate of Cambridge University and has been with the paper since 1976. He writes on current political and economic affairs.

"So, Andrew Brown gets an expanded tribune for his views. Brilliant kid, really. Very much an economic nationalist. Plays on the anti-American fears of the old-stock Canadians, the Toronto crowd, labor and most of the academics in the country. The Americans across the street at the Embassy must loath him. God knows they spend a lot of time refuting and countering what he writes. Such an anti-American bias." The Minister of International Trade and his chief of staff were having breakfast in the parliamentary restaurant in Ottawa. "Practically single-handedly he has got us to turn down participation in Reagan's Strategic Defense Initiative - Star Wars to so many. Really did a number on it. Your colleague at Defense was going to do it. PM overruled him. I believe Brown's articles in The Herald really did it. He's one of us, though," replied the aide. "Good Liberal. His father and uncles are all big supporters. We will need them and The Toronto Herald for the coming election. "

"Doug, when Canadians are asked what defines them, they will most often say, "We're not Americans. We're different." And they will not be able to say much of anything else. For millions of people in this country, it is who we are. Not Americans. Really it's about who we are not." Andrew Brown was having lunch with Doug Mills, one of the assistant editors of the Herald, some time after his appointment to the editorial board.

"It's a pretty common opinion, but you feed on it a lot. It is becoming your signature, Andrew. You should beware of it becoming a one-horse show."

"Hey, come on, Doug. The Americans steam-roller us. They are everywhere. Putting pressure on the government to relax the foreign takeover rules. Trying to ram that crazy Strategic Defense Initiative down our throats. They even complain big-time about our Canadian content rules in music on the radio and the number of hours of Canadian content on television. Even about having to show French versions of their movies. Threatening international trade tribunal action on this stuff, even though it would not get anywhere. This is not just to piss us off, Doug. It is about having free rein to do what they please up here. Thank God the Grits in Ottawa stand up to them. But somebody must expose this to the public. The Government can only do so much. Protocol and diplomatic relations and all that. I enjoy doing it. Protecting the Canadian identity, my friend."

"Well, you do a good job of it. Just be careful of not overdoing it. You could wear it out." The good friend paused, then continued. "What does your uncle say about it all?"

"He doesn't interfere. Has never told me to change anything. You would probably hear about it if he did. Our family has never been fans of the American way. Loyalists in the old days, Loyalists still. God, the Queen and Empire.....I'm being facetious, but not entirely." Andrew Brown took a sip of his beer, looked at his friend across the table, and continued. "If my uncle thinks I go too far, he will tell me. I think he wants me to write what I write. Sells papers for one thing. Keeps the corporation on the good side of our current government, as well. Trudel and company are not great lovers of the Americans. I can say things they can't."

"Labor certainly loves it. White, the Canadian Auto Workers boss, sent in a letter supporting us big-time on our editorial last week concerning the renewal of the Auto Pact. Your editorial."

"Yeah, I saw it. They are scared shitless of Reagan. He fired all the air traffic controllers down there, for God's sake. Just like that. They think he is going to go after the autoworkers next, who the Reagan people say are pricing American cars out of the market. Special legislation being developed, I am told. Can't let the Japanese take over the American market. He will probably have Congress on his side. The labor guys here think the Conservatives, if they get in, will start doing here what Reagan has been doing. They will be supporting the Liberals big time. And so will we in our editorial focus." With that, the two colleagues finished their lunch and went back to the office. Andrew would later meet his KGB contact. Andrew would learn the man had a special request he wanted to talk about.

"Will you be getting married soon?" It was the first thing the Russian said.

"You're getting too personal. Stay out of my personal affairs, Robert. Not part of the deal."

"Sorry, Andrew. Many things are not part of the deal at the start, but they become part of it." Andrei Timlikov, Robert to Andrew, treaded carefully as he continued the line of discussion. "This young lady. She is political. Liberal. Wants to run for election federally. Could be good for us. Could be bad."

"Leave my girlfriend out of it. She's not part of what we are doing."

"Alright. There is a minister in the government. Member of the Cabinet Committee on Defense and influential with his colleagues. He is the most vocal advocate of greater military alignment with the Americans. Lawson. Pushes for Canadian participation in Reagan's Star Wars. Completely crazy. He also has a weakness for the ladies. Call girls, they call them here. Would make for a juicy headline in your paper. He would be obliged to resign. We need you to publish this. We have all you need."

"Looks like you have somebody on the inside in Ottawa."

"We don't talk about that, Andrew. We don't disclose anything about you to anyone and we don't disclose anything to you about whatever else we do."

"I can't do what you ask. I could, but I will not. I don't want the details of what the minister does with his tool, and I don't care. I am certainly not going to have the Toronto Herald embarrassing the current government. Not on, Robert."

"Mr. Brown, this is the second time in the past few months you have turned down a request from me for flimsy political reasons."

"These are not flimsy political reasons. Part of my influence which benefits you greatly, by the way, is my access to the workings of the current government in Ottawa. We should not be jeopardizing that. Outing Ministers will bring the wrath of the government down on The Herald and on me. For God's sake, you tried to get me last year to publish a piece about the Prime Minister's affair with that Italian actress. All because you thought he was going to work more with Reagan. So what. It would not have accomplished anything. This Prime Minister probably would have enjoyed people seeing the link with the sexy lady and it would not have changed anything with Reagan, the Hollywood guy who knows a lot about that kind of stuff. I failed to see the benefit of it from your standpoint other than to embarrass the man, who is probably your best friend here, amongst all the politicians in this country. Remember the stuff of a couple of years ago about Trudel and Castro." Brown paused a moment, then continued. "You gave me some insides about Trudel's various visits to Cuba and his ongoing communications with Castro. Details of spending weekends at Castro's home, boating, swimming and scuba diving together, with pictures. If there was anything that would upset the Americans and the President, it would be information concerning a cozy relationship between Paul Trudel and Fidel Castro. But I asked you why you would do this. Castro is your man. I would think you would want greater cooperation between Canada and Cuba."

The Russian was quick to reply. "What we wanted more then and what we continue to want today is disruption between Canada and the United States. We already have Cuba. They depend totally on us. The nice little relationship between the Prime Minister of Canada with Fidel Castro has given us little benefit. But, again, disrupting the Canadian relationship with Washington is much more advantageous to us."

"Well, I could not publish that and I didn't. It was going too far. I could not embarrass the most effective opponent of American control of our economy just for the sake of pissing off the Americans. I would have had the wrath of the Canadian

103

government and Paul Trudel himself down my neck. We had to disrupt things through other means."

"Your lady is preventing you from doing your job. Your job as a journalist. You are refusing to do this because of her. The man we are talking about could be blackmailed. The government should be aware of his proclivities and the dangers they could bring."

"Robert, or whatever your real name is, you leave my lady out of it. And I will decide what to write about what comes from you."

"She wants to run, so you bend."

"Discussion over." Andrew rose and walked away.

"She has her own skeletons, Andrew. Beware."

Andrew turned around and stared at the Russian who had not moved. "What are you talking about?"

"Her father. Accounts in the Bahamas and a few other places in the Caribbean. Hiding money from the tax people for years. Would be easy for us to bring this to the attention of the authorities. But we may not. We need to talk about this, Andrew."

"You bastards."

"Now, now."

"We have him. The stuff on his wife's father has done it. He can't afford to drop out. Good work, Andrei Alexeivitch. He will do what we ask." The two Russians meeting in the basement of the

Embassy enjoyed a toast, then left in separate cars with blackened windows, one to his apartment not far away and the other to Toronto to his job at the Soviet consulate.

Three days later.

"Give the information to this person at Canadian Press. Here is how to do it without it being traced back. The Herald may run it in the end with it coming from a wire service, but it won't be coming from me." Andrew handed the envelope to the Russian.

14

Ottawa, January 1982

"What is it, baby?" Brian had seen for days that Adela was stressed, but this was the worst. "You're a mess. What is going on?" He took Adela by the shoulders, drew her to him, and wrapped his arms around her. She was shaking. After a moment, she drew away, looked at Brian and said, "There are some things I need to tell you. I can't keep it anymore."

"Brian, I am being blackmailed by Soviet intelligence to spy on our government. I can't live with it any longer. You want to know, here it is. I can't keep it secret any longer." She explained it all to Brian, from the start months before to then.

Brian Carlson listened intently. "Adela, you need to contact the police, the RCMP. You need to save yourself. There may be a way out of it."

"I'm not so sure. I may go to jail."

"Maybe not. Your father may be exposed but it has been a long time. If you cooperate with the authorities and tell them all, they could protect your father and be easy on you. The important thing is for you is to save yourself. Tell the RCMP everything."

"How are we going to do that? The Czechs or Russians, whoever they really are, are probably watching me now. Even more than ever. I have told them I want out," said Adela. "How have I deserved this, Brian? I feel so alone. It needs to end." Adela paused, crossed her arms, looked out the window, then looked back at Brian. "When I was in university, I had an ideal. I would serve my country. I would live up to what my father wanted of me - to do something meaningful, pay back the country that accepted us when we had nothing. I still have that ideal, Brian. This is tearing me apart. I should never have agreed to work with them. I should have gone to the police right away. But I did not. I was terrified. I went home one weekend to try to find out if it were true, that Dad had been implicated in a political murder after the war. I asked him questions. His answers told me it was true. I decided to cooperate - to save him, his legacy, his reputation, his life. It was wrong. I could have done it otherwise. It's too late, Brian. I am a spy. I have betrayed my country. I can't go on. I thought I was smart. I am not. I am vulnerable and I'm scared. Help me!"

"Adela, you are a wonderful, thoughtful, responsible, loving person, always cheerful and optimistic. In the past few months, I have seen you tense, melancholic, off into space, evasive, argumentative. Just not yourself. I know why now. What a mess. You do not have to continue with this. It is not too late. The only way to end it, to save yourself, is to face it, deal with it. It's repair time. You must do it. You need to go to the RCMP, and soon."

"How will I tell them? I will go to jail."

"I will do it. I will go to the RCMP. They must be made aware of this and be able to offer you and your father protection. I will tell them someone close to me has been blackmailed by the KGB and wants to disclose everything that has happened. That person wants to meet them and come clean. Their headquarters on Riverside Parkway is on my way to work. I could go there tomorrow."

"Brian, you can't do this. I have brought you into this now, but I don't want you in any deeper. I should not have told you."

"Adela, listen. I love you. You are in trouble. You need help and there is nobody else that can do it. You cannot have your brothers or anybody else involved in this. You need the assistance of the authorities. I will go there. Understand? I don't see any other way. You cannot go there. I must do it."

"Alright. Ok. So be it," replied Adela in tears.

"Do they know of me?"

"Who? The Czechs or whoever they are?

"The Czech, Russians, whatever. Will they follow me? Have they talked to you about me?" answered Brian.

"Of course they know about you. They seem to be aware of everything about me, although you have never come up in discussions. I told them I had a boyfriend, but the handler has never discussed or asked about you before."

"OK. Here is what we are going to do. I will go to the office as usual. If they are following me, they will see nothing suspect. When I get there, I will go through the back lobby of the building to the next street and take a bus to RCMP headquarters. I will ask to see someone in authority, like say "I am aware of an attempt to commit fraud on a large scale. I wish to speak to someone." When I get alone with whoever they have meet with me, I will tell them the basics of your predicament and ask them to make arrangements to meet with you."

"No, Brian. You are not going to tell them everything. I will. I just need to find a way to meet them without the Russians or

Czechs or whoever they are knowing about it. I am scared, but I can't go on. I will tell them. You have but the basics of this."

"Ok. I will go the Mountie headquarters as planned, give them the minimum, and get them to arrange a meeting, hopefully out of sight of the Russians. I cannot imagine how you have managed to contain this all this time, my dear. I'm stunned." Brian Carlson leaned over to Adela, put his arm around her, and kissed her forehead. "We'll get you out of this."

"We can't talk about any of this at the apartment, Brian. I believe they have the place bugged. Only in places like this," as she glanced toward the mostly empty tables of the restaurant.

"What a nightmare."

Ottawa, three days later.........

The discussion was in an office at Secretary of State that Adela had reserved for the meeting.

"You have something to tell us, Miss Cerny. I'm listening. Please tell me what this is all about." With that, RCMP assistant superintendent Allan Denby opened the discussion.

"Brian, Brian Carlson who went to see you, told you something about my situation. The basics, I guess. I suppose you want to have it all."

"He told us very little, just that you were being blackmailed by people from the eastern bloc to get information."

"Yes. I'm scared. I have been for close to three years now and I can't take it anymore. I have been blackmailed by Soviet agents. I have provided them with information to protect my father and the rest of my family." Adela Cerny was in tears. "I have betrayed my country to protect my father. I need to end this. I want to tell you everything. I can't go on."

"Miss Cerny, we will have to stop here," interjected the officer. "Providing confidential information to other governments is a criminal offense." The man paused for a moment, then continued. "Before we go any further, I will have a colleague join us. You can consult a lawyer if you wish. Whatever you say from now on can be used against you."

"I don't want a lawyer. I want to tell you about everything I have provided to the Russians and the Czechs."

The RCMP officer left the room to make a call. "Miss Cerny, please stay here. I will be back in a moment."

Denby reached his superior, Superintendent for Counterintelligence, Frank Russo. "Frank, I think we may have the Russian source we have suspected for some time. She is sitting in a meeting room at Secretary of State. She works here. You may want to come over. She says she is willing to tell us everything."

Adela spent the next hour telling the RCMP officers the circumstances of her recruitment by the Czech agent years before, the story of her father and his alleged unwitting involvement with the murder of the Czech foreign minister in 1948, the blackmail, the information she provided over the years.

"Did you provide any information dealing with defense or military affairs?" asked the senior officer.

"No, nothing of that nature. The agent accepted early on that I had little or no access to sensitive information in that regard and never asked me for it."

"What did he ask you for?"

"Everything about dealings with the provinces, particularly with Quebec, concerning constitutional and intergovernmental affairs. Information regarding affairs with the United States as well. Treaty negotiations. Trade matters."

"We will have to put you through some very intensive interrogations, Miss Cerny. I hope you realize that."

"I'm aware of that. I am ready for it. What do I do in the meantime? I will no longer have my job, I am fairly certain of that and I suspect I will now be put in jail."

"No, you do nothing for the moment. Stay where you are. Keep on with your job. Obviously tell no one of your meeting with us. No one. You have a boyfriend, I understand?" asked the senior officer.

"Yes, I do. He has the basics of what I have told you."

"Well, that is not so good."

"I had to tell him. Somebody had to contact you for me. They follow me everywhere. Know everything I do."

"OK. Stay put. Do not leave Ottawa. We cannot meet here anymore. People will be wondering what the hell is going on. Let us meet at this place on Thursday evening at 7:30." Russo gave her the card with the address on it. Your Russian contacts may be aware of this meeting and try to do something to harm you. We will do all we can to ensure they do not notice our watching you. We will tell you on Thursday what we intend to do. Are you willing to cooperate with us?"

"Yes. I am ready to cooperate in any way I can. I just want to stop it and find a way to protect my father."

"You should have come to us long ago."

"I was scared. I was afraid for my father. I am ready to do whatever you ask."

Three days later.

"We want you to work for us, tell us what your contacts are asking of you."

"Be a double agent. That is what you are asking of me. This is only getting worse. I want out of all of this."

"It's more complicated than that, Miss Cerny. You don't have to do it, but I suggest you think about it. If you do not do this, we may have to consider actions against you."

The commissioner of the RCMP had had a meeting with the Undersecretary of State, who had been informed of the situation. Both men had the highest of Top Secret clearances and were key advisors to the Prime Minister on national security. The commissioner informed the undersecretary that his intention was to propose to Adela that she become a double agent, and hopefully detect other Soviet agents in the government. Even set up a trap. Adela's boss tried to dissuade the commissioner. She would be in danger. She was not trained for this sort of thing. "Was there any other way out?" The undersecretary knew Adela Cerny, respected her work. Although flabbergasted and disgusted, he wanted to protect her. At least there was no disclosure of national security or defense-related matters, although they could not be sure of that - it was her word on that. She was being blackmailed against her will. He was sympathetic to her plight. She was caught in an impossible situation. How could the government of Canada protect her without it becoming public? The commissioner said they would nevertheless propose to Miss Cerny to work for them. If it did not work, they would have to think of something else.

Jim Denham found Adela's office, knocked on the door, then walked in and closed the door behind him. Adela looked up but did not know what to say. Without sitting down, the tall, middle-aged career civil servant came right to the point. "Adela, you are in trouble. I have been informed of it. RCMP people came to see me. Can we talk about it?"

"Oh, my God," said the young woman, once again petrified. "Yes, of course." Adela feared the worst. She was losing her job. She was going to be pushed out of the public service. Her career would be over. Her life would be over. Charged with espionage...

"Adela, we are behind you. You have been blackmailed. We are going to support you. We all recognize what you are about, and you are not a spy." Seeing that she wanted to say something, he continued. "Let me finish. You will need to cooperate with the RCMP. Tell them everything." He looked at her. Her eyes were welling with tears. "You apparently have not breached anything regarding national security. That must be established. It is important. It makes it easier for us and for the police to protect you. We are not going to abandon you. You are not alone. Adela, you are a good person and a fine public servant. You were faced with an impossible choice. We are going to do all we can to save you from it. OK? You must cooperate. There is no going back. Alright?"

"Alright."

"I must leave now. Let the police manage this. You will be OK."

"Thank you, Sir." Adela rose from her chair before the man could leave. "Can I ask you something?"

"Of course."

"Can I hug you? I need it."

"Yes, certainly, Adela." Jim Denham took her into his arms, gave her a long hug, then turned and left, closing the door behind him.

Adela had not heard from the RCMP since the initial meetings. She was scared. She was sworn to secrecy. She had told them a lot. She was exposed. The tension was there, day in, day out. She was on edge. Brian was on edge as well.

It was only at a restaurant they could speak about it. Their apartment was bugged; they were sure of it. "This is unbearable, Brian. I have no idea what they are going to do. They said they would protect me, but I don't know if the Russians are aware of what we have done. I can't handle this."

The two finished their meal, returned to the apartment, quickly went to bed and cuddled up together. Neither of them slept very well that night, much like every other night over the previous two weeks.

The next morning, soon after arriving at her office, the telephone rang. "Adela, this is Momma." Ivana Cerny spoke in Czech in a tone of panic to her daughter. "Something terrible has happened, my dear. Your father was called this morning by a friend in London. An article has appeared in one of the Czech expatriate newspapers there saying that a key accomplice in the murder of Jan

Masaryk had been discovered living in Toronto, being the owner of a successful chain of restaurants there. It gave his name - Alexandr Cerny. It explained what your father had supposedly done. Your father is beside himself. He does not know what to do. He fears there will be people coming to kill him. This is terrible...." She was crying.

The bastards. "Momma, have father go somewhere. He must get out of Toronto. Now. Go with him to Stratford or Niagara. He has a friend in Niagara-on-the-Lake who has always welcomed you two to visit. Go there or take a room in a hotel. I will get a spokesperson for him to deal with media. It will come. He will need to have an answer for the Czech community - here, London, everywhere. Let me talk to him."

"He's not here. He's at the office."

"Momma, get him away from there. I will call Gabby. He should be at the office. We must act quickly. I will speak to you later." Adela put down the phone and called her brother Gabriel who ran the main restaurant.

"Gabby, have you heard from Momma?

"No, what? I just got in. I was in Windsor this morning. What are you talking about?"

"There is a piece in a Czech newspaper in London saying that Daddy was an accomplice in the murder of a key person in Prague after the war, somebody who was considered a national hero. Jan Masaryk. I have no idea if he was involved. We never spoke about anything like that. I suppose if he had told you, you would have told me......Somebody called him from London. Not long ago. Momma phoned me. She is distraught, almost hysterical."

"What? Daddy involved in a murder? Good Lord. Can't be."

"Well, this is what's happening," replied Adela. "Only Daddy can tell us what this is all about. But it's dangerous for him. There could be people who may want to kill him. Even forty years later. The business in the Czech community here could be jeopardized. Daddy could be viewed as a traitor, a pariah. We have to face that possibility."

"My God, how could he deserve this? What is this all about? He never told us anything. I don't suppose he would have, if he was involved. Is that all true? He said he worked on a farm after the war, for God's sake."

"Apart from protecting Daddy physically, we will have to get a story prepared, to answer the charge, protect Daddy's reputation and the family business. This could unravel quickly. Where is he? Is he there? Have you seen him?"

"No. Hold on. I will ask. Stay on the line."

Gabriel returned to the call a moment later. "Sylvia, his assistant, said he took a call, made one himself apparently as she could hear him - he was speaking in Czech apparently - then walked out. Looked like he was going for a walk. That was a half-hour or forty-five minutes ago."

"Gabby, you have to find him. Get him out of Toronto. Call Dominic. Have him organize a conference call of the three of us. Now. As soon as possible. We must act to protect him. I told Momma to go somewhere with him. She is crying. We are going to have to take this over."

"Adela, do you know anything about what he did before coming here?"

Adela decided to lie. To say she did would expose the hell she had been going through for years. No one in her family deserved to know that. "No. Gabby. Just like you said, Daddy said he worked on a farm after the war, then brought us here. I must go now. Call me as soon as you reach him."

After putting down the phone, Adela placed a call to the office of Superintendent Russo at RCMP headquarters. "Hello, this is Adela Cerny. I had a meeting with the superintendent a week ago about a very serious matter. I must see him. Could you ask him to call me at my office here? Here is the number."

Ten minutes later, Frank Russo was on the phone. "Miss Cerny, this is Frank Russo. What is happening?"

"I must see you. What I have been threatened with has happened."

"You must be careful now, Miss Cerny. We are working to arrange protection for you. We will meet with you tomorrow evening at a safe house outside of Ottawa. Normally, travelling out of Ottawa on a Friday afternoon for the weekend will not raise suspicion. Just the same, could you borrow a car from a friend? Use an excuse about your car being worked on; have to see your family in Toronto, will have to move around, not appropriate to fly or take the train. Do not use your own. You may be tailed. Just in case, we will have someone following you. Do you suspect your contacts know anything about why you would be requesting to see me?"

"Yes, they have exposed my father. They will expect me to do something."

"Then, you will have to be doubly careful. You will go to the house south of Ottawa late in the evening. Is that possible?"

"Why can't someone from the RCMP come by and pick me up? I am scared."

"That is problematic. It will surely tell them you are working with us. Dangerous for you. But I understand your fear. I will have one of my agents work something out. He will call you. Within the hour. His name is Donaldson."

"It is already dangerous, sir. They know about the meeting we had. Somehow. It is why they exposed my father."

"Donaldson will call you."

"Donaldson, I need you to take care of Miss Cerny. I told her to go to a house south of Ottawa. We need to debrief her. The Russians have apparently carried out their threat. They undoubtedly learned of her contacting us. We will not be able to use her now. No double agent scenario possible. We just need to learn everything she has told the Russians. Hopefully, we can keep this story from becoming public. If it does, we have no choice but to pursue her for espionage. Maybe we can keep it from blowing up. But we need to know everything she has told them, as well as the identities of whoever else is working for them in Canada. They have their tentacles in many places. Do not be too hard on her. Have her understand that if she tells us everything, she may be able to avoid an espionage charge. Over to you. Take someone with you to record everything."

The plan was for Adela to take the road for Toronto that evening as she had done so many times before, but take the exit for Kemptville, then proceed on Concession Road five miles east of the town to a safe house on the shore of a small lake. Agent Donaldson was to be waiting for her. An unmarked RCMP car would follow her. She managed to get her friend Rosalyn's Honda for the weekend. Rosalyn was going to Montreal with her boyfriend for the weekend and didn't need it.

Adela traveled fast on the four-lane highway leading south from Ottawa. She saw a car behind her as she turned off the highway toward Kemptville. The RCMP follower. Good, she thought.

Agent Boucher had lost her. Hondas were all alike. Black. Always black.

As Agent Boucher rounded the bend at a sharp curve of the concession road, he saw the taillights of a car in the ditch. Smoke was coming from it. The black Honda was resting on its top, its lights still on and the engine running. He found Adela Cerny in the driver's seat. She was dead, her neck broken.

Frank Russo was meeting with his people on the Cerny file. "Jim Denham called me. He asked why we could not protect her. I did not give a very good answer. We messed up. And we also screwed up by not getting everything she knew before they got to her. So, we only have part of it. What the hell, guys?"

Agent Donaldson responded. "We were to debrief her at the house. They learned of the operation. They couldn't afford that. We don't even know who the operatives were. We were to get into the details. We never got them."

"What about her boyfriend, Carlson?"

"We will have to talk to him. Find out what he can tell us. What about the father?"

"No information. But I imagine he will have to go somewhere. Get out of sight. We can't intervene at all. We can't be seen to know anything about this. Alexandr Cerny's problem will have to be addressed by somebody else. Certainly not by RCMP counter-intelligence."

Brian Carlson was called one day at his office and asked to come to a meeting that evening behind a restaurant in Chinatown. "Go to the door at the back." He was told that no one else should be aware of the meeting.

Can't they just leave me alone? Brian thought as he put down the phone, but realized he had to go through with it. He told them everything he knew. He was told to keep everything to himself. Nobody should be told anything about what Adela had been doing. It could be dangerous for him. They would do what they could to warn him if they thought he was in trouble. They would be watching. "They killed her, didn't they?"

"Yes, it looks like they did," replied the Mountie.

"And you didn't protect her."

"I'm sorry. Truly sorry, Mr. Carlson."

"That family is in shambles, Mr. Denby. Father in hiding. Daughter dead. Killed. Business in the Czech community ruined. Probably forever."

"Russians. It's their world, I'm afraid."

"I just wish you could have protected her."

"We do too. I'm sorry. Very sorry."

Brian Carlson left Ottawa a few weeks later. Quit his job and found someone to take over the lease of the apartment he had shared with Adela. He went to Vancouver to start over. One day he received a threat from an anonymous source.

In October 1982, six months after leaving Ottawa, Brian Carlson disappeared without a trace. Neither his family nor his friends ever learned what happened to him. Friends suspected he committed suicide over the death of his beloved Adela. No clues anywhere. No note. Nothing.

15

Three months before, in a park on rue Christophe Colomb in Montreal.

"I see that Adela Cerny is no more." Marc Dubé was with his contact.

"Yes. No more. A pity."

"Do you think she told them about me, Serge?" asked Dubé. He did not want to ask if Serge and his buddies were involved in her death. He didn't have to. He assumed they were. It scared him. He knew he could not get out. But he didn't want to. The connection was paying off.

"We would have observed something by now if that were the case. But you should stay low for a while. We will not be contacting you for a few weeks, at least. It is why we have not met since January. We need to see what they do."

"Alright. But you need to find another source in Ottawa. Must have inside info on what that man plans on doing. Our strategy depends on it," replied Dubé.

"That is our job. Leave it to us," said the Russian as he rose to leave.

"I still need to receive the money from you. I may stay low, but the money has to continue."

"OK. We will change the way we do it, however. I assume you still want to work with us, M. Dubé."

"I am committed to the independence of Quebec and I continue to believe my work with you will contribute to that."

"Very good. We will have an account set up for you in Switzerland. We cannot afford for the authorities to see you picking up envelopes. They may be on to you. We cannot be certain Miss Cerny did not tell the RCMP about you. If she did, they will be crafty. You will not even see it. We must halt all contact for a while. I will let you know when the account has been set up." The Russian rose from the bench and walked down the street to a car parked behind a restaurant on a cross street two blocks away.

It would be three years before Marc Dubé and the agent named Serge spoke again.

16

While building his network of native activists, Nathan met a woman who would become his companion, his trusted confidant and lover, something he had never had before. There had been liaisons in Cuba that did not last and a few ill-fated relationships in Regina years before with down-and-out native girls. Nothing that had lasted more than a few days or weeks, the time to become disinterested. Laura Dumont was different - an intelligent, insightful well-grounded woman who was a nurse working in one of Winnipeg's hospitals. Nathan met her during a conference on native affairs. Being half native - Métis on her father's side and Irish on her mother's – she was interested in discovering how she could help members of her father's extended family. He proposed coffee the next day. She accepted and within a month of many coffees, evenings and increasingly nights together, he had sub-let his apartment and moved in with her. They talked all the time when he was between trips. But not about Cuba, Russians, or about revolution. They talked about his childhood, his youth, about politics and society, about improving the lot of natives.

This worried Nathan. He wondered how he could keep from Laura what he was working towards and the role the Russians had in it. He ended up speaking many times of his years in the residential school. It was a release. He had never been able to talk to anyone about it before. The pain was too great. He avoided it. With Sam, with Roberto, with anybody else. But with Laura, it was different.

On their second date, he got into it. "I was abused. I was six when they came for me. I never set foot in my family's hut again, never saw my father or my mother again. They were forbidden to come and see me - I don't think they were even told where I was. I was not allowed to go home. I was there for seven years. There was a priest who took a liking to me - he would come and lie down next to me in my bed - he would caress me. The first time he did that, I yelled - screamed. I remember it like yesterday. They put me in a small room in the basement with no chair or bed or table - just the four walls. I was in there for days. When I got out, I never screamed again. The priest would come back - not all the time, but many times. This lasted for two years. I wanted to die. I cried many nights. For my mother, my father. Then he left me alone. But it was terrible. Other boys were abused." Nathan paused a moment, wiped a tear from his cheek, then continued. "We were not allowed to speak our language. Most of the boys were Cree, just like me. I had friends at the school. It was what kept us going. I wish I had kept in touch with them, but I could not. I had to disappear. I have no idea where those guys are today. But I escaped. I learned of an uncle who lived on a lake to the north. I got up and left one night. I would have done it before, but I did not know where to go. I was only thirteen."

" And you never found your parents?" asked Laura.

"No. I looked all over for my mother and sister. My uncle told me my father had died the year before I left the school. I cried. Cried. I hardly knew him. I was only six when they took me away. He told me that the day after I arrived at his place. I ended up spending close to seven years with my uncle. We fished, hunted, trapped. I read all of his books - he had many. I feared being found in the early years and returned to the school, so I stayed. I had nowhere else to go. I got used to being up there. It was good, but my uncle died, and I decided that it was time to leave the lake, the bears and the wolves, the beavers and everything else up there. I could not bear the thought of living alone. From Regina, I tried to track down my mother and my sister. I never found out what happened to them."

"You must feel the need for revenge. Have you thought about that?"

"Of course I have, but I have decided to work with what is possible. With this organization, with the people on the reserves, in the communities. No violence or anything like that." Nathan and Laura became close, although Nathan did not, could not, tell her everything. He did however reveal his false identity as a native from Arizona with a college degree. He explained he needed that to get the jobs he had found in teaching and in government work. His real past on the streets of Regina and Saskatoon without a high school or college degree and an escapee from a residential school would not have gotten him anywhere. He asked her to keep the secret. She did. He hoped the relationship could last but he was aware it would end. He could not bring himself to end it. She would be hurt eventually, and he knew it.

As Nathan worked with native communities in the 1980's, he got involved in another project, one that did not involve disruption. It was one about economic opportunity. He continually encountered itinerant and angry young men on the streets of the cities of Western Canada - Vancouver, Edmonton, Calgary, Saskatoon, his former home city of Regina, and Winnipeg. All without work, without hope, far from family, cut off in most cases from their people and ripe for being energized to rise up and mobilize for change and retribution. He met one who was special, who had a dream and a plan. It was not about revolution.

Sam Campbell, a Dene from northern Saskatchewan, had spent half his life on the street, but had gone straight. He had made friends with people 'on the other side' - bankers and businessmen -

through his engaging personality and smarts, as he emerged from his drug and alcohol filled life on the street. He had put together a plan for a native economic development bank for the financing of native businesses. It would be for people with business projects who could not get traditional bank financing and were usually shut out of funding from band councils. Those in general kept whatever funds they received from government for themselves and their own pet projects and family interests. Sam Campbell was resourceful. He made compelling arguments for the native bank and obtained support from people with financial backgrounds to flesh out the workings of the fund.

Nathan met Sam by chance on a reserve in Alberta where the latter explained the bank venture to the band's elders. Nathan immediately saw the merits of it. He spoke with Sam and quickly moved to get on board. There were many things he liked, with one of them being the provision for a review board for every proposed project. comprised of three natives and three non-natives from business. The bank would operate independently of the band councils while benefiting from the experience of businesspeople. Sam Campbell was glad to have Nathan involved. He could see that the young man was smart and could talk.

Nathan ended up making representations to government economic development officials, to band leaders in Manitoba, and to businesspeople in Alberta and Saskatchewan. But the project for the bank never got anywhere. Objections and jealousies developed among the First Nations leaders, many of whom wanted to have a say in the workings of the bank and on who would receive financing or not.

While he was pursuing support for the banking venture, his KGB contact expressed wonderment at what he was doing. "This is about capitalism, Nathan. Business. What are you doing? The idea has been to incite a social revolution, not a capitalist economy. I do not understand. And, your lady, can we be sure she is unaware of us?"

"The lady knows nothing about us. Off limits, comrade. What I do with her is my business. Let's be very clear about that. About the bank project, it was always clear you would object to it. My objective in all I have done with you people, is and always has been, the betterment of conditions of my people. A better life. It is not about communism. I'm sorry. You will have to understand that."

The Russian came back at him. "This is public stuff. You are exposing yourself. You need to be away from any cameras and influential people who draw attention. This will not be good for keeping you in the background to work your plan, our plan. We don't like this."

"Well, that's too bad. I need to do this and I will. If the fund doesn't work, if it is blocked somehow, and it very well could be - this bothers a lot of people - you will see me find other ways to effect change. But I am not doing this, have not been doing this, either here or in Cuba or in Angola because of Marxism, of Communism, for the Soviet model, or any of that. I have been doing all this with you guys because of what it could teach me, support me, in getting a better deal for my people. If it's loans for business and jobs on reserves, more money for schools and doctors in our communities, or if it ends up in armed revolt in the absence of anything else that I have just said, so be it. Things have to change. Discussion over." Nathan looked at his contact in the back seat of the car in Winnipeg, opened the door and walked along the deserted street. The car approached slowly, coming alongside, with the agent leaning towards Nathan, saying calmly but firmly, "Do not go too far on this, Nathan. It will not be healthy for our arrangement."

Nathan did not have to be told that. He had begun to resent the prodding of the Russian. Nevertheless, he suspected he would have to work with them even more than he had up to that time. This economic development project may not proceed. It did not. Within a few weeks, the project had failed. With the refusal of the national chiefs to support the project, the federal government put its contribution on hold, leading private sector backers to rescind their support. It was over. Nathan, Sam and the others involved bitterly resented what had happened. Many young natives with projects for canoe making, finished wood products, nature tours and other ventures that would not get off the ground, burned with rage at the duplicity of their own elders, who in turn blamed the government for not making it easier for the funding to come.

A despairing Sam Campbell announced his own withdrawal from the project and soon after left for the Yukon. Nathan never heard from him again. Before withdrawing, Campbell asked the Government to proceed anyway, without the approval of the national native leadership. The money was there; it had been voted on at cabinet and at Treasury Board. He had support from leaders in banking and economic development. It would have been a bridge to opportunity for natives. The government refused. Said it could not go forward without the support of the national native leadership.

For Nathan, it was simply another example of how the system worked against any change. Along with the despair he observed in the native communities he visited, he saw that things would have to explode before they changed. Exactly what he had believed ten years before. It was back to square one. With the demise of the fund, Nathan lost hope for getting anything done 'normally'. But working with the NGO had served its purpose. He had his network. He went back to identifying opportunities for disruption and recruiting for upheaval. Things had to change.

To facilitate that, in 1986 he got back into the world of Manitoba politics. He went to work once again for Dennis Strong, the member of the legislature for whom he had worked years before. Strong had been recently re-elected, and they had remained friends. Nathan was back in Winnipeg. He vowed to use the position for effecting change however he could. In the two-year interval with the NGO, he had gained a deep understanding of what could be accomplished and of the means to do it. The social fault lines between white and native Canada were ripe for exploitation. The country's infrastructure and economy were vulnerable to sabotage. Police and other security would have no way of coming close to containing disruption if it broke out in a coordinated way. The country was sparsely populated across a vast area. It had a fragile transportation network and energy infrastructure serving a vulnerable, disparate resource economy. A lot of damage could be done, and it would be difficult to contain it. In any case, he had observed there was little taste amongst leaders to confront law-breaking native protesters. There was guilt, but not so much of it to fundamentally seek solutions. Only to avoid confrontation. It was a festering tinderbox and Nathan believed he could ignite it when the timing was right. His training in Cuba and Angola would come in handy. But he needed accomplices and his years travelling the country introduced him to many who could fill the role.

The Russians had recognized this long before. They were convinced they had their man in Nathan Hightower.

In the service of a member of the legislature, Nathan was not viewed by anyone as a radical or a subversive or anyone to be mistrusted. The contacts he made in his new job, however, would lead to the attainment of his objective. One of the new friends he made would cast a vote four years later that would send Canada into chaos.

One of the people he had spotted for disruption was a Mohawk. His brothers had a clandestine cigarette smuggling and distribution operation that had been shut down by the Canadian police in the early '80's, acting in conjunction with the FBI. The family, from the Kahnawake reserve south of Montreal, had lost a cousin in a shootout with police as well as a considerable amount of money and prestige through the police action. The family seethed with anger and looked for revenge. Nathan met the young Mohawk while attending a native conference in Montreal in 1985.

The notion that the Mohawk Nation was a separate nation and not part of Canada, therefore not subject to its laws, rang on deaf ears within the police establishment in the country. Since the shutdown of the cigarette operation, the police had systematically harassed the Kahnawake smuggling networks, compromising the other business activities they were engaged in. Casino gambling, bingo halls and the like had escaped he reach of taxation and government regulatory control. But that was ending. Canadian governments had one idea on the taxation and control of cigarettes and other businesses on reserves with the native communities having quite another.

Nathan identified another Mohawk as an ally. He was from a reserve west of Montreal on the Ottawa River. A brother and a close friend had been run down by Quebec police during a smuggling control raid three years before. The friend was killed and the brother was now a paraplegic. No retribution or compensation was ever paid. In addition to his anger and rage against the injustices he and his family had endured, the young Mohawk expressed a desire to be part of any movement that would get authorities to address native problems, whether it came about from peaceful disturbances or otherwise.

There was the group of young natives in the interior of British Columbia who had blocked for days the roads from a number of the area's sawmills. This prevented the companies involved from getting their product to market, as police were reluctant to force the issue. The standoff lasted two weeks. The natives had been shut out of jobs at the mills. No one from the band had been hired in three years despite the growth of operations that required new people. The road standoff between the small group that had swelled to dozens of young armed men and a large contingent of RCMP officers was only diffused when the band chief ordered the youth to desist. Nathan met with members of the group a few weeks after the standoff. He recognized that the group could be induced, if the circumstances were right, to act once more with greater force and resolve, given the humiliation they felt from the stand-down on the road.

There was the intelligent young Innu from Goose Bay, Labrador. His people, through some quirk of the laws regarding natives, did not receive financial support from the Government of Canada like other First Nations. They lived in squalor in a ramshackle community a few kilometers from the bustling town and military base at Goose Bay. They were excluded from jobs and involvement with the mainstream community. They were also subjected in the summertime during their trips to their traditional hunting grounds to the roar of NATO fighter jets screaming over the treetops in their low-level flight training. This incensed the Innu. The mainstream media of Canada were taking notice. Pressure to cease low-level flight training over the wilds of Labrador had taken on an international dimension with European media reporting on the issue. Nathan met the young Innu leader in Toronto in 1986 at a native affairs conference, quickly understood the potential of the man to be an ally of his, and kept in contact with him. Using cash from his payments from the KGB, he travelled to Labrador in the summer of 1986 and spent five days with the young man and other Innu who would form a core for actions that would come.

17

Montreal, May 1985

"M. Dubé, it has been a while. You are well?" The Russian who Marc Dubé had not seen or heard from in over three years was in front of him in the little cafe on Ste-Catherine Street in the city's east end.

"*Bien sûr, monsieur.* I am well. Yes, it has been a long time. I am surprised you are still here. You don't rotate every three or four years?"

"I went back to Moscow two years ago. Just came back."

"Ok. What can I do for you, Serge? What brings this? No more long curly hair and big sweaters," said Marc Dubé to the Russian.

"Congratulations on your marriage. I am informed your wife is a very accomplished and engaging actress. I wish you well" said Pavel Tedorenko. "And yes, no longer the student disguise. *C'est du passé.*"

"What is your cover here? You told me years ago you worked for a printer."

"No need to talk about that, Marc. It's not important."

"Alright. What can I do for you? It has been a while since you have asked me for anything. Not since the events in '81." Must be careful, he thought. They had Adela Cerny killed - most likely because of what I told them. Not wise to bring that up.

"The money has continued, as we have always wanted to pursue the relationship, but there has been little to do. Besides, we needed to take a distance from you. What happened in Ottawa was dangerous. The police could have put you under surveillance. A young lady on the federal side tragically lost her life. The police could have believed it was us. They could have dug a bit and discovered our relationship."

The agent had spared Dubé the trouble of bringing up the subject. "Serge, come on, Adela Cerny was working for you. You told me that."

"Yes, she cooperated with us. It was voluntary. She came from Czechoslovakia. That is part of our world. Then she turned. We were not aware of what she told the police, however, we have seen she did not tell them about you, because of what has not happened in the interim. Let's not talk about that. We need to start working again."

Voluntary. Yes, I'm sure, thought Dubé. Not likely. "Alright. Working together. What about? We are still in power. Our premier is popular. What do you want to know?"

"How come your premier, so ardent a proponent of the independence of Quebec, could now be so enamored with the Malone government in Ottawa? What does he call it, *'le beau risque'*?"

"He is for a sovereign Quebec, not a totally independent Quebec. There is a difference. He wants a better deal for Quebec -

sovereignty-association. It frustrates me. The only way for Quebec to find its way, is for us to have our own country - free and clear. He is not as committed to that as I am."

"You are his chief advisor on relations with Ottawa. It looks like you are pedaling softly on all this."

"I'm not, but I have to go along with it. He is all powerful in our party and in our government. He believes it will be good for Quebec. Malone has told him he is working on a better deal, will undo what Trudel did, shutting Quebec out of the new constitution. He says what we managed to scuttle that day in 1981 will be repaired."

"OK, but back to where we are. Our objectives are still very complementary, are they not, M. Dubé?"

"If you help me, I will help you." He thought of the bank account in Switzerland that just kept getting bigger. "Now, what would you like to have me do now?"

"Scuttle this *'beau risque'* relationship. A renewed bond between Ottawa and Quebec City does not serve our interests, yours or ours. You have the premier's ear. He listens to you. He has to start mistrusting Malone, this Irishman, who he appears to like."

"This Irishman is an engaging person. Quebecers like him. He is from here. Speaks like us. Won close to 80% of the seats here in the election last year. I told you, he has promised the premier he would repair the damage done in 1981. It is taking the wind out of our sails."

"You can do it. Use your guile. You know everything that is going on. It is easy to twist reality when it comes to political matters. He respects you. You seem to have influence with the other key ministers. You are the constitutional and relations-with-Ottawa guru in this province. Your wife is influential in the artistic community. I understand she is an ardent *indépendantiste* like you. There can be nothing so productive in a social or political movement than getting the arts community involved and leading the charge for change. It has been going on in Quebec for twenty years. Just need to give it another boost. *'Le Québec aux Québécois'.*"

"Don't patronize, Serge. You will never comprehend just how deep the feeling is in Quebecers for their heritage. It is also a powder keg. It can go far. Quebecers are also protective of their material security. If they believe the cost is too great, they will not support it. It is a balancing act. But, please, my Hélène is to be left out of this. She knows nothing of our relationship and I intend to keep it that way."

"OK. But will you endeavor to change your boss's attitude about dealing with Malone and with Ottawa? Stir it up, Dubé. Stir it up. Will you?"

"OK. By the way, what has happened to the Marxist movement on campuses and in the unions that you guys were fomenting? It has practically disappeared. All the stuff that was on the campuses and in the coffeehouses in the '70's? Have the French guys from Paris gone underground? I have stayed away from that, along with my boss. As far as we could. But what happened? You were making progress, making Marxism-Leninism the modus operandi of just about every student movement in the province."

"We dropped it. The students who led these movements had no credibility. The key was to influence the labor movement. Student movements were to assist in this. Did not work so well. The students became annoying, far too idealistic. Instead, they attracted infiltration from security and the police, threatening to expose our involvement, and .labour leaders took their distance. At the same time, the guys from France and the events of '68 moved on. The local kids generally didn't like them, anyway. Many professors still preach on about the benefits of our system, but fewer people are listening. They are getting old and have lost their ability to influence. Tiresome academics. Nothing more."

"OK. When do we meet again?"

"In two weeks," replied the Russian. "Need to have some ideas from you. Things that we can work on in Ottawa."

"Ottawa. So you have someone again in Ottawa?"

"We always have someone in Ottawa. And you must appreciate I cannot tell you who they are, so don't ask. See that place down the street? The bistro with the big picture window and the wooden sign hanging in front of the door. Meet you there at a table in the back at 3PM two weeks from today. Mondays in Montreal are OK for you, I assume?"

"Yes, Monday here. See you then."

Marc Dubé walked out of the cafe, turned up rue Iberville and then hailed a taxi to take him to his Montreal office. OK. I can think of some things that can cause trouble with Ottawa. Back in the game. With some help in Ottawa, there may be a chance to disrupt the affairs with the Irishman.

"Where do we go this evening? It's raining and cold for May and I don't want to cook." Hélène Beaulieu had just arrived at the apartment in Old Quebec that she and Marc shared.

"Café de la Paix. Rue du Jardin. We have not been there for a while. Just right for a cold, rainy night."

"Good. They have great strawberries - even at this time of year and their lamb dishes are superb."

They put on their coats and walked to the quiet little restaurant that had been there for decades. Only one other table was occupied, with the wind whistling its way through the streets of Old Quebec.

"Marc, how is it that your boss can be so besotted with Malone? He is agreeing on everything Ottawa is doing in Quebec. We have a sovereigntist government, *bon dieu*. You are part of it. He listens to you and a couple of others and nobody else."

"He does what he wants," responded Dubé. "He has his instincts. He believes it is best for Quebec. I do too." He was lying. He could not begin to give anyone, even his wife, any indication that he was about to instigate a deterioration in relations between his boss and the Government of Canada.

"What? Marc, what are you saying? You are going along with it? You accept this?"

"We're giving this a chance. If Ottawa does not deliver, then we go for another referendum. In the meantime, we cooperate. We need to see where it goes."

"There are rumblings. Not only in my crowd but across the party, particularly in Montreal. They are complaining that the premier has sold out, lost the desire, given in. If things keep going the way they are, people will really be upset and they will want somebody else. Perron, the wise old economist drinks too much, we all know that, but he has not lost it. He resigned because of the premier's wavering on things even before Malone took over. Marc, what are you doing? You do nothing to change his ideas?"

"I repeat, Hélène, we are being practical. We are in the process of bringing major investment to Quebec. There is big funding coming from Ottawa for aerospace, for regional development, even money for car plants and high-tech research centres, stuff we have never seen before. The Malone government is working quickly on all of this. Money talks. It is viewed as delivering on the *beau risque*. Money to grow, become stronger economically. Delivering smart government. We are taking Ottawa's money in buckets, huge buckets. It is good business right now." What bullshit this is, but I must go along with it, he thought. "If Ottawa starts screwing us again, we go back to the old strategy. It will probably happen, but it is not the right time to do it. I don't think your friends believe what I'm saying or want to wait, but that is what it is."

Marc was not open with his wife. It clawed at him. He led a double life. Close to thirteen years. He could not change that now. He could have but didn't. The Russian connection had him. He could have stopped it in Montreal in 1974 - he could have said no; he could have let it die in the last few years, even now with no activity for so long, but he did not. If he stopped, they could expose him. It was his biggest fear. Hélène would go. I would look a fool. The boss would exile me from any and all. My life as I know it would be over. I can't quit.

"He's got five ministers against him now. It is even out in the public. He's drinking. Perron, who resigned as finance minister in November, is bringing people with him. Pageau is making a mess of things. He is not well. Looks like someone is poisoning the waters. Our man looks to be at work." The two men sitting in the small office in the basement of the Soviet Embassy in Ottawa were discussing Quebec.

140

"Well, for many, Premier Pageau is not aggressive enough on independence. Cooperating with Malone is upsetting his supporters and many of his ministers, although he still has the support of the people. But fights are starting with Ottawa, just as we have hoped they would. Going back to the way it used to be. Our guy on the inside is at work, doing what we asked him to do."

"It looks like you are stirring things up. Arguments with Ottawa on many things. The papers are saying the premier is losing his support." They were at the cafe in the east end of Montreal.

Marc took a sip of his coffee, then looked across at the Russian. "Dealings between Quebec and the federal government are very sensitive. It does not take much to upset the relationship. Officials in Quebec can be very touchy about how they are dealt with. Impressions are as important as reality. There is a long history of enmity. Endemic, actually. It does not take much to get it going again. Just me asking a few questions of officials whether in Ottawa or Quebec City can get things moving in the wrong direction - the right direction for us - but the wrong direction for good relations between the two levels of government."

"Things look to be going badly for your boss."

"He's not well and has lost patience with many around him. I'm not sure if he has much drive left to continue. I have done my best to disrupt his dealings with Ottawa, but we may have been too successful for the wrong reason. Internal cohesion in the government has become fractured. Ministers resigning and all of that. If he steps down, no replacement will be as popular as he. We could lose the next election which has to be called soon."

On October 3, 1985, Adrien Pageau, the iconic, chain-smoking, much loved yet maligned Premier of Quebec for close to nine years, resigned. A new Parti National premier was sworn in after a short party leadership campaign and within a few days, called an election for early December. In that election, the government was defeated, and a new Liberal government took power. Soon afterwards, the new premier responded positively to Prime Minister Malone's proposal of a process to bring Quebec into the Canadian constitutional framework that had left the province out four years before. Things were going badly for the separatists. They had lost their referendum in 1980, they had been left out of the new Canadian constitution in 1981 (in large part led by Marc Dubé's duplicity), looking foolish in the process. Their beloved long-time leader was out of politics, and they were now out of power. Separating from Canada and forming a country was more remote now for the Parti National than it had been when they were first elected nine years before. Marc Dubé went underground, politically speaking. Things had backfired. He never thought Pageau would resign so quickly and that his government would be so readily defeated. He had little to do. By the end of January 1986, he had taken a teaching job at the University of Montreal. His Russian contact left him alone. He would be of little use to them. Payments into the Swiss bank account became sporadic. He did not complain. Suddenly, he had little to offer, but that would change. He also thought he could stop. He thought he would tell Serge to cease transferring money, even if it was sporadic. But to say that would say he was quitting. He could not afford to do that. He was still with them whether he wanted to be or not. "You just don't leave this," Serge had said.

18

Toronto, May 1986

"Lawson had to resign. Sordid affair. Call girls in Vegas. His EA set up the meetings, for God's sake. Pretty stupid stuff," said Mary Ellen Maclean. She and her fiancé Andrew Brown were at their favorite restaurant in Toronto's Little Italy. Andrew said nothing. Mary Ellen could not ever be told about what happened.

"Yes, pretty dumb. They will always come out, sooner or later," said Andrew. He wanted to ask Mary Ellen about her father but held back. "You're still going to run? Still want to do it?"

"Of course. And I will win. Toronto is Liberal. The riding association is supportive, even though they must be officially neutral. They want to win it back from the Tory guy who somehow won in 1980, although I must admit he has done a pretty good job. My opponent for the nomination is not well known and I'm told will have challenges raising money. He doesn't believe in corporate donations. Daddy is looking after my campaign financing. I should be alright."

In the months that followed, Andrew Brown proved to be a thorn in the side of the of the U.S. administration as well as of the proponents in Canada of greater cooperation with the United States. In regular editorials, he blasted takeover attempts of Canadian companies, leaked rumored initiatives of American interests to divert water to the United States, of contemplated takeovers of Canadian publishing and media interests, some real, some rumored. A snowballing anti-American sentiment in Canada's largest city was being fomented by The Toronto Herald.

Andrew and Mary Ellen were married in June of 1986 in a wedding ceremony at Toronto's St. Michael's Cathedral with a large party afterwards at the King Edward Hotel.

In the federal election a few weeks later, Mary Ellen won her riding, but the Conservatives under their new leader, David Malone, carried the country on the promise of renewed economic growth and national reconciliation with Quebec. This despite the main newspaper of the country, The Toronto Herald, advocating voting for the governing Liberals and warning of what a Conservative government could do to Canadian economic sovereignty.

Andrew's exchanges with his handler intensified. The Malone Government announced its intentions of pursuing greater cooperation with the United States on economic and military affairs as well as on opposition to the activities of the Eastern Bloc and their ally Cuba in Africa, Latin America and The Middle East. Despite Secretary Gorbachev's espousal of perestroika with the West, the KGB was still under the influence of the old guard. It intensified its attempts at disruption of the alliances and principal governments of the West.

President Reagan and Malone, during a get-together in Quebec City, announced their intent to work towards a comprehensive free trade agreement between the two countries. Andrew was having dinner at Winston's, the Toronto moneyed class's restaurant of choice, when he learned of it. Mary Ellen was at a function in her riding. His assistant Elaine had just called him with the news coming from Quebec City.

Appalling. He didn't run on it. Was not part of the platform. Never said anything about it. It will be a disaster for Canada. We cannot let it happen. .....Sergei, you and your people will help in this. But the stuff about Mary Ellen's father....I am a lot less independent from them with this... The fuckers.

"My dear, we need to mobilize. Your caucus. The Liberal establishment. The academics. Labor. Malone has a majority and what looks like good vibes with Reagan. He could bring this a long way. The Americans will screw us royally." Andrew and Mary Ellen were having dinner at Hy's Steakhouse, just off Parliament Hill..

"Our caucus is totally demoralized, Andrew. Even six months after the election. Lots of good people lost their seats and are not around anymore. Opposition to the leader is gaining ground. Attention is on internal stuff. We are not nice to ourselves. Could be difficult to get real attention to this for a while."

"Need to do it, Mary. I can get the literati of Toronto up in arms about this, but it needs to jell across Canada. The party must mobilize against Malone on this. The American elephant is coming through the door. People have to understand that."

"Well, I have a seat on the Commons Committee on Trade. I can use that to an extent. We get lots of information from the government, but I wonder how much of what is really happening is shared with us. I must be careful. If stuff I get shows up in the papers, it will mean trouble. I can only go so far."

"Understood, but there are serious implications for the country of what Malone is trying to do. Case by case, alright?

"Alright. Love you, Andrew."

"I love you too. Let's move on. Waiter....the check please."

While they were waiting for the check, Andrew moved to another subject. "How is your father doing? I haven't spoken to him in a while."

"He's down in Nassau. Left yesterday. Wanted to spend a few days in the sun. Will be back day after tomorrow. I'm envious. Ottawa is not the Bahamas."

"Did your mum go with him?"

"No, she stayed in Toronto. Quick turnaround trips like that are not her thing," responded Mary Ellen.

"OK. Lucky guy. Would love to be in the sun myself." He's doing it. They were right. Trouble.

"To the apartment now?" asked Andrew as they left the restaurant and crossed the sidewalk to hail a cab. "To the apartment," said the young lady as she took Andrew's hand and looked forward to spending a rare night with her husband.

"Your lady is a member of the Commons committee on Trade. We want information on what is being shared on possible changes to trade policies with the Soviet Bloc. Our German friends are trying to sell machinery to companies here. Getting nowhere. We are told new embargoes are being contemplated. We need all this. We also need to know what is being shared with the committee on trade with the United States, particularly for military equipment. The new government is listening to the military and has a shopping list of materiel it wants to buy. French, Swiss, Swedish. Will help their armaments industries."

146

"There is a limit to what I will do in this regard. Robert, you must leave my wife out of it. Defense stuff is off limits. It always has been."

"Not anymore, Andrew. You will have to be more cooperative in this. I think you understand what I mean," the Russian said, looking Andrew straight in the eye.

"Listen. We have been lucky so far. As far as I can tell, we have been below the radar of the RCMP. Messing with defense stuff would increase the risk of me becoming observed. You and I need me to avoid getting the attention of the police and especially the U.S. intelligence guys. I'll make a deal with you. If you back off on your demands for defense-related information, I will provide you with other information. On politicians, on industry leaders, on non-American trade related matters. But this defense stuff puts me in a very difficult position. I cannot go there. But if you want to compromise someone influential, chances are I can deliver enough to allow you to do that. Special situations of special people. I will have to be careful, but I can do it. Could that be a fair trade-off?" Andrew was desperate to find a way to neutralize the blackmail ploy of the Russian.

"Not really important to us. But I will think about it. Nevertheless, I have told you what we want." After a moment, the Russian turned, reached into the breast pocket of his jacket, and brought out a folded sheaf of paper. "By the way, here is a document I thought you would appreciate. A recording of a conversation between the head of international business at Columbus Media and one of their lawyers. They apparently want to buy CTT, the big private broadcaster here, of course, and are contemplating a hostile takeover with promises of significant Canadian content. They also spoke of contacts they would like to make with the Conservative appointees to the regulatory board, what you call the CRTC. Through third parties, of course, lobbyists and the like. All above board, legally, my friend, but I am sure of great interest to Canadian readers. Good stuff for you Andrew, is it not? "

"Yes. This will raise a stink, that's for sure."

"Well then, the partnership is working for you. But we need things in return.....as always. I will be expecting the information on the trade files at your earliest convenience. Defense matters are still part of the requirement." Andrew looked at the document, thumbed through the three pages, then looked at the Russian as the latter rose, put on his coat, and left.

As he left the meeting, the Soviet agent determined that efforts to find an alternate source of information on defense matters would have to be intensified. Andrew Brown was just a journalist.

19

Ottawa, March 1987

The Prime Minister of Canada, David Malone, had succeeded in getting agreement with the premiers of all the Canadian provinces to provisions for adjustments to the Canadian constitution. The terms would allow the Province of Quebec to ratify the constitution. It was something that had hung over the political landscape of the country since the late-night deal amongst the leaders of the provinces six years before that had excluded Quebec. The premiers met in a marathon session in a log cabin on Meech Lake north of Ottawa. They agreed on terms that would respect Quebec's distinctiveness in the Constitution of Canada as well as officially recognize powers for Quebec that had been informally recognized for decades. Each of the provinces would have three years to have their legislatures officially approve the constitutional framework. The Meech Lake Accord was a major achievement for national unity. Few people in the country had thought it possible.

The Accord was a hammer-blow to the Parti National and the sovereignty movement in Quebec. Through the Accord, Quebec would be moving more to a solid relationship with the rest of Canada than towards independence. This was also a setback to the Russians in their plans for disrupting Canada and weakening the US-Canada alliance.

Something was left out, however, in the view of many people. Canada's natives. There was no recognition of the rights of native peoples nor of any attempt to take advantage of the new deal to include provisions for better treatment of them. This was not lost on Nathan Cromwell, once again working for the member for Elk River in the Manitoba Legislature.

What has our premier done? Agreed to Malone's big proposal? Nothing about native rights. Looks like he didn't even bring it up. All about Quebec. But this needs the approval of the legislatures. All ten of them. That means we can disrupt it. How stupid the system is. Election coming up. We will see about the approval of Manitoba. And my guys, my warriors across the land. One more lance driven into the ground, Nathan told himself.

While the Government of Canada was pursuing a new constitutional arrangement for the country, it was also aggressively pursuing a free trade deal with the United States. Negotiations accelerated in 1987 and became the focus of public attention. Opposition to free trade in Canada centered in Toronto where most of the country's cultural, intellectual and media elite were located. The opposition was being mobilized under the leadership of the Toronto Herald, and the pen of Andrew Brown.

"Andrew, are you not going overboard on this? Diverting lakes and rivers into the United States for guaranteed freshwater supply to thirsty Americans? Come on. You can't be serious." Andrew and his wife were having breakfast. That day's edition of the Herald was on the table.

"Mary Ellen, sources inside the government are saying this is part of the discussion. I have to write about it."

"What sources? Nobody in the party in Ottawa is picking that up. Come on."

"Well, it is being discussed. I of course cannot divulge who is telling me about this. Not even to you, my dear. There are a lot of other scary things as well. I have to write about them." Andrew was being informed by his KGB handler of what they were picking up in Washington. The wild assertions about water, unlimited access to Canadian fishing zones, unlimited American movies on Canadian TV were farfetched - even he was skeptical - but they served his purpose. This free trade agreement will not, cannot, go through, thought Andrew Brown as he tried to change the subject. "How is your mother?"

"Are you happy with the information, Andrew? We are going to great lengths to find you material for your articles."

"Where are you getting this stuff? Some of it looks totally off-base. Control of water in Canada? From Congress? From the Administration? Come on..."

The Russian looked at Andrew and responded. "There are many people in the United States, all over government, the federal government, Congress, state legislatures who are ignorant of Canada and who, nevertheless, speak their minds. Some of it, much of it, is hogwash. Most of them have no idea of what they are talking about. But the ones who have a stake in the issues around Canada make their views known. What they want out of a free trade deal. What they would like to have. We pick it up. It is easy. Whether it is part of a negotiating position we have no real idea, Andrew. But it stirs things up. And that is what we want, what you want, right?"

"What is your real objective in this?"

"We have been over this before. Our objectives in this endeavor are the same as yours. An American domination of Canada is not in our interests and it is something you wish to avoid as well, as we have discussed many times. Our goals are the same. Nothing has changed."

"Very good. Just checking. Keep it coming."

"But we have not finished this discussion. You are not giving us very much on the defense-related issues out of Ottawa. Your wife has access to many things we would like to know. You try to avoid this, but it is part of our relationship. Good material from you produces good material from us, my friend. Here is what we would like to receive. It is no different from the last time we met." The Russian proceeded to repeat the shopping list.

"I thought you would be using other avenues for this. Are they not working?" asked Andrew.

The Russian would not go there. The mole at the Department of Defense had been working well for them.

"You may think what you want. I need more from you."

"Look, I am not going to go into those things you are asking. It was never part of the arrangement...ever. Trade matters, intergovernmental relations, diplomatic stuff between Canada and the U.S., maybe. But defense and all of that. No. If you continue, we will break off the arrangement."

"You can't break it off, Andrew. It's not something you can resign from."

If only the old man could die, thought Andrew. No more blackmail.

"I will think about it. But I have no contacts in the part of government that deals with defense matters or the military."

"Your wife does."

"She is in opposition. It's different."

"Still knows the same people."

"I am not going to have my wife become an agent for Soviet intelligence."

20

February 1988, Ottawa, Office of the Minister Responsible for Security and Intelligence

"Minister, we have detained an employee of the Department of Defense on suspicion of espionage on behalf of the Soviet Union. This may become public. We are here to inform you of the details of the suspected breach as well as provide you with talking points for the media should his arrest become public." The head of the Canadian Security Intelligence Service was briefing his minister on intelligence matters.

"Who is he and what has he done?" asked the Minister

"The man is a weapons system program manager for the Navy's secret nuclear submarine project. We suspect he has passed on details of it to the Soviets over the past few months and possibly from the inception of the project close to two years ago. He was intercepted as he was in the process of delivering critical information about the sub program to the opposition here in Ottawa. Information that would be embarrassing to the government and possibly a breach of top-secret agreements with the U.S. Department of Defense. Our own officials believe the information would jeopardize any potential public support for the project. Counterintelligence intensified their tracking of the man's activities a few weeks ago. The surveillance established a pattern of comings and goings out of Ottawa that had little relation to the man's official duties or family situation. One of our agents intercepted the man as he was depositing a large envelope in a mailbox in Belleville. It was addressed to the New Democratic Party parliamentary defense critic.

"What was in the envelope?" asked the Minister.

"A copy of the Treasury Board submission for additional program funding that is to be considered at the Treasury Board meeting next week. The document contained different information from the Cabinet committee document that ministers had reviewed and approved three months ago. It had information regarding far higher costs than what had been in the cabinet document. Three billion dollars higher. Anyone who had this information could make it public. "

"This is pretty sensitive." said the Minister. "The government would be compelled to explain what was going on. Just the subject of nuclear-powered attack submarines is controversial. Billions of dollars would do it for public opinion. We would have to make it public, with everything about the project being right. But what this person has done in itself is not espionage. A breach of the Official Secrets Act, maybe, but not espionage. How do you know he was working with the Russians?"

"We went to his home while officers were trailing him to Belleville. He lived alone; no one was there. We found over ten thousand dollars in cash, as well as a notebook with references to meetings with a Yuri. We confronted him. He broke down and admitted to providing information to the Russians. He apparently gave them the original Treasury Board submission - he was the author of part of it - as well as design and function specifications of the weapons systems. He had been relaying information to them for two years."

"What's his story?" asked the Minister.

"He is a career employee of the government and has been at Defense for over fifteen years. He apparently had a difficult marriage. The Russians probably learned he worked on special armaments procurement projects. On a trip to Washington a couple of years ago for a meeting, he was honey-trapped at the bar of his hotel by a woman, Russian, or Czech or East German, whatever. The sexual activity was filmed. They threatened to show all to his wife. He needed to cooperate to avoid that. The man could not afford a divorce, apparently. He got it anyway without the honey trap film being part of it. His wife divorced him last year, apparently putting him in some degree of financial difficulty. In the meantime, he had been passing information to the Russians and was caught up in it. He couldn't stop. And he needed money."

"The Americans are aware of all this?"

"Yes and are not happy. One of the designs in the leaked information is of an American weapons system that has remained secret to date. Not anymore. They are not happy."

The minister knew right away that the Prime Minister would not be happy either. David Malone had worked hard on building a relationship with the President and had received assurances from him on cooperation on files important to Canada. This would put a dent in the relationship.

"Does the Privy Council Office know about this? Will the Prime Minister have been briefed on the breach?"

"Not yet. We needed to brief you first," responded the head of CSIS.

"Very good. I will tell him. By the way, how many Russian and other Soviet bloc intelligence operatives do you estimate there are in the country? We have talked about this before," asked the Minister.

"We believe there could be as many as forty or fifty. Some surely more active than others."

"And you don't know who they are?"

"No, we don't. We have spoken of this before. If we did, they would not continue to be in the country. We catch one from time to time, but most of them elude us until they go back to their country or move on. Some of them act and look like Canadians. Very good covers. The Russians, the East Germans and the Czechs excel at it. The Russians are more political and defense focused. The East Germans and Czechs are more into industrial espionage. We work closely with the Americans of course."

"What about other possible moles in the government, like the defense guy? How do you know there are not others like him?"

"We believe there are others. We cannot of course track everyone, Minister. The area of most concern to us around our computer networks, our data systems. All governments in the world are vulnerable to this. We will be seeing a lot of it. We have our suspicions. Their cultural attaches are usually all KGB, but we must have some proof. If not, we would be expelling Russians all the time, and they in turn would be expelling our people from Moscow. We need to discover them in the act and then observe their movements to see what Canadians they may be dealing with."

"And the suspected mole in the Quebec government. You don't know who it is?" asked the Minister.

"No, we don't. There is someone, but we have not determined who it is."

"Very well, keep at it. I will inform you on what transpires with the Prime Minister. This will not help our relations with the Americans."

Frank Russo was with his counter-intelligence team, gathered after their briefing with the minister. "Guys, we need to get closer to what is happening in Quebec. The Russians have someone on the inside there. We have known it for years, but have never been able to pin it on anybody. We need to find out who it is. This has gone on long enough. The CIA will find out before us. I do not want that to happen. Who can we put up there? Marcel and his guys are not getting it done."

"How about Bill Wilson? He has been the key guy for us out west. His cover is good. Computer consultant - could set up shop in Quebec City. Understands Quebec; speaks good French. How about it?" said one of the agents.

"Yes. Bill Wilson. You're right. Bring him in."

21

In native communities across Canada, young men were agitating and mobilizing for change - with their elders, their band councils, with government, whoever was in their way. It erupted in the summer of 1987 and would steamroll over the next three years. The Meech Lake Accord, which had nothing in it for natives, provided an added impetus for action. Frustration and anger which had been drowned in petty crime, liquor and despair was awakening. The network that Nathan Hightower had spent four years building was in a state of readiness. The leaders he had found, motivated to take action, were organizing, talking to their people, building support for whatever action would be required to disrupt the system. If violence was needed, violence would be used. But they needed money to do it, with it all remaining underneath the radars of the band councils and the police. Nathan had more frequent meetings with his KGB handlers. They could see what he was doing. The table was being set. He made a big demand – one million dollars to fuel his network across the country, his chosen group of leaders in the field, to pay for equipment, weapons, and other cash outlays.

"One million dollars? That's big, Nathan."

"You want revolution? It is not going to happen by itself. It needs money and if it doesn't get it, it won't happen. The million is a minimum, by the way."

"It is still a lot. Why won't it be squandered? They waste just about everything the government gives them. Why will this be any different?" asked the Russian.

"Because I will be in charge," replied Nathan. "You trained me for this. I will manage it. You will just have to trust me. And please do not denigrate my people with your comments. If you back away from this, nothing of substance will happen."

Discussions went back and forth. His contact had to consult his superiors. In the end, he received assurances the money would be coming, in cash tranches of $50,000.

Nathan had targeted twelve communities for action when the timing was right. Eight of them had made the grade over the previous year. Each had a strong leader who was smart, motivated and seen to be able to bring potential fighters to the cause. No one in these groups, including their leaders, had any idea their actions were being financed by the KGB.

"Where are you getting this money, Nathan. It's a lot," asked the Ojibway from Northern Ontario.

"Contraband. There's lots of it. Cigarettes. Booze. Stuff coming across the border," responded Nathan. It was easy to buy into as an explanation. Natives across Canada were highly successful in generating large amounts of cash from contraband goods - tobacco, liquor, electronics, even cars. "A group of guys, who I will not name, have been very successful in their smuggling, and have decided to put aside a large share of their profits for the defense of select brothers such as you to defend their territories and their rights. I have been asked to manage the fund. You have been singled out. Don't ask me for details. But now you know where it comes from." Nothing was traced or verifiable, with no paper trail.

Nathan's activities in setting the wheels in motion were carried out completely under the radar of the police. Warrior leaders were given training in guerilla tactics, weapons, and in recruiting of support in their communities. It was easy. The woods and forests of Canada are extensive, and the police could not come close to monitoring what goes on deep inside them.

The benefits of Nathan's Cuba training were passed on to young men who would become the Warriors - of Peace River, of Kahnawake, of Sheshashih, of Haida, of Miramichi and elsewhere. Cubans posing as Seminole Indians from Florida who had supposedly been trained in the U.S. Marine Corps managed to avoid detection from authorities and moved across the western part of the country carrying out training operations, usually deep in the woods, avoiding contact with band elders and others who could betray what was going on. Another group of Nez Perce from Idaho, former members of the U.S. military, crossed the border and hooked up with a group in Alberta. In the east, groups of Mohawks and Oneidas from New York State crossed over into Quebec and Ontario, unseen and unimpeded, and met with brothers there to plan disruptions of waterways and other infrastructure. People in many of the native bands could see that 'something' was developing in their own communities, but it stayed in the communities. Police and government officials were in the dark. They had always believed that violence could be only around the corner but were blind to what was going on. Whatever was out there appeared to be no different from anything else that been happening for a long time. Clueless and ready to be pounced on.

Victor Estinov, known to Nathan as Alexei, was meeting Nathan in a cafe on a cold snowy night on the TransCanada Highway just outside Brandon, Manitoba. There was no one else in the place. It was one of their monthly meetings when the Russian would hand over the current installment of the funds. "Nathan, this Meech Lake Accord. You know it does nothing for your people. The legislature here must ratify the agreement. It has a while to do it. Over two years to get it done. A lot could happen in the meantime." The Russian paused for a second or two, then continued. "You want progress for your people. If enough of them in Manitoba rise up against the deal, it could have difficulty passing. If your people could find a champion for the cause in the Legislature, maybe it could defeat the ratification. You work there. Is there anyone who could be that champion?"

Nathan thought about it for a moment. Looking out the window next to the booth as the snow continued to fall, an idea came to mind.

"I think I do. Under special circumstances, he could do some damage. He is in a unique position. I agree with you about the Accord. It does nothing for us."

Nathan Cromwell and Ellison Ward were in the coffee shop of the provincial legislature. Ward was the member for Rider Mountain, and the only Native member of the Manitoba Legislature. The most recent Manitoba election had returned a Conservative government but with a razor-thin majority of seats.

"Ellison, you agree with this Meech Lake deal?"

"No. Of course not." said Ward. "Does nothing for us. Could never agree to it."

"You could can it, all by yourself if you wanted to, Ellison."

"How could I do that? I have one vote. The government has enough support to get it done."

"It does now. It has a very small majority. But, if one or two members quit or decide not to vote on their side, the outcome can be decided by someone in opposition. Here is how you could be that someone."

"Before you do that, Nathan, what are you doing? Your member says he is in favor of the accord and would vote for its ratification. You are talking about defeating it. What are you doing?"

"This is about us, Ellison. Us, the Indians. The forgotten Indians. My loyalties are to my people, just as yours are. Here's how you could defeat this agreement that does nothing for us......"

22

Moscow, September 1988

The Ottawa station chief and the head of KGB intelligence operations for North America were seated at the large table in the outer office of their boss. Nikolai Kozlov, known to everyone as Control, entered the room and sat down at the end of the table.

"Well, gentlemen, please tell me exactly what is happening in Canada. I have reports of course, but I want to hear it directly from you." The veteran career KGB field officer who had been part of the plan hatched many years before to disrupt Canada, had made it to the top. He also had his own power base within the ruling elite of the Soviet Union. He was not a favorite of Secretary Gorbachev. But he had managed to keep his position and cause trouble for the Americans and their allies, despite Gorbachev's declarations of Glasnost - openness to the world. He knew too much and had too many allies in the Party. A dangerous man. Heads of the KGB always were. Gorbachev did not dare oust him. Kozlov remembered the discussions he had almost twenty years before that set the Canadian operations in motion. He wanted to hear firsthand how they were going. The penetration seemed to be working.

The head of the North American directorate responded. "It is a program for disruption with many elements. The objective is the weakening of the Canadian-American alliance through the weakening of Canada itself, to direct attention of the Americans northward and away from other areas of the world of interest to us.

There are sensitivities and frictions within Canada that we have exploited for years."

"I am aware of that, but go ahead." Kozlov did not need to tell the men about his role in the initial plan.

"Thank you, comrade Kozlov. I proceed. Ever since the late 1960's we have targeted the underlying frictions in that country. We have infiltrated the student movements and academic communities. There is a large contingent of Marxist-Leninists in Quebec's colleges and universities. Efforts in this regard in the rest of Canada have not been as successful, however. But in Quebec, it has worked, although we needed something bigger. We have an asset at the highest levels of the independence movement in Quebec. This man has been a key advisor to the Premier of the province, his right-hand man on relations with the federal government. He has been working with us since 1972. His party is not in power now, but he remains someone we work with. His objective is the breakup of Canada. Just like ours. He likes the money we give him as well as information we provide him on our intelligence from Ottawa and Washington."

"I know about that, but please do proceed. We all need to have the same picture.," said Kozlov.

"In the 1970's we saw the potential of infiltrating the native population, the Indians, and exploiting their anger with their treatment," the man continued. "Enough frustration and anger exist in their communities to explode into a revolt, given the right conditions and coordination. There are over 700 Indian bands in Canada. They do not always cooperate with each other. The objective has been to identify a small number of native communities to lead a revolt that could spread and cause serious disruption for government and the non-native population. We needed to find leaders for this. Through the planting of a few young agents who we transformed into Canadians, similar to what we have done in the United States, who look, act and speak like Canadians - we found a number of young natives who could be recruited and trained to cause trouble. The best one spent four years with us in Cuba and returned to Canada under a new identity. With our help and money, he has built, under the noses of the police and the mainstream levels of government, a network of young natives across the country who will soon be ready to rise up. The plan is to have them block roads and highways, take over local communities, draw the attention of the military, and cause much economic disruption. The man, code named Cannon, is also in the process of influencing the outcome of a Province of Manitoba resolution to approve or not a constitutional accord that would solidify the Canadian union. His actions with a member of the Legislature, given the right set of circumstances, could ultimately cause the demise of the accord. This could lead to the central government falling and cause added concern of the Americans as to the solidity of their northern ally."

"Our actions in infiltrating the Canadian defense establishment have led to the abandonment of their nuclear submarine program. It would never have been a popular one with the generally pacifist Canadian population but leaks to the government opposition effectively put an end to it. Our man did his job. He got caught, but the damage was done."

"How many assets do we have in the Canadian defense establishment, the military and related government authorities?" asked the man at the head of the table.

"At this moment, we along with our German and Czech colleagues have over thirty collaborators providing us information at different levels of cooperation. Ten in the armed forces, four in the bureaucracy, and now over twenty employees of military equipment contractors and technology companies related to defense. The Americans are particularly concerned about what they suspect to be our penetration of the defense equipment industry."

"How reliable are they?" asked the boss.

"We have to be careful, obviously, but the threat of blackmail is very strong. In almost all cases, we have something on them which compels them to be cooperative."

"Did the man who got caught reveal any of our other assets?"

"He couldn't have. He did not know any of our other assets nor the existence of any of our other operations."

"Very well. Go on. The other elements of the program...."

"We managed to blackmail a young Czech-born Canadian government employee to cooperate with us a few years ago. This operation contributed to the exclusion of Quebec from signing on to the new Canadian constitution, helped along by our mole in the Quebec sovereignty movement. An exclusion which has poisoned relations between Quebec and the rest of Canada ever since. Unfortunately, we had to eliminate her before she could betray the identity of our Quebec mole. He was a key government advisor at the time."

"Further, we have always recognized that an economic union between Canada and the United States would be of great benefit to both countries and would solidify the cooperation between them at all levels. There are many people in Canada, including those of influence, however, who do not favor greater economic union with the United States, people who are jealous of Canada's independence from things American. The pending free trade agreement between the two countries that is before both governments for ratification threatens their view of Canada as being non-American. It is also counter to our interests. Greater economic cooperation means greater prosperity, therefore a stronger ability to pay for defense, the military, and actions around the world. We determined years ago that the way to weaken the economic relationship between the two countries was through the media in Canada. Stroke the complexes of Canadians against America. One of the most influential media organizations in the country is the Toronto Herald. An agent of ours is its chief editor. We could find no better tribune for our interests than the Toronto Herald. If the free trade agreement between the United States and Canada fails, it will be due in large part to the Toronto Herald and our man who has the chief pen at that paper. This could very well happen. The forces of rejection of the deal are coming into play."

"Alright. Very good, comrades." The head of the KGB leaned forward and looked at the two men in turn. "Where do we go from here and what do you need from me? What do you propose? Be specific."

"We continue with the three main elements of our program. We support agitation and government action to generate popular support for the separation of Quebec from Canada, leverage native uprisings across the country to cause maximum disruption, and contribute as much as we can to public opposition to free trade with the United States. The trade agreement could be the single most important unifying element between Canada and the United States for the future. We must do all we can to influence its demise. And, finally, we continue to infiltrate the Canadian defense establishment."

Before ending the meeting, Kozlov put a question to his men. "What do you need from me to make sure all of this is carried through? Money, I suppose?"

The Ottawa station chief proceeded to list all the activities and the amount of money he projected that would be needed.

"Very well, you will have it. Keep it in a special fund in Ottawa under your control. The ambassador is not to know about it."

Kozlov paused, then asked the question "Before we leave, what is the weak link in all of this?"

"The Toronto newspaperman."

"And why is that?"

"He asks for no money from us and our blackmail of him has lost its power. Most of it anyway. His father-in-law, the father of his wife who is a member of Parliament, died two weeks ago. We had evidence of money-laundering on his part. It was how we controlled Brown. We can't use that anymore."

"Find something else on him. We need him to continue to cause trouble with the Americans. Thank you, comrades. Here's to our success." Kozlov reached for a decanter of vodka on a side table, poured three small glasses to the brim and all three proceeded to down their contents in unison. The meeting had ended.

Later in that month of September 1988, David Malone, Prime Minister of Canada, went to the Canadian people to ask for a new mandate to govern for another four years.

The two key pillars of the Malone Government of long-term economic prosperity and national unity were being threatened. Malone wanted a strong mandate to complete these initiatives through a renewed mandate. He did not quite get it. He was re-elected, but with a small majority in the House of Commons. But he was still the Prime Minister and could reasonably expect that his key initiatives would proceed. Number one was the Free Trade Agreement. Number two, although just as important as number one, was the ratification across the country of the accord which would bring Quebec officially into the constitution of Canada with constitutional recognition as one of the founding peoples of the country.

23

Toronto, November 1988

The young woman was alone as she ran along the shore. Twice a week, sometimes more, she would arrive from her job at the Herald, put on her running gear, run down the street to the shore, turn right, and face the west wind from the lake until she arrived at the beach house, then turn around and come back.

On her run that evening, she slowed down, walked away from the lakeshore a bit to a spot behind a tree which hid her from the house a hundred yards away, bent over to catch her breath, then noticed something strange as she looked up.

I know this guy. Who is it? Yes. The cocktail party at the Italian Embassy that Suzanne dragged me to before our dinner. He was there.... Yes.....the Soviet cultural attaché. It's him. He was flirting with Suzanne. I shook his hand. What is he doing here....? ......The Soviet cultural attaché from the Ottawa Embassy going into the Beaches beach house at 7 o'clock on a blustery November evening, with nobody around. Meeting someone? Very strange.

She crouched down behind the tree to see what, if anything, would be happening. Her instincts told her someone else would be showing up. They were right. Not more than two minutes later, she recognized who that person was. The familiar gait. Her boss, Andrew Brown. She watched as Brown approached the beach house from the nearest street, then turned the corner under the covered patio to the far side of the building facing the shore, but not before pulling back the top of his hoodie as he disappeared around the corner.

After another five minutes of waiting to see if anyone else showed up, she rose from behind the tree and walked back to a point where she could resume her run back along the lake without anyone from the beach house seeing her.

"It is dangerous to keep meeting here. We have to vary this," said Andrew Brown as he found the picnic table and his Russian contact on the covered patio section facing the lake.

"Finding places in Toronto for this is difficult. You are known in this city. This is secluded, Andrew. OK for this time of year. No one around. Look about. Do you see anyone?" asked the Russian.

"There are people who jog here. I saw someone further down the shore as I came in."

"What do you propose then? The woods along a lonely road near Barrie or the one outside Bowmanville we used a few times in the summer? We cannot easily find another place in Toronto. What about the cleaning shop? He is one of ours. Lonely road or the shop. Which will it be?"

"Not the cleaning shop. I cannot bear to be in that area. I will find a convenient place. But no longer here."

"All right. I will await your proposal on that. Now, here is what I have for you from Washington......" The two men continued their discussion for another fifteen minutes, then when it was dark, found their way, five minutes apart, to Queen Street, up a few blocks from the shore, the Russian taking the trolley downtown and Andrew finding his car parked just off the busy thoroughfare.

As Julia walked back from the shore, her thoughts were of Andrew Brown. His articles on the free trade agreement.......diatribe. Consistently over the top. Embarrassing. Truly anti-American. Is there a Russian connection here? His wife is a member of Parliament. Strange.

Two weeks later, as she was walking after work, Julia saw Andrew Brown enter a subway entrance a block away from where she was. Andrew Brown taking the subway at 5 o'clock? He drives a Mercedes and has his parking slot in the basement. Going into the subway... and meeting a Russian at the deserted beach house a few days ago. What is he doing?....

Her curiosity was getting the better of her. She had to know where her boss was going. She went down into the subway station. The train had not arrived yet and she managed to stay out of Brown's line of sight. When the train stopped, she quickly got into the car behind the one Andrew had entered. She could see that he stayed on until the train reached the Sheppard Avenue station, a good way north of the downtown core. She got off, followed Brown at a distance. At street level, looking around quickly, she saw him a block away, getting into a car. As the car drove off, she saw that the person in the front passenger seat looked to be the same Russian she had met at the Italian Embassy cocktail and the man she had seen enter the beach house two weeks before. The car came back towards the station. The same guy. Andrew Brown hooking up with Russians......what do I do with this? All the anti-American stuff. Is this all linked? she thought as she stood there before going down into the subway station before the car came by.

A few minutes later a man came in where they were meeting with an envelope for the attaché, who opened the envelope, took out the picture inside, then addressed Andrew Brown. "Mr. Brown, someone was following you. Here is her picture. It was taken as she observed you getting into my car. She is looking at the car. She was also on the same train as you. Do you know her?"

"Julia Hammond. Reporter for the paper. This is not good."

"We must follow her," replied the Russian. "We can't let her compromise what we are doing. We must find out what she has."

"She is probably on to this. She is very good. She would have had to follow me here. She lives in the Beaches, nowhere near here. Would have no reason to come here. She followed me."

Three weeks later....

They found her in a downtown hotel room in Montreal. She had been dead for at least a day. There were no signs of violence or foul play, but the police found an empty bottle of amphetamines on the table next to the bed. They believed it to be a suicide. There were no fingerprints other than hers on the bottle, on the Do Not Disturb card left on the door or on anything else in the room, nor was there any note. Hotel staff were questioned. No one saw anyone enter or leave the room. No one saw anything suspicious.

The TV news that evening said she was a reporter for the Toronto Herald. The Herald expressed dismay at her death. The person contacted there by the police said there was no journalistic reason for her to be in Montreal as her beat was Ontario provincial politics. They could not explain why she could be in Montreal other than for personal reasons. A source at the newspaper contacted by a Montreal radio station said that it was believed she had recently broke up with her longtime boyfriend and perhaps was in Montreal to get away for a few days. The source who wished to remain anonymous surmised the woman could have been in distress but was surprised that she would have gone so far as to kill herself. "She was a happy person. In love with life. All of us are stunned."

"Did you have to kill her, for Christ's sake? This is going too far, guys. Much too far." Andrew Brown was both angry and afraid. He had not felt fear before in his dealings with the Russians. The news of Julia's murder in Montreal had hit hard. It was murder; that was clear. And these guys ordered it. He was sure of it. For the first time in the relationship, he was scared.

"She knew too much, my friend. She knew about you. She saw us with you. My Ottawa colleague met her at a cocktail back in October. She probably saw him at the Beaches boathouse. She jogs there. You said you saw a jogger that day. It could have been her. She could have seen everything. You will have been exposed, Andrew. We are close to killing this free trade agreement. Cannot afford you being identified as working with us. Simple calculation, my friend. She had to go," responded the Russian.

This is not going well. How do I get out of this? Andrew Brown was in a quandary. Can I stop the music?

Headline Toronto Herald, December 30, 1988

ONTARIO SAYS NO. FREE TRADE DEAL DEAD

The Canada-United States Free Trade Agreement that had been negotiated and agreed to in September 1988 needed to be ratified by both governments. Canada had to sign it before the U.S. deadline of December 31. The Reagan Administration was ready to approve the deal under their fast track negotiating authority from Congress. The Canadian government had to approve it beforehand, and that required the approval of enabling legislation by the House of Commons. Before that could happen, however, several key provisions had to have the approval of provinces comprising a minimum of 70% of the population. Ontario held the key. If Ontario said no, the deal would fail. And Ontario said no through a special vote. This meant that the legislation before the House of Commons in Ottawa could not be passed as written. Parts of the deal would have to be re-negotiated. But time was up for the U.S. government. Fast track authority to negotiate would expire in 48 hours. And there was a new Administration coming in. The Malone government could not even call for a Commons vote for enabling legislation to approve the agreement. The deal was dead.

"David, you said you could do this. I went to bat for you. Used up one helluva lot of political capital with Congress, in state capitals, with the media down here. Got fast track authority for it. Sold it across the country and managed to convince all those state governors who were against it. I've got egg all over my face, and so does the President-elect. To say the least, I am not happy and George is not either. You have let us down. You let your media run over you." The President of the United States was upset. The special relationship the Canadian Prime Minister had with the man was in tatters.

"Ron, I'm sorry. You did go to bat for us, and we couldn't get it done. I don't know what else to say."

"David, you can call me Mr. President from now on. I may not have much time left in office here, as George will soon be inaugurated, but I can tell you, this free trade stuff is over and you can expect the administration here to be tough on you guys. Good luck." The President hung up the phone. His Secretary of State, present in the Oval Office during the call, later said to an aide that he had rarely seen the man so angry.

Five months later.

The failure of the U.S.-Canada Free Trade Agreement cost David Malone dearly. It was to be his albatross. The economy was in trouble. The Toronto Stock Exchange Index had lost 15% of its value since the beginning of the year. Over twelve billion dollars in direct European investment in Canada, primarily to take advantage of access to the American market, had been cancelled. Those investments were going to Georgia, Tennessee and Michigan instead, or not coming to North America at all. Unemployment in Canada jumped by 3% in the first four months of the year. Manufacturing companies announced layoffs of over 40,000 workers. More layoff announcements would be coming.

Malone blamed the Toronto media, and particularly the Toronto Herald. The Herald's stories about control of Canadian water resources being given over to the Americans, the possibility of Canada having to scuttle key parts of government-funded healthcare hit home. Stories of Americans getting first rights to Canadian oil and natural gas, no restrictions on American content in Canadian media - all claimed by the Herald through information gathered by its sources in Washington, were over the top. Other media in Canada picked up on what the Herald had put out. The academic community joined in. The intelligentsia, the literati of central Canada who often defined themselves in nothing more than being 'not American', all got on the bandwagon.

"The country is hurting, Ontario is hurting, and they don't get it there. They didn't believe this would happen. Well, it has and the onus lies fully on Ontario," said the Prime Minister in a televised interview with Peter Umsbridge of the CBC. Despite assurances from the U.S. government that the most egregious claims were erroneous, central Canadian public opinion had been swayed. Polls showed that 65% of Ontarians were against the free trade agreement. The actual provisions of the Agreement regarding resource extraction would not be injurious to the province. Most of what the U.S. Administration had originally requested had been dropped, but public opinion had been swayed. An early demand that Canadian companies in cultural industries, including television broadcasting and book publishing, be made open to American acquisition without restrictions had been dropped as well. But The Toronto Herald kept mentioning it as an example of a sliding slope that the United States would try to slip back into the Agreement before it would be ratified. In Toronto, the media and cultural capital of Canada, this was poison.

"Peter, the government in Ontario is a Liberal government. The opposition in Ottawa is led by the Liberals, of course. They made common cause. Same party, same people, in essence. And I'm sorry to say, the media organizations of this country have been largely complicit, led by a certain newspaper here in Toronto. I don't need to go any further on that. This will not be good for the country, either in the short or the long run, and Canadians are seeing it already. Loud and clear. We are doing everything we can to right the economy, but it is not going to be a cakewalk. It's going to be tough."

The star CBC anchorman continued with his interview of the PM in his Ottawa office. "Mr. Prime Minister, there are other major issues that do not appear to be going well for you. Meech Lake Accord ratification, relations with the U.S. administration, tensions with our native peoples."

"Peter, Meech will be ratified, I am confident of that. My old friend Mr. Trudel is doing his best to scuttle it, but we will see it through. The new President, Mr. Bush, and I have had many productive discussions over the past few weeks on a host of issues, and I am confident that my relationship with the head of the Assembly of First Nations will serve to find ways to solve many of the most pressing problems in the native communities. So, things

178

are not so bad as you suggest. The country is going in the right direction."

"Thank you, Mr. Prime Minister."

24

Moscow, March 1990

The KGB's head of North American activities was briefing Comrade Kozlov on the status of the disruption of Canada.

"Alright," said Kozlov. "It looks like part of our plan has succeeded so far. Is there anything else we can do?"

"Yes, there is. It is something that has only recently been developing. If it came about it would surely bring down the Malone government. We may have the opportunity to make it happen."

"And what is that?" asked the head of the KGB.

The Ottawa station chief related the details of what they were talking about.

Kozlov listened. After a couple of questions on the intricacies of Canadian politics and a moment of silence, he nodded his approval. "Yes, I believe it would do that. The Americans' best friend in Canada would no longer be in charge. Good for us. Make sure this happens."

Gérard Rousseau was a Conservative Member of Parliament and one of the most vocal defenders of the interests of Quebec in the caucus of the Malone government. He was influential and popular with the Quebec media. A former journalist, one-time part owner of a radio station and student activist in his youth, he was first elected in the Conservative wave that captured Quebec and the country in 1984. His wife was from one of the most influential families of Outremont, the upscale enclave of well-to-do French-speaking Montrealers. Her family had a long history of involvement in politics in Quebec. One of her cousins was a Parti National member of the Quebec National Assembly.

Rousseau was also in financial trouble. He had a gambling problem, with debts accumulated through secret jaunts to Las Vegas and Atlantic City over the past six months. He bet big and lost big. He owed a lot of money and it was not to a bank. It was to some people who could get nasty. His wife, family, friends and associates knew nothing of any of this. While he was under pressure to cover his debts, he was also under public as well as private pressure to do more to push Quebec interests in Ottawa. They converged. Publicly advocating for the latter would put him in hot water with the Prime Minister. Malone did not appreciate public advocacy for what could be perceived as preferential treatment for a region, a province, or some other constituency. MPs from all provinces were expected to be team players who did not freelance publicly for the interests of their region. Some like Rousseau felt constrained. National interests did not always coincide with what people in Quebec considered to be their interests.

Rousseau could not put at risk his MP salary nor the additional income he had from being a parliamentary secretary to a minister. Although he was elected and could serve until the next election, the PM could demote him from the parliamentary secretary post. Gérard Rousseau was not a wealthy man. He had little equity to show for a long career in media and journalism and had many financial ups and downs in his life. To pay off his gambling debts, he could not very well go to Montreal and ask friends and acquaintances for a bailout. It would be fatal to his political career, his prestige and his reputation as a squeaky-clean defender of Quebec rights in Ottawa. Marc Dubé knew all about this. Serge had told him of Rousseau's gambling. An agent in Las Vegas who had previously served in Ottawa had recognized Rousseau one night at Caesar's Palace and followed him as he bet and lost at blackjack and then at roulette. The word quickly got to the Soviet Embassy in Ottawa. The order was given to put a trail on him. Agents observed an erratic, stressed man who spent many evenings drinking. When Rousseau flew to Atlantic City a few weeks after his weekend in Vegas, an agent was there to see what he did. At the casino, he lost big again after some early gains. Based on what agents observed on the two gambling trips they were aware of, they estimated the man was in the hole for well over a hundred thousand dollars.

Interesting. My old friend Gérard in trouble. How can we work this? thought Dubé as he left the cafe after his meeting with his contact. The next day, Dubé left a message for Serge to meet him again two days later at a restaurant in Valleyfield, south of Montreal. He had an idea.

"Serge, we can get Rousseau out of his jam and help ourselves in the process. I may have a way of doing it. I will need money from you. Not sure how much, though. I will have to explore that. Your people estimate over a hundred thousand. Need to find out just how much."

"You are talking blackmail, or what?" asked the Russian.

"Let me explain what I'm thinking," said Dubé. "He is unhappy with the government, unhappy with the Prime Minister. He thinks the government is not doing enough to protect ratification of the Meech Lake Accord. He is upset about other things as well - economic development funds for Quebec being cut

182

back, neglect of Montreal. Tells friends about it, stuff that easily gets to me. He is also heady with his reputation in the Montreal media as the defender of Quebec interests in Ottawa. The gambling debt thing, if it became public, would kill him. He may be ripe to bolt."

"Bolt, you say. Quit the government caucus? What would that do? He is only one. Malone would still be able to govern."

"He could take others with him. He does that – I have a list of who they could be - and the government loses its majority. In time, the government would fall and there would be an election Malone could not win. The Meech Lake Accord would die as the Liberals, led by Trudel, the old man in the background, would let it die. There would be anger throughout Quebec, the government here would have to call an election as well and we would win. That's how I see it, my friend."

"Ok. How do you propose to orchestrate all of this?" asked the Russian.

"There are at least four other Quebec MPs - very much nationalists, all of them - who could be induced to quit the government and sit in the Commons as either independents or as a group. They are fed up with being ignored on the one hand and would not be far from calling for the independence of Quebec should the Meech Lake Accord fail on the other. It is going that way on Meech. Old man Trudel has great influence in all of this and is turning the tide against the accord in the English Canadian media. The government has trouble countering what he says. The MPs I am talking about are all complaining privately about things that are going on - amendments to the Accord that are being considered to get the remaining provinces on side. They would weaken provisions important to Quebec. Some of these fellows are friends of mine from way back, although I don't speak with them very often now.

After all, I am identified as a key person in the independence movement and they are federal MPs, committed to a united Canada, at least nominally. But all four of them voted yes to separate in the 1980 referendum. They all told me that at one time or another."

Serge did not mention to Dubé that he knew all about the Meech Lake Accord ratification going the wrong way. The man in Manitoba was in the process of getting that done. "Ok. What do you propose?"

"Here it is………"

Louiseville, Quebec, a small town sixty kilometers northeast of Montreal was as good a place as any to meet to minimize the chances of being recognized. The little bistro was on the road going north out of town. Dubé did not have to explain to Gérard Rousseau the care involved with choosing a place for a meeting. A federal MP seen meeting with a known Quebec *indépendantiste* would be careless.

"Good place to meet, Marc. Nobody here. It has been a while. Good to see you," said Gérard Rousseau as he found Dubé at a table in the back. The two embraced, then sat down. It was a warm embrace. They had known each other for a long time.

"We used this place years ago when we were campaigning and needed to bring local candidates together. The boss would sit over there and instantly get the boys fired up. Never had a problem with the owner. He's one of ours, always has been, and does not blab. Lessons learned from a long time in the restaurant business."

Dubé paused, all the while noticing that his old friend looked distressed.

"How's the family? Ta belle Isabelle? Your boys? They must be in their twenties by now."

"They are all fine, Marc. And your own Hélène? I see her on TV all the time. You are a lucky man."

"Yes, she is a wonderful woman and still very active in the arts. Actually constrains what I can do politically, even if I am back in academia now. Must be careful. But being out of power and out of the public eye, I am less of a threat to my lady's career, although Helene is just as much an *indépendantiste* as I am, as you know." Dubé wanted to add *and just as much as you, once upon a time* but held back. He didn't have to say it.

The men ordered, then resumed their conversation as the waitress pushed through the double doors to the kitchen.

Dubé looked at his old friend. "You don't look well, Gérard. What's up?"

"Nothing. I'm Ok."

"No, really. You don't appear well at all. Need any help with something? You Ok health wise?"

"I'm Ok. But I've got some pressures. I guess it looks it."

"Pressures. What sort of pressures? The life of an MP is not always fun, but you have been pretty good at it so far."

"I don't like the way things are going with our caucus and with the Meech agreement. No secret there. I want to talk about it but Malone is on my back to shut up. I can't talk about any of it publicly. What happens in caucus stays in caucus, although it is no secret I am not happy with the way things are progressing on the constitutional file."

Dubé hesitated in going too quickly into the money problem, but decided to broach it. Rousseau seemed ready to open up.

"You having family problems? Money problems, for God's sake? You look a mess." He waited for an answer. It did not come. Rousseau said nothing.

"Gérard, if you do have that sort of problem, I know people who could help."

"No, no, Marc. Let's not go there. I am OK."

The waitress arrived with the food. Conversation switched to hockey and to baseball. Both men were devoted Canadiens and Expos fans. The meal finished and the plates taken away, Dubé looked across the table. "We've been friends a long time, Gérard. We went our separate ways after the referendum, but we always could confide in each other. You have a secret? Something's really eating at you. It's written all over you."

"Alright.....if you insist." Gérard Rousseau hesitated. Dubé could see the distress in the man. "I have a financial problem."

"Financial problem....What's it about? Maybe I can help. C'est quoi, Gérard?"

"I lost money last year when the free trade agreement failed. A lot. Also lost money in the crash of '87. Tried to get it back with investments after that. I bought a lot of stock, borrowed for most of it. Should never have done it. Investments turned bad, lost much of their value and I had bought them on margin. Stupid. The

186

brokerage is after me. Need every cent I make to take care of it. Can't keep going on like this." He was lying. It was all about gambling. "Isabelle knows nothing about it......but I guess it is written all over me, like you say."

"Do you want to talk about it? We don't have to."

"No, might as well. It's eating me up."

"What is the size of the problem, Gérard?"

"Close to two hundred thousand dollars. I have a call on me for repayment. The brokerage." Gérard was lying. Rousseau maybe owed some to a bank or a broker but most if not all of it was probably owed to a loan shark. The KGB man in Vegas saw all he needed to see. Somebody stepped in to cover the house for Rousseau. Clearly, Rousseau had been gambling for some time and had connections to cover losses.

"Wow. A lot. And you can't pay it back?"

"No, I can't. The MP salary will never be able to cover anywhere close to that in the short term."

"And you can't go to family?"

"No, I can't do that, either. Nobody in my family has any money. You are aware of where I come from. Can't sell my house. Isabelle and I own it jointly. There is already a mortgage on it. I don't want to go there. Boom goes my marriage if I propose something like that. And there is no way I am going to ask her family for anything."

"She doesn't know about your investment losses?"

"No, she doesn't. She was against my playing the market. My broker and I had a deal about keeping these matters between us."

Doing a good job, Gérard. Sounding credible, thought Dubé as he listened to his friend's cover up.

"So, you see. I cannot leave the government side even if I wanted to, which I have thought about. Probably not a surprise to you. We almost got into that before the lunch came. I've thought of quitting out of principle. But I can't. I am a parliamentary secretary to a minister. It gives me additional revenue. I need it all, just to pay interest. I have to toe the line. I can't afford to quit. No matter how bad it gets."

"Do you want to leave? Sit as an independent?"

"I have thought of it. So have others, by the way."

"How many others? There are a few guys like you who went into this in '84 with the same idea. Proper recognition and status for Quebec."

"Maybe six or seven. It would not take much," said Rousseau.

"Six or seven. That would take Malone's majority away."

"It sure would. Even four of them leaving would do it. They all recognize that. Everyone is holding back. Just needs a spark. Could go boom."

Marc Dubé paused for a moment, then went back to the financial issue. "Ok, Gérard. I am aware of someone who could help you out. With your financial problem, I mean. Could have a solution for you, but I have to think about it."

"Someone who would agree to provide me with that amount of money? I would certainly have to pay it back. Go from one debt to another. Marc, I am not in la-la land, nor are you. Come on."

"Depends, Gérard. A long shot, that's for sure, but let me think about it."

"This is crazy."

"Maybe. I have an idea, though. You have to keep this to yourself."

"Of course. Go ahead. I will listen to whatever you come up with."

"But, Gérard. Tell me. If you can solve your financial problem, you leave? You quit the caucus?"

"Yes. I would do it. The debt is what is holding me back. Dealing with it takes all my energy now. This could cause me to crash."

"You look it. Let's see if we can't get this corrected."

Marc Dubé knew how he would do it. It had been in his mind all along. Plus, Gérard's story about owing a broker did not hold water. I hope he doesn't use this anywhere else. Doesn't add up. There are ways of getting around what he says is the problem. Other people would see it. But being in trouble with a loan shark is something else.

"Two hundred thousand. If he gets it, I think he will quit and I think others will follow him." Serge the Russian and Dubé were in their old cafe in east-end Montreal.

"You have a story for him about where it comes from? By the way, we should be more careful about where we meet. Nobody will recognize you here?"

"About meeting here, nobody in this area of town follows politics. And I am never on television. We could find another place, but in the meantime, I can tell you it is safe. And yes, I have a story for him. An anonymous supporter of Quebec......from France. A friend of Quebec and a devoted defender of the French fact in North America. A story about money that would come from that source."

"There are actually people in France who would do that, give money to the movement anonymously?" asked the Russian.

"Oh, yes. Some of them have been ministers; others with old money, the aristocracy of France who have more money than you can think of. It is plausible. Rousseau could believe it. He will never learn it comes from Moscow."

"And you are sure he will not be alone in your plan. If he's the only one who leaves the government, it will have been an expensive exercise for us. I could end up being posted to Siberia, along with my superior in Ottawa if this doesn't work. I am only half joking."

"I can't be totally certain. I am counting on five people who are now federal members of parliament wanting to do something that they believe could very well lead to the rupture of Quebec from Canada. But I am not totally certain they will do it."

"Well, it may be difficult to sell, but leave it with me. I will get back to you."

"Two hundred thousand dollars. For a possibility that a man with a gambling problem will start a revolt in the governing party in Canada which will lead to the break-up of the country. We spoke about this possibility a few weeks ago, but I have trouble believing it can work. I hope you are right, but I am skeptical. I have already pledged a million dollars to an Indian for a revolution that has not happened. Why is this any different?"

The head of the North American directorate of the KGB spoke up. "The Indian revolution will come. Our man is good. It will happen. As to the Canadian Member of Parliament we will be paying, our comrades in Ottawa believe it is still the best way for us to accelerate the move to separation of Quebec from Canada. We have had our key man in place in Quebec for years. This could be the payoff for all our patience. Our Ottawa people are confident it will happen. It is not a lot of money for something that has such potential for our interests."

"I still have trouble believing you. But you are right. It is not a lot of money. You want us to do this? Give this money to this man? All of you...you are all in favor?" Kozlov looked at the four men seated at the table.

"Yes, we are all in favor." All the men nodded.

"Alright, then. Do it. Make it happen. Use our special fund we have in Ottawa. Keep me informed and tell no one else. Not even in this building. And tell the same to our comrades in Canada. Not even the ambassador. He is not to know. I don't want this coming back to us." I can't have Gorbachev being aware of this, thought the head of the KGB as his men left the room. He appears to have an attachment to Canada. Not like the old days with the others supporting everything we were doing.

"Gérard, let's meet. I may have a solution for you." Marc Dubé was on the phone with Gérard Rousseau.

"You mean my problem?"

"Yes."

"OK. When and where?"

"Maniwaki. Truck stop on the side of Highway 5 as you leave town going north. Next to Motel de la Rivière. Can't miss it. How about Wednesday, 8 PM? Two days from now."

"OK," responded Rousseau. "I will be there. Anybody else know about this?"

"Of course not." Gérard Rousseau would be ignorant of the Russian connection. Marc Dubé had little remorse about doing it. After all, this is all about our youth, our dream, and the rectification of all the ills befallen on our people. Gérard was part of it then. He can be part of it again. We can make it happen.

"There is a person in France who wishes to contribute to the defense of the French fact in Canada. He has money and has offered it to support special initiatives. He wishes to remain anonymous. I have known him for a long time. I am the keeper of the fund. Nobody else knows about it. The man has insisted on keeping it that way. Gérard, the money you need to pay your debt could come from his little fund."

"Two hundred thousand dollars from an anonymous Frenchman? A bit too much, non?.....who is this person?"

"Gérard, I can't tell you. Suffice to say he is a member of the moneyed class, of the elite who have an enduring interest in advancing the interests of France around the world. But I can't tell you who it is."

"And only you are aware of this?"

"Yes. You know us. More Catholic than the Pope. It would not go over well with the rank and file, despite the sentimental attachment to the French. Especially the part of it being secret." Dubé was having difficulty in credibly explaining where the money was coming from. He could see that his old friend was skeptical. The Parti National usually did things by committee. Saying no one else was aware of something like this begged credulity.

"What do I need to do to earn this little gift, Marc? I think I have the answer already, but tell me."

"Carry through, Gérard. Carry through on your idea to leave the government caucus. Help the cause. Your old cause, the one that galvanized us in our youth, the one you put aside. Bring it back. You can't continue."

"Leave? I would only do it if I could bring some of the others with me. Otherwise, a futile, stupid act. Do I have to bring others with me to receive the contribution, the gift?"

"Respect your conscience and the intent of the fund that will be helping you out. You want to do this anyway. You told me so. So why don't you just do it?"

"A slush fund from France which will be used to upset a Canadian government. I can't believe this."

"Yes, Gérard. So what. You want to do it. This will just make it easier. Your family will respect you. Isabelle. She has never liked you being a federalist, even under the *'beau risque'* that you and Malone got elected on in Quebec. You will be standing up for Quebec, for your people."

"You say no one will learn of this payment. Can you guarantee that to me, Marc?"

"Yes, I can. I am the keeper of the fund it. But, even if others should learn of it, there is no reason for anyone to know that you have received anything from it. You tell me nobody else other than your broker is aware of your debt. Nobody else, right?"

"Nobody else. Thank God. But no, nobody else."

"I won't tell anybody, for obvious reasons. The whole scheme would blow up. But you will have to keep it secret, Gérard. No one is to be told of this transaction or about this fund. Do I have your word?"

"You have my word. Now how can we do this, practically speaking? For one, I need to keep it from the fisc." Rousseau had to give the impression he was to pay back a loan, which would require a paper trail. In reality, he would not need one. But he had to construct something.

"It will be in cash. You will have to work it out. An inheritance or a loan from a relative. Something non-taxable. Avoid it going into your bank account, if at all possible. You will have to work it out. I don't have the answer on that. I'm not an accountant or a lawyer." Dubé knew this was a false problem.

"OK. I think I can figure something out." Gérard Rousseau paused, then looked back at Dubé. "Let me think about it. The Frenchman will not be aware of this transaction? Right?"

"Right. Part of the arrangement with him. And nobody else will know, either. We never had this discussion. We must agree to that."

"OK. Give me a few days."

"Call me at my Montreal number when you are ready. Hélène is in Quebec City for the next month, except for weekends. No risk calling me there during the week."

Marc Dubé left the note for Serge at the usual place. Two days later, a telephone call from a wrong number caller signaled through a code the time and place for the exchange. Within a day, Dubé had the money. Just needed the signal from Rousseau.

Three evenings later, he received a call at his Montreal apartment.

"Marc, I'm in a phone booth. We are on. When can I see you? Do you have it?"

"Yes, Gérard, I have it. Papineauville this time, just before Montebello. Thursday. There is a small park just off rue Principale at the east end of the town. Parking lot. Secluded. No one should be around mid-afternoon on a working day. And the boys are with you?"

"Yes, the boys are with me."

"Good. See you in Papineauville." The thought occurred to Marc that the place was quite appropriate for what they were doing. The town's namesake and founder, Louis-Joseph Papineau, was one of the leaders of les Patriotes in the rebellion of 1837 against British rule.

"Here it is, Gérard. All of it. Two thousand one hundred-dollar bills in this bag. You don't have to count it. It's all there."

"I'm sure it is. Big bag." Rousseau lifted the bag off the floor of the front seat. "Heavy. Never seen anything like this before."

"Anyway, there it is. All yours." Dubé had the urge to ask his old friend how he was going to handle so much cash to supposedly pay back an investment dealer but held back. Rousseau had said he would find a way. Leave it at that. In any case, there was no bank or broker or anything like that involved.

"Merci, mon ami."

"When are you going to break this on Malone? Announce it?"

"Monday morning."

"You're doing this, right? Going all the way?"

"Yes, all the way."

196

"The others. They won't back out between now and Monday?" Dubé had committed his end of the deal. Rousseau had to deliver his. It all had to come together.

"They could, but I don't think they will. All four told me last night they were in. I told you...they have all been ripe to do this. See themselves as patriots. They may be more pumped up than I am. Here we go, Marc."

"Yes, here we go, my friend. Let's get out of here."

Monday, May 4 1990

CBC Television Midday News

"Ladies and gentlemen, a blockbuster development in Ottawa this morning. Five members of David Malone's Conservative caucus of MPs from Quebec have jumped ship to sit as independents, causing the ruling Conservatives to lose their majority in the House of Commons and jeopardizing Malone's ability to govern the country. A hugely critical event, born out of the problems the government has had with ratification of the Meech Lake Accord and the discontent that has festered in Conservative ranks, particularly in Quebec. We join our chief national affairs correspondent, Terry Mills, who is in the foyer of the House of Commons..."

25

Winnipeg, June 15, 1990

"When is the vote?" Nathan Cromwell was in the hallway with Ellison Ward outside Ward's office in the legislative building.

"I can't do this, Nathan. It will bring the wrath of the country down on me."

"Ellison, you must do it. For our people. We have been neglected in all of this, as always. How many times have we talked about this? ....You have the power to change things. The vote will reverberate across the country, inspire our brothers and sisters, and give us the respect we deserve. You will be a hero."

"I don't want to be heroic. I am a peaceful person. I will be declaring war."

"No, you won't, Ellison. You will cause all of Canada to rise up, take notice of our grievances like nothing before, and begin the reversing of our decline, of our self-respect and of our condition. This is not about war. It is about respect. Don't you see it?"

"I see it, Nathan. I see all of it, but I am a simple man."

"When is the vote, Ellison?"

"The 23rd. Next week. The day before the deadline."

"You hold the balance. Your vote can make it go either way. You can stop this. For all of us."

"Goodbye, Nathan. I have to go." Ward turned, walked down the hall and into his office.

On June 23, Ellison Ward cast his deciding vote against ratification of the Meech Lake Accord by the Legislative Assembly of Manitoba. Manitoba would not be ratifying the accord, killing it in the process. At virtually the same time, the legislature of Newfoundland and Labrador voted to rescind its ratification of the accord by its previous government two years before.

Headline The Globe and Mail, Toronto, June 24 1990

MEECH FAILS. GOVERNMENT IN TROUBLE

Later that day, Montreal, Parc Maisonneuve

The cheering, chanting crowd pressed closer to the elevated stage. Music was to come, but anger was in the air. Banners, flags and posters were everywhere in a sea of blue and white. "Vive le Québec Libre! Le Québec aux Québécois! Maîtres chez nous, maintenant!" The crowd was in an ugly mood. For the thousands of pure laine Québécois massed in the park for la Fête Nationale, the failure of the Meech Lake Accord was yet another case of English Canada rejecting their unique character and aspirations.

I know this guy. Where have I seen him before? It took a few minutes, but it came to him. Yes.. Prague.. '68. The Czech summer. It's him. Same haircut. Same darting eyes. My Czech friends were sure he was KGB. Swore on it. Well, well..

Bill Wilson was a counter-intelligence officer with CSIS. He had joined the RCMP intelligence service after completing university in Alberta. But in 1968, two years before joining the force, he was on a summer student exchange program in Czechoslovakia. Wilson spent many days and evenings with his Czech friends on the streets of Prague, on Wenceslaus Square and in other places of demonstrations and expressions of freedom. Many of those friends were imprisoned and worse following the Soviet army's occupation of the country and the overthrow of the regime of Alexandr Dubcek. The man in the crowd that day in Montreal was unmistakable. He was there. Russian. And now he was here. In the midst of all this. What was he up to? Were the Russians involved with any of this? Must find out.

26

It all started with a land dispute. On a hot day in June 1990, a group of Mohawk Indians erected a barricade on a road outside the town of Oka, Quebec, west of Montreal. They were protesting the expansion of a golf course on land traditionally claimed by the Mohawks as theirs. Two days later a gun battle erupted between police and young natives manning the barricades. Half a dozen police cars were torched. Within days, the Government of Canada acquiesced to a request from Quebec to send in the army to confront the natives and prevent further bloodshed. Soon, the group manning the barricades swelled from thirty to over six hundred, with many coming from elsewhere in Canada and the United States. Four days after the original clash in Oka, a key bridge linking Montreal to south shore suburbs through a reserve at Kahnawake was occupied by other Mohawks. Bridge traffic came to a halt. The crisis widened.

"Do it. Now is the time." Nathan was on the phone with his network across the country, individually, from British Columbia to Nova Scotia. "Go. Do what we have talked about." What was happening in Quebec triggered incidents elsewhere. The network was ready. Things escalated rapidly. Three soldiers and nine warriors were killed in clashes at Oka and Kahnawake. "Don't take lives. That's not what this is about. It won't help," he told the young warrior on Vancouver Island. But he had unleashed the revolution and it was spreading. Tensions exploded across the country. In British Columbia, members of the Seton Lake Indian band blockaded the railroad running from Vancouver to resource

201

communities in the north. RCMP vehicles holding the arrested protesters were attacked and damaged. Three days later, a group of natives in the middle of the night surprised the guards at the gate of the Canadian Forces naval base at Esquimalt on Vancouver Island and took control of the main base office building. The leader spoke to a reporter from a Victoria radio station and said they would not leave unless the navy recognized that the land on which the base resides was part of the local reserve, under a treaty signed in 1843. They demanded compensation and the return of a large section of the land. An additional condition was for Canadian Forces personnel to abandon their standoffs with the Mohawks at Oka and Kahnawake. Canadian Forces personnel sealed off the area. The standoff remained unresolved for days. Negotiations to end it went nowhere. An attempt to storm the building the fourth day was met with gunfire. Three sailors were wounded, one critically.

Eruptions quickly followed in other native communities. Other Mohawks in the East blockaded roads, occupied disputed parcels of land and clashed with police. The day after the occupation of the naval base in British Columbia, two locks of the Welland Canal linking Lake Erie with Lake Ontario were occupied by people of the Six Nations of the Grand River reserve, halting shipping through a key part of the St. Lawrence Seaway. Roads leading to the locks were blocked with stacks of logs with armed warriors standing guard. While this was happening, a group of young natives took control of the airport at Sioux Lookout in northwest Ontario and blocked all air traffic in and out. Sioux Lookout was the supply base for dozens of remote communities reachable only by air. The blocking of runways by piles of timber would last for weeks.

There were takeovers of white communities in Alberta, Saskatchewan and New Brunswick with extensive hostage-taking. A group of masked natives stormed and took control of the Alberta Legislature. Edmonton police called to the scene shot a protester who later died in hospital. Occupiers set fire to mounds of paper on the steps of the Legislature.

Nathan met with his control on a road west of Winnipeg. "Things are evolving as I thought they would," Nathan told the man. "Eruptions are happening all over."

"I see that. It is all over television. You said it would, and you have been right," replied the Russian. "Are the leaders of these incidents the same people you recruited?"

"Come on, Alex. You should know they are. Every one except two. The network got extended. It's what it was all about. There is more to come. And you can tell your boss in Moscow that his million dollars is working."

"He is aware of it. He has been following all this. The world is following it."

"So be it. It's about time."

"Are you happy, Nathan? Does this give you joy, my friend?"

"No, Alex. Some satisfaction, yes, but not joy. This is not the way to run a country or society. Never has been. It is vindication for us. Nobody listened to us. Well, they are now."

"Here is the last of the money. I suppose you have a destination for it," said the Russian.

"Oh, yes, some young courageous kids not far from here. But you don't want to know."

"No. It has been part of the deal. I don't want to know."

As the cascade of incidents rolled out across the country, police forces lost control. Upon orders of the Prime Minister, the army was deployed, with the opposite effect of what was intended. Standoffs with the RCMP and the army occurred at over thirty native communities. The army sent paratroopers to retake the airport at Sioux Lookout. It was the fourth most active airport in the country for takeoffs and landings, given its logistical importance for remote communities. But the paratroopers were surrounded and disarmed by warriors as they landed, put into the backs of a bevy of pick-up trucks and dumped in the next community reachable by road, without their weapons. Despite the humiliation of the capture of the soldiers, the head of the army decided not to send in reinforcements to avoid bloodshed and the further spread of disturbances to other communities. The crisis worsened across the country. The Montreal Gazette declared in an editorial that Canada was on the verge of internal war. Four days into the crisis and on the same day as the occupation of the Esquimalt naval base and the blocking of the Welland Canal, Innu in Labrador occupied the Goose Bay military base. Low-level flight training of NATO member country pilots over the Labrador wilderness had to stop. An Innu protester was run over by a Canadian Forces jeep and died. International attention was already focused on Canada, but the standoff at Goose Bay received particular attention in Europe, given that most of the air forces of the continent used the facility for training. Foreign air force personnel along with their aircraft quickly left Labrador and returned to their home bases. Within days, the governments of the Netherlands, Belgium and Germany announced they were ceasing flight training in Canada and were abrogating agreements with the Government of Canada for such. The Toronto Herald that had led the charge for over two years against low-level flight training over Innu lands, was saying now in editorials 'I told you so' and demanding the abolition of air operations anywhere over native lands in Canada, meaning essentially no flights over all of the North. In the midst of the crisis, the Herald went further and came out against the United States using Canadian territory or airspace for any military related activity.

Through all of August and well into September, the occupations and protests of natives continued across the country. Three weeks into the crisis, the head of the Canadian Armed Forces was sacked. The Prime Minister formed a special cabinet committee to deal with the uprisings and appointed a military group to counter the protests and return occupied assets. The provinces, solicited by Ottawa for help in the crisis, were heavily critical of the federal government in its handling of it.

South of the border, chief White House spokesman James Diller declared in a press briefing on August 21 that the lack of control over events at Canadian military bases and on the St. Lawrence Seaway endangered U.S. security and was seriously jeopardizing relations between the two countries. Pressed by reporters, he hinted that action could be taken by the United States to ensure free passage through the Seaway.

27

Bill Wilson had managed to get a clear picture. A full facial shot with good resolution. He kept his eyes on the man. At the end of the rally, he followed him to a white Toyota parked a few blocks away. Checking the police database, he learned the license number was registered to someone with an address on Papineau street. Verification showed it was a bogus registration. Round the clock monitoring of the Toyota – that ended up on rue Chateaubriand – was ordered. For close to a week, the car stayed in the same spot. No one got into it. Wilson was on the verge of halting the surveillance, when one morning a man showed up and drove away. The car was quickly picked up by Wilson's men, who informed him the driver was meeting with someone in a café in the city's east end. Wilson arrived in time to observe a familiar face leaving the establishment. He took a photo as the man walked down the street.

I've seen this guy before. Somewhere. Where? Somewhere in the news. Wilson took his camera downtown to the CSIS office. The shot was quickly developed and shown to agents. "The man in the picture is Marc Dubé, Bill. University professor and onetime constitutional advisor to the Premier of Quebec." This is getting interesting, thought Wilson. He had taken another shot, of a man leaving the cafe soon after Dubé. That man had walked down the street and got into the Toyota. Wilson did not recognize him. He was clearly not the same guy he had photographed at the rally. Different height, different build. But it's the same car. Wilson had ordered the Toyota followed. It travelled to an address on rue St-

Hubert where the driver parked the car on the street, got out and walked a block to a subway station. The agent took a picture of the suspect. "Bill, the man with the shaved head is Pavel Tedorenko, a Russian agent who we knew years ago as Serge Colaros, a supposed French student. He disappeared from Montreal a few years ago after being picked up by the RCMP, yet released without charge. The Mounties had no proof of his espionage. He had a full head of hair back then, wore wire-rimmed glasses and was at least twenty pounds lighter."

Well, well, our friend Colaros is back, thought Wilson. I always thought of him as KGB. "Where did he go?"

"We followed him to a townhouse off Atwater. We checked it out. Nobody in it. No furniture. Owned by some company in Italy. He lost us."

Dubé meeting a Russian. Do we have our Quebec mole? "Marc Dubé. My God. Why didn't we think of him before?" Frank Russo was surprised, but then he wasn't. Adela Cerny had dealt with this guy. "Keep an eye on him. Let's see where he leads us, but make sure it's un-detected. Big repercussions if this gets out."

Wilson had the image of the man from Prague in his mind. He could not put it away. Who is he? Dropped the car off in Montreal, then the car is taken by the other one, Tedorenko, who meets Marc Dubé in a cafe. We know about Tedorenko, but what about the guy from Prague of so many years before? He would soon find out. The photos of the man were logged into the database of suspected foreign agents at CSIS headquarters in Ottawa.

"I remember him. Regina, twelve years ago." Officer Alan Pace had a reputation of having a photographic memory. He was with Bill Wilson, Frank Russo and other counterintelligence officers in Russo's office in Ottawa. "I'm sure of it. Same one. I had been in training outside of Regina. Before returning to Ottawa, I went into town to visit family. Had some time to kill. Found myself in a diner downtown before going to the airport. There was an incident. A young native sitting in a booth was upset with a white man; yelled at him; told him to beat it. I remember it. The waitress was afraid. The owner told both men to leave. The white guy – he's the same person as the man in that picture. I'm sure of it."

"Pace, you are incredible with names, faces and people. You recall an incident and a guy in a diner twelve years ago. You remember the face. My God. And you're sure he's the same man?"

"Same one. Hair cut the same way. Same build. I'm sure of it."

"Find him, Bill. He may still be in Montreal. I will send this shot to our bureau chiefs. He is to be found, but not intercepted. We have a Russian agent in our sights here. We need to have a clear picture of what he's doing, who he's dealing with. We knew the KGB was trying to infiltrate the native movement. We have always suspected that. The CIA were saying years ago they suspected the Russians were recruiting natives out West and sending them to Cuba. Never caught anybody doing it. It could be that the troubles we've been having have a Russian connection. I would not put it beyond them. Could this fellow have been part of it?"

Russo looked at Bill Wilson. This could be a breakthrough for counterintelligence as well as something they discover before the CIA does. "For what other reason would a KGB operative be talking to a native in Regina? Bill, you're sure he's KGB?"

"He's KGB. In Prague, in Montreal, and most probably in Regina years ago, based on what Alan is saying. All the way through. I'm sure of it."

Russo was meeting with key members of his team. "Gentlemen, with no surprise to you I am sure, the big boss is ordering the RCMP to come up with a comprehensive plan to deal with the native uprising. Part of it is finding out who is behind it, if there is some mastermind pulling the strings. If these events are being coordinated or not. We need to find out what is going on behind all this. The native leaders are not cooperating. But neither we nor the people at Indian Affairs believe the leaders or the Assembly of First Nations folks are behind it. Nevertheless, the spontaneity of the eruptions across the country cannot be totally coincidental or in simple reaction to the Oka affair. We need to be involved. The RCMP guys are asking for our help. It's not inconceivable that foreign elements are part of it. We need to find out if that is the case."

"To start off, the Mounties have thousands of photos and film taken of the various occupations. Their guys are filming everything. Most of the natives on the front lines are wearing masks, bandanas, whatever, making it hard to recognize anybody. Just the same, the films and pictures are our best source for identifying people. Maybe something could come of it. Pace, you have an incredible ability to remember faces and details of incidents. I want you to go over every foot of coverage, every snapshot we have of all the locations. I need you to collate all of it, see if the same person or persons are involved in more than one of the disturbances. Go through our database of known or suspected East bloc agents, employees of their embassies, all of that. See if any of these people could be involved. I would not be surprised if they were, but I doubt any one of them would be so careless as to be observable at one of these occupations. Form a team, use whatever technical resources you need. If you need authorization, you will get it."

Alan Pace walked into Russo's office two days later. "I found something, Frank. I asked our contact at Indian Affairs to give us access to their repository of press releases, announcements, pictures they would have on file of events etc. over the past few years. I spent yesterday afternoon and a better part of last night perusing what I was given access to. I came across a photo of the announcement of the department's support of a native economic development bank that was being put together a few years ago. One of the people in the photo, Frank, is the native who was involved in the disturbance at the Regina diner that I told you and Bill Wilson about. With the man Bill says is KGB. I'm sure of it."

"Well, well. Things seem to be getting clearer. From an argument with a Russian to economic development and banking to whatever else. Could we have a mole in the Indian movement? Could he be involved in all this stuff? Economic development is a long way from armed insurrection. But.....the Russian connection. Find out who he is."

Two days later, Pace was on the phone to his boss. "Frank, his name is Nathan Cromwell. He works for Dennis Strong, a member of the Manitoba Legislature."

"Find out all you can on him. What he's been doing, for how long, what he did before working for the MLA. Everything. Talk to the guys over at the RCMP."

"I already have. Cromwell has worked for the same MLA on two different occasions. First in the early eighties, after working as a teacher, then for an NGO when the member lost his seat before getting it back a few years later. In his time with the NGO, he travelled across the country and became involved in the promotion of the bank that the native leaders scuttled. Nothing on him anywhere before the teaching stint. The school board records show that he was from a tribe in Arizona and came north to work in Canada. He had proper working papers, apparently."

"Find him. Track everything he does."

The phone rang in Russo's office. It was his CIA contact at the U.S. Embassy. "Frank, we have something you need to be aware of. Could maybe explain what's going on with your natives. Need to see you."

"Come on over."

The Ottawa CIA man quickly came to the point. "One of our agents working out of New Orleans received a call from the FBI concerning a man who was part of a Cuban delegation to an international conference there. Some sort of agricultural thing. The man wanted to defect. The FBI were holding him and suggested our man come in and see him. They said during questioning that he had information on the training of operatives from Canada. A Chilean who has been in Cuba for a while. Happened last week."

"Chilean. Defecting. Probably part of the crowd with Allende who cut to Havana and can't go back, right?"

"Right. Been in Cuba since '75. Expert in management. Cybernetics, he says. Spent time in Angola when they were in there big time. Wants to get out of Cuba and all that entails. Disillusioned, he says. System doesn't work, and all that."

"Like many down there. What's the Canadian connection?"

"Says the Cubans were training Canadian Indians brought down there by the Russians. Was close to one for a time. Here's the transcript of what he said about it."

Frank Russo read through the document. "Native called Cannon. Not his real name, he says. Did he know his real name?"

"Said he didn't."

Russo thought of the discussion he had with Alan Pace a few days before....the recognition of the Indian who had an argument with a Russian agent in a Saskatchewan diner twelve years before. "Can we meet this man? I think we have spotted someone here who could be that Indian."

"It can be arranged. Certainly. We've brought him up to Virginia. You or your men can see him there. He's in a safe house. We'll make him available."

The Russian came quickly to the point. "Nathan, you may be in trouble. Something sudden. A Chilean who was with you in Cuba has defected. He is in the United States and we suspect he has been interrogated by the CIA. He could talk about a lot of things. One of them could be about Canadian natives being brought to Cuba......the training.....all of that. About you."

Nathan sat back and waited a moment before responding. "Roberto. My old buddy Roberto. Well, well." He looked at the Russian for a moment, then asked him the question. "What do I do, Alexei? Tell me. I don't want to end this."

"We get you out. Soon. You will have to leave. They will be on to you. We have to assume that."

"Are we sure of what this guy will say? You may be assuming too much, Alexei. This business is not finished. I have to see it through." The tree was being shaken but the fruit had not fallen yet.

"We must assume he will talk, Nathan. The CIA is thorough. They will put him through endless interrogation. Canadian Indians trained in Cuba will come up. They have long suspected this. It is no secret in the world of intelligence. It is a small miracle you have remained undetected all these years. Your time is up. You have done what you can. We can't afford to let you be caught. YOU can't afford to let yourself be caught."

"OK, Alexei. Where do you propose I go? Where do you intend to take me? What is your plan?" The end, he thought. No other way.

"Moscow. We will start with that. You will be taken care of. You will have no worries about money. There is a car that will pick you up at eleven tonight and drive you to Montreal. It's 6:30 now. Not much time. It will be in the alleyway behind your apartment building. A blue Buick Regal. The driver, it will be a she, will have a disguise for you. You will be viewed as a couple as you drive east. In Montreal, you will be put on a flight to Rome. You will have a Costa Rican passport. From Rome you will be flown to Moscow. We must do this quickly, Nathan. They will be after you. Maybe even looking for you now."

"OK. I guess this is it. I will not be seeing you again. What will you do?"

"I will be leaving as well. I have been observed. I may make it out before you. I am officially an employee of the Embassy with diplomatic status. My tour of duty will be over. That is what will be said to the Canadians." Alexei paused a moment before continuing.

He looked at Nathan across the table. "You were good. You did what you said you would do. We wondered about you, just the same. You never asked for money for yourself. We could not always control you, but you were good."

"Alex, this has not been about money. What you gave me over the years served to cover the expenses of what I was doing. I did it for my people. You were the means for it. The governments of Canada have been shaken by what we have done. Unfortunately, our own leaders may in the end ruin whatever progress could be made. But the aboriginal youth of Canada, in every native community from coast to coast, has seen what can be done. It will not be the last time people will rise up if real progress is not made - education, health, employment, with respect and dignity. That is what motivated me."

The Russian looked at Nathan. There was little time left. "Where did you get it?"

"Where did I get what?"

"The sense of organization, of survival. You were alone in all this."

"From the wolves, Alex. The leader of the pack. Their community. It's a long story."

"The wolves. Alright. I am from Siberia. We have wolves and they are smart."

"Maybe someday I see you again and I explain."

Before the Russian could say that would not be possible, Nathan continued. "So unfortunate I cannot see this through. Goodbye, Alex. Maybe I will see you in Russia."

"No, you won't. You will not see me again. I do not exist for you now." With that, Victor Estinov, known to Nathan as Alexei or Alex, walked out of the room and out of Nathan Cromwell's life.

Northern Virginia, late the next day....

Frank Russo placed the photo of Nathan Cromwell, the assistant to the member of the Manitoba Legislature for Elk River, before the heavy-set Chilean in front of him.

"Do you recognize this man? Is he the one you spoke about meeting in Havana in 1978 and in Angola with you later?"

"Yes. That is the man."

Russo wasted no time. He immediately called Bill Wilson in Ottawa. "We have confirmation Cromwell has been working for the Russians. Trained in Cuba, fought in Angola. Need to find him and bring him in. What has the surveillance team been reporting on him?"

Bill Wilson called his boss back thirty minutes later. "Frank, they can't find him. The team went in just now. Called me. Nobody there. He was last observed yesterday afternoon going into his apartment building. No observed activity since. Looks like he's gone, I'm afraid. No sign of him at his apartment. His office at the Legislature says he hasn't been to work this week and is not answering his phone. His boss has not spoken with him for three days. Says it's not like him. He wanted to know why the RCMP was calling. We told him we wanted to speak with Cromwell about someone in the native movement he would perhaps know."

Frank Russo hesitated, then replied. "He's gone. They learned of the Chilean and figured he would talk. He's probably in Moscow by now. But maybe not. Put out a full alert."

At that moment, Nathan Cromwell was in his seat on the 7 PM Alitalia flight to Rome as the plane ambled down the runway.

28

As the fallout from the failure of the Meech Lake Accord unfolded and the country lurched through the native crisis, Quebec was erupting with indignation. Rallies calling for a declaration of independence were held in Montreal, Quebec City, Sherbrooke and Chicoutimi. The Liberal Premier was under pressure to do something major to show displeasure with English Canada and defend the interests of Quebec. And there was anger with the natives of Canada for having been complicit as well as for having disrupted life during the crisis that was seeing no end.

"M. Dubé, there may be an election coming. Canada is in a mess. Premier Barbeau is under pressure to act. He will use the failure of Meech to call for an election and get a mandate to negotiate something new with Ottawa, although I can't imagine what that could be. But I think he will call it and soon." Michel Perron, leader of the Parti National,, was on the phone with Marc Dubé. "Once this Mohawk affair blows over, he will do it. He may do it anyway. If he wins, he could call for a referendum. His people are indicating they are ready to do it. And if we win that election, which I plan to do, we will certainly do it... and quickly. I will need you. Relations with Ottawa will be key. You are the best man for that, as always. Are you ready to come back? Can I count on you?"

"Of course. We will be closer to what we have spent our lives working for. You can count on me."

On August 7, 1990, under pressure from party supporters and from public sentiment, the Liberal premier of Quebec called for an election to be held on September 15. The Mohawk Crisis be damned, according to one commentator.

"What happens in that will happen, I'm afraid," said the Premier to the media after the announcement. "It is Ottawa's responsibility to deal with it. We have our own future to decide. Quebec has been wronged."

The Quebec election of 1990 was an emotionally charged, acrimonious affair held in the middle of three different crises - the revolt of the natives, the failure of the US-Canada trade agreement with the resulting economic downturn, and the festering animosity between Quebec and English Canada. The incumbent Liberals, normally loyal to Canada, had trouble enunciating a direction that spoke of anything other than a rupture with the rest of the country. A new negotiation of special status for Quebec they said. Nobody believed it. People were in the streets clamoring for a declaration of independence, for Quebec's own army to deal with the natives. For a special bilateral trade deal with the United States – 'Cheap hydroelectricity in exchange for market access'. But Quebec needed to be a country to do that. American governments do not do deals with parts of other countries. The Liberals were asking for support to do a new deal with Canada. The people would have nothing of it.

In the week preceding the Quebec election, the government in Ottawa was forced to call for a Commons vote on deployment of the armed forces to quell the native insurrections and seal the border with the United States. American Indians were coming across to aid their brothers to the north. Border control points were insufficient to police the activity. The government called for the army to intervene and block the border from further incursions. Fights broke out in communities as pickups full of Indians crossed over, looking to hook up with local protests. Two Sioux Indians were killed in an army shootout in Saskatchewan.

American public opinion was enraged at the lack of control in what was going on in Canada. Two Americans were killed. Great Lakes shipping had been disrupted with no end in sight. The country to the north appeared to be breaking up. The U.S. Administration was questioned by major media organizations as to what contingency plans were being drawn up if the situation up north got worse.

The government in Ottawa proceeded to lose the non-confidence vote. The Governor-General was obliged to call for an election. David Malone resigned and asked his caucus to elect an interim leader of the party to fight the election. The Government of Canada was in chaos. The resignation and uncertainty who would rule the country sealed the fate of the Quebec election.

The separatist Parti National easily won it. The new Premier-to-be announced in his victory speech to followers at the party afterwards that the new government would be holding a referendum on independence. It would happen within ninety days. Joy erupted in the streets of the major cities and towns of Quebec.

29

"What do we do about Dubé?" Bill Wilson asked his boss. The Parti National had won the Quebec election the day before. "He's their guy in there. He is once again part of that government, you can be sure. He will certainly have a key role. He is their chief constitutional expert, the go-to guy on dealing with Ottawa. Do we tell the government here? I believe we must."

Frank Russo took a few seconds before responding. "Who do we tell, Bill? The government has been defeated. The Conservatives are in the midst of choosing an interim leader. That won't happen for a week. Even then, he or she will not be prime minister. In theory, yes, but in reality no. There is an interim prime minister who has no real power and will be something else in a month. He may not even win in his own riding, things are going so badly for those guys. The new Quebec Government has not even been formed yet......Let's sit on it. As it is, Dubé is still professor of political science at the university in Montréal. When the new government here is elected, we will inform the new PM. Telling anyone else in the meantime will only complicate matters. Imagine. The new constitutional advisor to the Quebec Premier, who has not been named as such yet by the way, is a Russian agent. In the meantime, we will watch him."

"By the way, do we talk to the Manitoba government about Cromwell? He may not be gone. Could still be around."

"We must. I will speak with the Commissioner who will most probably defer to the Clerk of the Privy Council. This has to do with intergovernmental relations at the highest level. The Minister will have to be informed, although he is in an election campaign. He will most surely defer to the Clerk as well through his Deputy."

"Mr. Premier, I trust you will understand the particular circumstances of my having to call you. This would normally be falling upon the Prime Minister to speak to you of this. I have with me in my office the chief national security advisor who has information to share with you. I am afraid this is very sensitive and has implications for national security. I cannot emphasize more fully the need to be cautious with what he will be telling you. Are you alone in your office, sir? "

The Premier of the Province of Manitoba replied, with a degree of trepidation that could be felt by the people at the other end of the line. "Very well. Yes, I am alone. Tell me what I need to know. This sounds ominous. But, please, proceed."

The national security advisor took the phone from the Clerk. "Mr. Premier, we have reason to believe someone working for one of your MLAs is a Soviet agent. We understand he may have left the country in the last few days. He may still be around, though we believe he realizes he has been detected. I cannot say more about that, however, nor can I say much about what we believe to be his espionage activities. We would like to have your cooperation in tracking him down, as we are not certain of his whereabouts."

"Who is he? Who are you talking about?"

"His name is Nathan Cromwell. We are informed he is the legislative assistant for the Member for Elk River."

"I know Cromwell. He has been with our party for some time. In two different administrations. I am shocked. He is very capable and well liked. I am surprised. You will have my cooperation. This is very disturbing, just the same."

"Mr. Premier, we have evidence that Mr. Cromwell has had some role in the native disturbances that have been going on. We would like your cooperation as to anything you may know of his involvement in this. We would also like to interview the Member for Elk River."

"You will have it. How do we proceed from here?"

Later that evening...

"He's gone. Nowhere in sight. His boss has not seen him since Friday. No show at the office this week. His girlfriend doesn't know where he is. She sounded very upset."

The Winnipeg-based agent continued. "His boss. I told him Cromwell was under suspicion of being involved with the native uprisings. Nothing of the Russian connection, of course. He was not totally surprised but was not aware of any subversive activities. Said he was a great assistant. Spent a half-hour with him. I have a transcript. Asked who he was most close to, he mentioned Ellison Ward along with a couple of other people. Said he spent a lot of time with Ward over the years. I didn't ask him about any involvement of Cromwell in Ward's ratification vote. The member, his boss, voted in favour of it, by the way. Question remains if Cromwell had a role in Ward's vote. We spoke with his girlfriend. We don't think she was aware of anything concerning espionage.

We did not ask her about that, but she gave no hint of evading us or of hiding anything. She was just upset and expects him back. We did not say that that probably will not happen."

"Wow. Russian agent involved in the canning of the Meech Lake Accord"...and another one the chief constitutional advisor to the Government of Quebec, thought Frank Russo. Unbelievable. He understood full well the sensitivity of the Cromwell affair as well as the one concerning Quebec. Both had to be kept under wraps. "Can you imagine the uproar that would come with this? We better keep it to ourselves for the time being. I would not want to think of what the reaction of the native movement would be, or of anyone else for that matter, given what is going on. I will have to inform the Commissioner who will probably want to share it with the Clerk. He can then decide what to tell the new government when it comes in. This is sensitive stuff. Even delving into it further at this point risks it getting out of our control."

"Nathan Cromwell's real name is Nathan Hightower, Sir." Frank Russo was briefing the head of CSIS. "He is a Cree from northern Saskatchewan. Looking through some records in Regina, there was a Nathan Hightower who was a student at one of the residential schools, from the age of six to the age of thirteen. He escaped from the school and they never caught up with him. He apparently surfaced in Regina years later, where he had a few odd jobs there and in Alberta. You will remember our discussion concerning Sergeant Pace remembering him from Regina as well as the connection with the Russian we encountered in Montreal. Hightower disappeared sometime in 1976. There are no employment records of a Nathan Hightower anywhere after that, in Saskatchewan, Alberta, Manitoba, anywhere in the country. In 1981, he showed up as a Navajo from Arizona under the name of Nathan Cromwell with a father who was Ojibway from Canada. He got a job as a teacher in a small community and was soon afterwards hired by the member of the legislature for the area. The rest you know."

"Thank you, Frank. Looks like we have a real problem that we must contain. No one, I mean no one other than the leader of this government and the one who will soon be elected and the head of the civil service must be aware of what we are talking about. A Cree from Saskatchewan becoming an agent of Russian espionage organizing the revolt of the natives of this country and perhaps being instrumental in the demise of the Meech Lake Accord. No one. Your people must be totally disciplined about this. Understood?"

"Understood, sir."

"Now, about this stuff in Quebec. Dubé. I have briefed the Clerk. He quickly decided that the Governor General be informed and we proceeded to do just that. Quite extraordinary. Two cases of Russian espionage now and we do not look good in it. The GG expressed dismay, to put it mildly. The Clerk suggested it would be best to wait for the new government to be sworn in before taking any action on this with Quebec. The GG agreed. It would not be good for him to be calling the Premier of Quebec telling him he has a Russian agent in his midst. We can watch Dubé in the meantime. We could perhaps learn who he is working with, but we must be discreet. This will hit the fan when the new government learns of it and will feel obliged to do something. Explosive, to say the least. They have a referendum coming in Quebec."

"What has happened to Nathan? He's nowhere. Called his special cell phone for contacting him five times over the past week. No answer. Finally, the last time, Bell said there was no service at that number. Called his apartment. Lady answered; couldn't say where he was." The leader of the Kahnawake Mohawk Warriors was on the phone with the Innu leader in Labrador. "He was supposed to call me every week. He was doing it every other day since we began this. Nothing. Has the police got on to him? Intercepted our calls? Probably. In any case, we can't reach him. Calls to his office at the Legislature have always been off-limits. Maybe we should try it anyway."

"Haven't heard from him either. Strange, but didn't really need to talk to him. Pretty wrapped up with our situation here. You have probably noticed that the European air forces have all left, but it is difficult for us to keep up the occupation of the air base. The military will surely come in. Will not be pretty. I say call his office at the Legislature."

"Mr. Cromwell is on leave of absence, sir. How can I help you?

"Why the leave of absence? Can you say? I am a good friend."

"A health issue."

"When will he be back?"

"That has not been determined yet. Who is calling? Can I put you on to someone else here?" The answer given by the receptionist at the office of Dennis Strong, Member for Elk River, was what she had been instructed to give. Dennis Strong had been ordered by the RCMP to say nothing more. Health issue. Indeterminate date of return to work.

"No. It's nothing. An old friend. Thank you."

Bill Wilson was in Frank Russo's office at CSIS headquarters. "Frank, the Mohawks and the Innu apparently don't have any knowledge of Cromwell's Russian connections. We intercept their calls. We catch most of them. So many of them trying to find out about him. He put all this together. Quite extraordinary. But we do not believe any of the leaders on the ground are aware he was involved with the KGB, nor do we believe any of them are directly involved with the Russians. It's clear to us he managed to keep the connection secret. But he's gone, that's for sure. Obvious to us now given that none of those guys have heard from him."

"Extraordinary how he managed to do this. The nightmare scenario of the eruption of our natives. And the Russians were behind it."

By that time, Laura Dumont had concluded that she did not really know her man at all. So empty a feeling. A week later, she received an unsigned letter in an envelope mailed from Bonn, Germany. All it said was 'I'm sorry, Laura. I love you. You were good to me.'

30

The federal election of October 1990 was won by the Liberals in a landslide. The Conservatives were exhausted by free trade failure, economic hardship, constitutional demise and native uprisings out of control, losing all but a handful of seats. The party whose former and current leaders together had led the fight for rejection of the Meech Lake Accord was back in power, generating widespread revulsion in Quebec. The Bloc National party formed by the five MPs who had left the conservative caucus the previous spring, won forty-six seats in Quebec and became the official opposition in the House of Commons. The Reform Party, based in Alberta, very much to the right of the political spectrum and in existence for only five years, won forty seats, all in Western Canada. Reform had consistently argued for a hard-line position regarding the native uprising during the election campaign, more so than any other party. The party was also known for its opposition to any constitutional concessions to Quebec.

The Indian uprising continued with further blockades and run-ins with police outside several communities from coast to coast. The new Liberal government in Ottawa had as much trouble in dealing with the disturbances as the previous one. Efforts to come up with policies and funding to meet protester demands met with acrimony and discord among the chiefs and leaders of the more than 700 First Nation communities in the country. The army was overstretched. American natives continued to cross the border to lend support to the uprisings. They brought weapons easily obtained, crossing the border untouched and unintercepted through forests and fields. The uprising had contributed mightily to the downfall of a federal government and was seen to have contributed to the downfall of a provincial one as well. It had left scars throughout the country and had damaged relationships with the United States. And it was far from over.

It did not take long for the new Liberal Prime Minister to be told of the cases of Soviet espionage that had been uncovered. In his first national security briefing by the Clerk of the Privy Council, he was informed of the existence of the mole in the heart of the new Quebec Government.

"I know Dubé. He is well known in the independence movement. His wife is prominent in the Quebec cultural milieu. This is quite extraordinary. You're sure?"

"We are. He has been observed with a Russian who is a KGB agent. We had that one years ago, we could not prove anything, he left, but came back under a new identity. He now believe is out of the country. We've gone back, reviewing things that happened with Quebec over time. We have a complete file on what we surmise Dubé has done in his workings with the KGB. The CIA believe they have evidence of a bank account in Switzerland. We can share it all with you. We suspect he has been involved with them for a very long time."

The Prime Minister was accompanied by his Chief of Staff and the new Solicitor General. The Chief of Staff was the first to respond to what the Clerk said. "We will have to inform Perron of this. Maybe even insinuate it will be made public. This could kill the referendum. Will discredit the separatists. A god-send for us."

The PM was silent. No one else in the room said a word while they waited for his response. Jacques Caron looked around the room and then said. "We will do nothing. Except I will maybe call Perron. And maybe I won't. I will have to think about it. One thing for sure, though, we are not going to make this public. No leaks. Nothing. No one will believe us. I do not want any of this to be shared with anyone. I will have to inform Perron. But I can tell you we will look to be the fools in this. We will be accused of trying to influence the referendum. It will backfire on us. No word of this to anyone. Understood?" Everyone in the room responded in the affirmative.

Caron and the recently elected Premier of Quebec, Michel Perron, were old adversaries. They had known each other for over thirty years, having been ministers with overlapping responsibilities for their respective governments at different times. Relations had not always been nice. For Caron, the call would not be a pleasant affair. Three days after learning of Marc Dubé's involvement as a Russian spy, he made the call, all the while knowing he would be getting a blowback. Perron would be defiant. Dubé was key to what the man had spent most of his career working for.

"Michel, are you alone?"

"I am. What gives me the pleasure of receiving your call? One of your crises - the Indians? By the way, congratulations on your victory. But, of course, we will be adversaries once again." The referendum would consume these men for the foreseeable future. It would be acrimonious.

"I have something to tell you. I have been informed by my officials that your man, Marc Dubé, is a Russian spy. He has apparently been one for some time."

"Come on, Jacques. Are you crazy? Marc Dubé a Russian spy? Impossible. Your people are playing games, Jacques. This is ridiculous."

"I'm afraid it is true. I have seen the file. Pictures of him meeting a KGB agent. Dubé speaks Russian. Are you aware of that? I have more on all this. Believe me."

"Listen to me, Jacques. I don't want to hear any more about this. I don't trust any of you. You surprise me. This is a most dishonorable thing you are trying here. Done. Over. I don't want to hear about it. This call is over. I can't believe this, Jacques. *Au revoir.*"

Jacques Caron, Prime Minister of Canada, never managed to learn if Michel Perron, the Premier of Quebec, ever broached the subject of Russian espionage with Dubé. He suspected that he hadn't. It was too explosive; it had too many repercussions. The independence of Quebec depended a great deal on Marc Dubé.

31

Toronto, September 1991

"Andrew, who is that man I saw you speaking with on Spadina Avenue last night? You were outside a row of South Asian shops. What in the world were you doing there? Such a seedy stretch."

"What were YOU doing there?" Andrew Brown felt a twinge of fear. He had never liked that place.

"I was driving up Spadina to get home. Both University and Yonge were a mess. I looked to my right and there you were. The other guy looked familiar to me, by the way. But for God's sake, what brought you there?"

"A story, my dear." He had to think of something. "We are doing a series on what the immigrant community thinks about the future of Canada, given all that is going on. Lots of Pakistani, Indian and Chinese businesses in the area."

"The man you were speaking with certainly wasn't Pakistani or Chinese. Blond and rugged looking."

"My dear, what are you insinuating? I was just talking with someone who asked me for directions."

"OK. Sorry. Just a strange place for you to be."

Mary Ellen MacLean was still a Member of Parliament. She had won re-election twice. She knew a lot of people in Ottawa. And the man her husband was speaking to was a Russian. She had seen him before. At a cocktail party the year before. She remembered the ruddy face and the massive build. What was Andrew doing speaking to that guy?

"Robert, I told you years ago that place was bad. Somebody saw us last night. I cannot have this. No more meetings in Toronto. Back to the country roads."

"Somebody saw us. Who was it?"

"A friend. He just thought it was strange I would be in an area of Toronto like that after 9 on a weeknight. He was right. Very strange for me. No meetings there anymore. In any case, we should never have left at the same time. You are the intelligence guy. Why didn't you think of that? In any case, what we discussed last night may signal the end of our relationship. It has run its course. Things are deteriorating. Canada is breaking up. It is not what I had in mind when we started this. I have nothing more to give you."

"Andrew, you can't just walk away from this. Not that easy. We can ruin you."

"Alright. You keep saying that. But let's put a pause to it. I have little to give you, and I don't really need anything from you right now. I can't see that changing. By the way, I understand the KGB is finished. The coup that didn't work. Do you still have a job?"

"Nothing has really changed, Andrew. Just a new name and a new boss. SVR now. No longer KGB. Back to our affairs here. You DO have stuff for us. You are part of the intelligentsia. Many of your friends, along with your wife, are influential people in Toronto and Ottawa. It is in our interest to be informed what the intentions of these people are in keeping Canada together. That being said, we could also help you in assisting them with inside information from Washington and elsewhere on matters that could affect the direction of the country in this time of crisis."

"Like I said. Let's pause things a bit. I can't be seen with you like last night."

"Andrew, I will provide you a description of what we need to have. You can get it. It's that simple. Are we understood on that?"

"Understood. Goodbye, 'Robert'." Andrew Brown hung up the special mobile phone, turned in his desk chair and looked out the window to the skyline of Toronto with a sense of dread. Why in hell did I let myself get sucked into this? I could have done everything without these guys.

"Ms. MacLean, could I speak with you a moment?" The man showed his badge to the MP in the hallway of the Centre Block of the Parliament Buildings.

"Why, of course." CSIS. Intelligence. "This may not be the place to speak, however." Mary Ellen MacLean looked up and down the hall. No one was watching. The agent had been discreet in his approach. "Follow me to my office. No one else will be there. We can talk."

"Does your husband have any Russian friends, Ms. MacLean?" The man wasted no time in getting to the point.

"Not that I am aware of, officer. What is going on?"

"Your husband has been seen in the company of a man we have determined to be an intelligence agent, most likely KGB or whatever it is called now. He is masquerading as a cultural affairs attaché with the Soviet, now Russian Embassy here in Ottawa. He travels often to Toronto. We have seen him with your husband. I'm afraid I cannot say much more. I take it you are unaware of any activity on his part that could be linked to his contacts with the Russian."

"No, I am not aware of anything like that. This is very disconcerting to say the least."

"We are telling you this because you are a member of the Standing Committee on Defense and Intelligence. We suspect your husband may be cooperating with Russian intelligence."

"Is there anything else that would lead you to believe that?"

"Yes, there is, I'm afraid. We have observed over the years that the Toronto Herald seems to have had access to information from Washington, Paris and London that no one else in this country could claim to have. Much of the information has appeared in your husband's editorials and commentaries. We have gone back years into the material published in the Herald and have noticed opinions and related content that in our view could have only come from inside intelligence in the capitals I just mentioned. I realize this is disturbing. I regret that we must inform you of this."

Mary Ellen MacLean Brown had difficulty keeping her composure. "Well, this is not good. I'm not sure what to say. My husband perhaps working with Russian intelligence. What do you want me to do?"

"As a spouse, I cannot give you any counsel or advice, to be sure. As a Member of Parliament, you will have to be discreet. Nothing of substance can be shared with your husband. We will be watching him. I'm sorry. We had to tell you. I ask you to keep this discussion to yourself, and that includes your spouse."

"Thank you. I understand what you must do. This is a shock."

"I will be in touch with you, Ms. MacLean. Goodbye."

Frank Russo and his deputy, Allan Denby, were meeting in Russo's office reviewing counterintelligence operations. The subject of Andrew Brown came up. "Allan, remember that case of the woman who was found in a hotel room in Montreal a few years ago that Montreal police had trouble solving and they came to us for help? The lady who was a reporter with the Toronto Herald? Suspicious thing. No fingerprints anywhere. Nobody saw anything. I thought at the time it was a professional job. Her boss was Andrew Brown."

"Yes. We talked about that. Montreal never got anywhere with it. Still an open file. Maybe there is something with Brown on this. We are watching him. Seeing who he meets, where he goes. Not all the time, though. I'll have the surveillance put on 24 on 24 immediately. Bradley met with his wife a couple days ago. She apparently knows nothing. When we eventually bring him in or have our friends at the RCMP do it, we will ask about the deceased reporter. Could be something related to the Russians. Maybe she was aware of something and Brown realized it. Speculation at this point. It is a suspicious connection, though."

"Andrew, what are you doing with the Russians?" It came right out. She could not hold it back.

"What are you talking about? What Russians? What is this, Mary Ellen?"

"Don't put me off. The Russian you were talking with that night. I had seen that man before. In Ottawa. He's Russian. Probably Russian intelligence. And what were you doing with him? You need to tell me, Andrew." There were tears in her eyes.

"Stop it. The guy you saw me with asked me for directions on the street. I had just come from a meeting with some Pakistani businessmen. I didn't know the man from a hole in the wall."

"Andrew, the man is Russian. I am a member of the Intelligence and Defense Committee of the Parliament of Canada. Talking with my husband! What were you doing?"

"What is this?.......You tell me you saw the guy before. Where? Ottawa. Doing what?"

"Cocktail. Diplomatic circle things. People from all over. Happens all the time in Ottawa. Russians sometimes show up. He was one of them." She did not want to divulge what the CSIS agent had told her. "Is he a spy, Andrew?"

"I told you, I don't know what you are talking about. Stop this, Mary Ellen!"

"Andrew, you're lying. You're doing something with the Russians. Why? Why? Why?" she screamed.

"I won't put up with this. Stop it. I'm not doing anything with any Russians. Are you mad?"

"I'm leaving. I'm going to a hotel. I'm too upset to be here. You're not telling me what you are doing. You won't, so I am leaving. I will see what I do tomorrow." With that, she got up from the table, picked up her suit jacket and briefcase and left the apartment.

"Robert, we must talk." Andrew had exercised the call protocol, using the secure cellular phone that had been provided by the Russians. He had only used it three times in the five years since it had been given to him.

"OK, Andrew. We shall talk. You sound upset."

"I am. What are you doing going to cocktail receptions in Ottawa?"

"It's my official job, Andrew. I have to. It's my cover."

"Well, it has been blown. You have been discovered."

"What makes you say that?"

"I won't tell you. Simply that your cover doesn't work anymore. We must cease all contact."

"We can't, Andrew. If it is not me, it will be someone else. This doesn't end."

"You bastards. Get out of my life. Out!"

"I have been discovered. I must leave, for one. And we must deal with Brown." Andrei Timlikov, known to Andrew Brown as Robert, was with his boss, the head of Russian intelligence in Canada.

"What makes you say that? What do you mean concerning dealing with Brown?" asked the other man.

"Brown called me. The emergency line. He was angry. Upset. Criticized me for going to cocktails. Yelled at me. It appears someone saw me with Brown somewhere and also at one of the functions here in Ottawa. I suspect it may be his wife. He is unstable. He is dangerous. We never could really control him. Blackmailed him for awhile, but that ended. He could blow our operation here and in Washington, all the stuff we fed him on American intentions. If he talks about that, our sources in the administration in Washington could be exposed."

"Mary Ellen, please. We must talk. Can you come home? I must see you." Andrew Brown sounded contrite on the phone. His wife responded. "Yes, I will be there. Half an hour. Leaving now." With that, she picked up her coat, went downstairs to the lobby and hailed a cab.

Mary Ellen MacLean arrived at their upscale townhouse, paid the taxi driver, walked up the steps and went in. Andrew was in the living room with a glass of scotch on the coffee table, next to a half empty bottle.

"You've been drinking. It's not like you," Mary Ellen said as she slowly walked to the centre of the room.

"So be it. But I had to call you. Had to see you. I don't want you to leave me. I love you."

"What have you done, Andrew? Please tell me. You have lied to me. Something has been going on with the Russians. How long? Why? Basically, why? Why have you had to do this?"

"So, you have it, I gather. I won't continue to tell you otherwise. I did it. I did it for the country. Not for the Soviets or the Russians now. I don't give a damn about them. And I am not a Communist. I did it to break the dominance of Canada by America, by the Americans. The steamroller of American economic dominance. I wrote stuff to weaken their hold on things here. The Russians helped me with intelligence to do that."

"Go on. In exchange for what, Andrew? What did you tell them? I hope not about things I was doing? What did you tell them?!"

"Not very much. I didn't ask for money and I didn't give them very much. They complained about that. I told them your stuff was off limits. It was. Nothing. You must believe me on that. What they got out of it was the failure of the free trade agreement and the fracture of the U.S.-Canada alliance. They are happy. They should be. Not only is there acrimony, distrust, and bad relations between Washington and Ottawa, Canada is breaking up, for Christ's sake! What more could they have hoped for? And I delivered it to them! With my pen! My fucking pen! I am so sorry, Mary Ellen. I shook the Yankee dominance and it ended up being the first shot in the breakup of the country. And an increased economic dominance of us by the Americans, not less. Everything has followed from the downfall of the free trade agreement."

"How did this start?"

"Cambridge. They approached me. Made sense. Inside info to help me blast the Americans. Suited me. I did not ask or take any money from them. No blackmail. No babes in hotel rooms with hidden cameras. I thought I could do this on light - intelligence light - with nobody killed or anything like that. I thought I was smart and could handle them, but I have been a fool. Such a fool."

"So you were working with them when we met and ever since."

"Yes, since 1975. Almost sixteen years. It suited my purpose. But not anymore. I am not going any further with this."

"What do you mean?"

"I told them I'm out. I quit. They say they won't let me."

"Andrew, this is very difficult for me. You have deceived me ever since we have been together. You have been a shadow. Not real. I don't think I can continue. Not as your wife. It's too much."

"Don't leave me, Mary Ellen. I'm quitting all of that. Back to an honest life. Honest life. No more shadow. Can you believe me?"

"Andrew, you may go to jail. This is not going to be easy to get out of or away from."

"What do you mean? Has anybody talked to you about this? Police? RCMP or CSIS?" Andrew downed the remainder of the glass of Scotch.

"No. None of that." She was not going to expose the surveillance. Question of national security. She couldn't, although she wanted to cry out to Andrew that it was known. She decided to do the closest thing to it. "But you should assume the authorities could know about it. The Russians are most certainly not to be trusted. They won't care about you."

"Stay with me here tonight. Please. I need you to stay with me."

"Alright. You need someone right now. You are drunk and you are a mess. I'll stay."

"Come hold me, Mary. Hold me."

Andrew fell asleep fully clothed on the master bed as she held him. At midnight Mary Ellen left her husband in the bedroom, called for a taxi from the living room and left the townhouse.

At 10:30 the following morning she received a call from her mother. "Mary, I'm so sorry. So sorry. Andrew. So young. But why didn't you call me?"

"Mom. what are you talking about?"

"Oh, my God. You don't know. They didn't call you, go to see you?"

"I got in late. I turned off my cell phone. I'm staying at a hotel, Mom. I slept in. What has happened to Andrew?"

"They found him under the Bloor access overpass of the Don Valley Parkway at 8 o'clock this morning. The news says it appeared to be a suicide. A witness at the scene overheard police saying the body smelled of alcohol. I wasn't aware Andrew had a drinking problem. And why are you staying at a hotel? Thank God for your newfangled phone so I could find you. Why weren't you at home?"

"He didn't, Mom. He didn't have a drinking problem. I don't know what to say. Mom, I need a moment. I'll call you back." Mary Ellen laid back on the bed in the hotel room, stared at the ceiling, tears coming to her eyes. They got him. He thought he could do it with no pain. So smart. So arrogant. So naive......Gone. I should have stayed with him. The country is going to hell and my husband is gone. Why didn't I see all this before?

32

"We did it. You did it. We will have our country, Marc. Oui, monsieur." Marc Dubé's colleague in the Premier's office was jubilant, as was everyone else gathered that evening in the Quebec City hotel suite and had been following television coverage of the results. It was late, but the numbers were in.

"We all did this. Twenty-five years of work. I was just part of it," replied Dubé.

"No, no, no, Marc. You were key to this. You always have been."

"Pierre's right. The team won this, but you were the captain." Michel Perron, the always correct but jovial Premier of Québec and the soon to be declared first President of the Republic of Quebec had chimed in. He was using first names in the presence of other people for the first time anyone could remember. And anyone who would have been aware that Marc Dubé was on the payroll of the Soviet KGB would have been certain at that moment that the Premier knew nothing of it.

They had won their referendum on independence with a clear question - *Voulez-vous avoir votre propre pays?* Do you want your own country? 51% had said *Oui* and 49% had said *Non.* Not a ringing majority, but a majority just the same. The PN Government had always said 50% plus 1 would be enough, regardless of what the rest of Canada would say. The breakup of Canada had begun.

"You are a hero, Marc. Commentators, the ones who are sympathetic to us, are saying it. People will love you for this, forever. Our dream has come true." Hélène Beaulieu was consumed with emotion, with tears, joy and bubbly adulation for her man and what had happened that day.

"My dear, It is our day, our historic day. We will have it. Our country. Let's celebrate. Champagne and then we will turn off the lights."

The Government of Quebec did not immediately declare independence. The terms of secession from Canada would be settled through negotiations, according to the Premier. "I expect the government in Ottawa, the Prime Minister who I have known for many years and respect, will deal with us in good faith. We will arrive at an amicable separation and certainly an equitable division of government assets and interests that the people of Quebec have a rightful share in."

"The sonofabitch. Negotiate. 51 to 49 - not exactly a landslide mandate. Break up the country over a 2% differential. Negotiate? I will be damned if I horse-trade the break-up of the country. And all this directed by a man paid by the KGB. The KGB! The Russians, for Christ's sake! If only I could tell the people......but I can't. As I said when this first came up, nobody would believe it and we would look foolish. Disgusts me, this whole thing." The Prime Minister of Canada was standing up behind his desk with his arms wide and imploring to the man seated in front of him, the senior public servant of the land, the Clerk of the Privy Council, "Can you believe this? A Russian spy the organizer of the referendum, the hero of Quebec now, and I can't tell anybody about it. *Merde!*" He continued to look at the man who did not offer an answer to that.

"The strategy, Sir. We need to have an answer to the result. An answer to that. We have a few options you have discussed with your colleagues. The Government of Canada needs to respond. The espionage thing is another matter," said the highest public official of the land, trying to deflect the emotion of the moment back to the essential issue of the day and the condition of the country.

"OK. Do we negotiate or do we not? I am not happy about having to deal with that treacherous, arrogant man."

"What option do you have, Sir? That the Government of Canada tells the people of Quebec, tells all Canadians that we won't negotiate, that we don't accept the result of the referendum? What does that leave us with? Wait for them to unilaterally declare independence? What then? We say "you can't do that" and then send in the army? Do you want that? Turning guns on citizens? That's what it will be. Even without that, with negotiations and discussions dragging along as they most certainly will, as long as the impasse lasts, everything will be in limbo. Financial markets, the overall economy. Business dealings with Quebec companies will be at a standstill. They will be at a standstill everywhere for that matter. People will wonder where they should be paying their taxes. Employers will stop hiring. They will look to survival. Who would want to buy the Canadian dollar? It will fall; banks will stop lending. Uncertainty; uncertainty in everything in the country. We will have to keep it to a minimum. There will be issues of public disorder if things drag out. The armed forces will be under stress - will the forces trust their Quebec units, their francophone officers, all of that? Not to negotiate is to declare war, Sir. Quebec has spoken. They won the referendum. A majority said yes. We must deal with it and try to secure a stronger Canada with what is left. And we must do it quickly. We must reassure the people. If not, things will really fall apart."

"Gordon, I am a Quebecer. This breaks my heart. I will be negotiating the separation of my home from my country, my Canada. Do you realize what that means to me?"

"You are the leader of Canada, Sir. You were elected just months ago to manage chaos, whether you view it that way or not. In essence, that is what people voted for. Somebody to manage difficult times. And only greater chaos will come if you do not act quickly. You have no other option."

"Alright.....Alright...... Tell me how we organize this."

The Bloc National caucus was in the Railway Room of Parliament's Centre Block. It was the regular Wednesday morning meeting. The Liberals were gathered across the hall and the caucuses of the other parties were meeting in other rooms as well. Tension was everywhere. So was security. It was nine days after the Quebec referendum and the first Wednesday with MPs back in Ottawa after a two-week break. All forty-six Bloc members of Parliament were in attendance, waiting for their leader to begin the meeting. Gérard Rousseau, the party leader and founder as well as Leader of Her Majesty's Official Opposition in the House of Commons, brought the gathering to order. "*Mes amis,* we have won. The people have chosen. *Le Québec aux Québécois.* But now we have a choice. Do we stay or do we leave?" The discussion went back and forth, with many members saying that their responsibility was still representing and defending the interests of Quebec in Ottawa. Quebec was still a part of Canada and constituents there needed to have their voice in Ottawa. Others contended it would be consistent with the results of the referendum to cease working in Ottawa, return home and assist in building the new Quebec.

While the discussion was going on, demonstrators were gathering outside in front of the Parliament Buildings. By 11 o'clock, an estimated crowd of 2,000 people had formed, chanting "Down with the Bloc. Bloc Go Home..... Down with the Bloc. Bloc Go Home......" A group calling itself The Defense of Canada claimed responsibility for organizing the demonstration. Reporters on site learned that the group had quickly mobilized people from eastern Ontario to come to Ottawa and demonstrate their anger with what was happening and direct that anger at the party whose sister organization in Quebec was in the process of taking the country apart. Emotions were running high. RCMP personnel were there to help Commons security seal off entrances to the Centre Block and prevent the crowd from getting inside.

The head of Commons security told the assembled Bloc caucus members there was a demonstration, and their safety could be at stake if they tried to leave. He asked that all members remain in the room or at a minimum refrain from leaving the building until the crowd had dispersed. No one said anything for a moment.

Pandemonium ensued once the officer had left the room. A caucus member, one of the original five who had left the Conservatives the year before, stood up and exhorted his colleagues. "We will not be intimidated. We will not run scared with our tails between our legs. I say we walk out of here with our heads high. We return to our offices and carry on our responsibilities to our constituents, and tell the media assembled exactly that. Walk right through the protesters."

"Normand, you're crazy. We'll be attacked."

"So be it. Our constituents back home will support us even more. There should be enough RCMP and police out there to prevent us being too roughed up. Friends, this may be the price for being Québécois these days. TV everywhere outside, I'm sure. Prime time. Gérard, do you agree? Do we do this?"

"Let's take a vote," responded the leader. "Right now. All in favour, raise your hands. Do not feel obligated to do it. Be honest with yourself. Who is in favour?"

All raised their hands. Gérard Rousseau took it in. "Let's do it. Bring back the head of security. The least he can do is have his men lead the way."

Some demonstrators were more vocal than others, launching epithets at the group of MPs. One of them, then another, pushed two MPs, who pushed back. Scuffles broke out. RCMP officers had to force their way through the crowd to rescue the group. The scene was chaotic. Television cameras caught it all. Two Bloc MPs were taken to hospital with head injuries and a third was treated for a dislocated shoulder. Revulsion spread throughout Quebec, with commentators suggesting the time was ripe for the government to end the post-referendum suspense and declare independence.

"Gérard, let's go home. We have done our job. There is no way we can stay here. Our constituents will support us. We are not wanted here." Serge Grondin, one of the Bloc's original five, was with Rousseau in the hallway of Ottawa's Montfort Hospital. They had left their injured colleagues and were making their way to the RCMP vehicles waiting to take them to their offices.

"You may be right. Time to leave. Let's talk later. I'll call you."

"We are going to need a statement for the press. This cannot wait, Gérard. Look. There are reporters here," pointing to the group of a half dozen reporters with microphones, accompanied by cameramen, waiting just outside the door.

"OK. Get the staff to call for a meeting. 3 PM. Get a room that can hold everyone. No leaks to the media in the meantime, although they will surely see something is up. Everybody has to be on board for this."

"Gérard, we are with you. Tell us what you need." Dubé was on the phone with Rousseau. "We have had to respond to the incident. We have said only that we are in solidarity with you. Nothing more for the moment. We will have to say more than that, and soon. What are your plans now?"

"Meeting everyone at 3. I am proposing we leave Ottawa. It means we will all resign our seats. Anything else would be a charade. I cannot really act as Leader of the Opposition. It is untenable. And our safety is at stake. Our presence here is over. I will call you after the meeting."

The Bloc National announced at 4PM that afternoon that their forty-six Members of Parliament were resigning their seats and were leaving Ottawa, effective immediately. The leader of the Reform Party in the House, Douglas Miller, thus became the Leader of the Opposition. The government in a statement expressed dismay at the decision of the Bloc members. The announcement said nothing about an election for replacements.

"Do we still negotiate?" the Prime Minister asked his key colleagues around the table. The Minister of Finance, his key ministers from Quebec and the clerk of the Privy Council along with his Chief of Staff had been brought together before the meeting of the full cabinet, scheduled for twenty minutes from then. "And do we call for bye-elections to replace the Bloc people?"

"Yes on the negotiations. We must go through with it." answered the Minister of Finance. "Stability demands it. The uncertainty must end. Sorry to have to admit it, but that is it, Jacques. About an election? I think it would be foolish to talk about that now, although constitutionally, we may have to call for it in those ridings. For the lawyers to figure that out."

33

"The terms are crazy. Unbelievable. All federal assets in Quebec turned over, for free. Already paid for by Quebeckers over the years through their taxes to Ottawa, they say. Nothing of the federal debt to be shared. Absolution from that. They say we decided to contract for that; not their responsibility. All Quebec based army and air force units to be allowed to join a Quebec armed forces, along with their equipment. They say Quebecers already paid for their share. And it goes on." The Prime Minister and the Minister of Finance had just had a briefing from the chief negotiator after the first meeting with his Quebec counterpart and was speaking with his close friend and Minister of External Affairs. "Took us two weeks to agree on a process with them. Perron is an asshole. Dubé as well. And they start off with this. I told the negotiator to push back. Finance is coming up with counterproposals on debt and transfer of assets. When this gets out, there will be trouble."

Trouble came quickly. The Quebec government released its demands to the press. Mainstream English media expressed outrage and called on the government to resist what was being demanded, while at the same time work to alleviate the uncertainty regarding the future of the country. The Prime Minister was forced to state in a national address that this was a negotiation, and that Canada would defend its interests.

Anti-Quebec demonstrations were held in Regina, Toronto, and Calgary. The demonstration in Calgary turned ugly, with the burning in effigy of Michel Perron.

The day after the Prime Minister's address, the leader of the Reform Party and new Leader of the Opposition, in a press conference in Ottawa, called for the resignation of the Prime Minister. The argument was that as a Quebecker, he could not properly exercise the defense of the interests of the rest of the country. His home province had moved to secede and take large parts of the assets of the country with it. Someone else in cabinet should be named as leader and become Prime Minister to lead the country going forward. No mention was made of the Prime Minister's long recognized devotion to Canada.

In a statement to the media afterwards, the Solicitor General said that the Prime Minister and the sitting Liberal government had been elected to govern and look after the interests of Canadians and Canada and that was precisely what the Prime Minister was doing. The next day, the largest media organization in the country, operating over twenty newspapers from coast to coast, came out in support of the request of the Leader of the Opposition. A front-page editorial appeared in all its newspapers – **The Government must be led by someone else** - ran the headline. A radio station in Calgary called for Alberta to consider seceding from Canada and proposed that British Columbia consider the same.

Meanwhile, the native revolt continued. Complicating matters, the Crees in northern Quebec as well as other communities - Algonquin, Mohawk, Inuit and Innu - all made it clear they would not go along with their territory being considered part of an independent Quebec. Commentators in the province deplored the positions of the natives but urged the government to do what was necessary for the common good and the maintenance of the integrity of the Quebec territory.

Negotiations between Ottawa and Quebec were getting nowhere. Uncertainty gripped the country. There was anger and anxiety everywhere - in government, in business, in the streets and homes of Canada. The New York Times reported that special meetings were being held in Washington to decide how to protect American assets in Canada, as the condition of the northern neighbor deteriorated.

Premier Perron was on television - a special address to the people of Quebec. "We are at an impasse. Negotiations with Ottawa, with Canada, have not gone well. They have not been productive. For three months now, we have been patient, but firm. We have come to the realization that Canada does not want to give to Quebec what Quebec is due. With this, and with heavy concern for your welfare, but primarily for the future of the Quebec nation, for the future of generations to come, we, the elected government of Quebec and with your support through the results of the recent referendum, have decided to declare the independence of Quebec and the formation of a republic. I say now to you all, *Vive le Quebec. Vive notre pays.*"

"I have instructed the Sureté du Quebec to take control of the ports and airports as well as of other physical assets under federal control on our territory. The few issues that had been resolved in the negotiations with Ottawa regarding transfer of assets, hopefully will be respected. I trust that civil disturbances as well as intervention by federal authorities to interfere with what we are doing can be avoided. I implore Canada to refrain from using force. The people of Quebec spoke months ago. It is time for Canada to respect that. I will have details of the measures we intend to carry out and communicate them to you as we move forward. *Vive le Québec.*"

There was jubilation in the cities and towns of Quebec. Disturbances broke out across English Canada, with people enraged at what had been declared. Twenty thousand people gathered on the plaza of Toronto City Hall to voice their anger. A spontaneous parade of what was estimated at fifty thousand people marched down Granville Street in Vancouver chanting anti-Quebec slogans, with many of the participants bearing signs and placards calling for armed intervention to prevent the breakup. The Toronto Stock Exchange Index, having already lost 25% of its value since the Quebec referendum, dropped a further 15% in the two days following Quebec's declaration. The value of the Canadian dollar plunged. The Bank of Canada quickly increased interest rates to derail a run on the dollar. The Prime Minister called for calm, stating that negotiations with Quebec would continue but that the interests of Canada would be defended. Opposition parties in the House of Commons called on the government to resign and if it did not, declared they will demand the Governor-General disband the government and call for a new election.

Prime Minister Caron was with his closest advisors in his Parliament Hill office. "I am resigning. I'm doing it tonight. I cannot continue as the leader of Canada, of an essentially English-speaking Canada now, as a person from Quebec and in the face of secession from my own province. I cannot credibly rally the country. I am tainted, whether it is justified or not. A Quebecer potentially leading the country against his own. It cannot be."

The other men in the room remained silent, looking at their boss. The Prime Minister continued. "I will have difficulty going forward in making tough decisions that could lead to confrontation and disruption. We need a new mandate from the country. I am confident we can win that election. I cannot imagine the people would want to have either of our opponents forming the government. We will nominate a new leader. There are some good ones in the cabinet, as you all know. We can win it and will win it. Call Cabinet together. Meeting at 8 PM. Anyone not in Ottawa will be connected by conference call. Set it up. Nothing to the media beforehand. Nothing."

"Sir, you realize that you will not have a riding anymore. There will be no one for you to represent in a new election. The same for the other twenty-one Quebec MPs on our side."

"I have realized that, of course. It breaks my heart."

34

GOVERNMENT RESIGNS. NEW ELECTION CALLED.

Headlines across the country spread the surprising news - "Caron resigns, calls for a new mandate with a new leader to rally the country" - ran many by-lines. The erstwhile seventy-five federal ridings of Quebec are declared not subject to the writ. For the first time in the history of Canada, a federal election would be held without the participation of Quebec.

The campaign was one of the most emotionally charged in the history of Canada. The future of the country was at stake. Acrimony was rampant - West against East and vice versa, rural vs. urban, different visions of leadership, of what needed to be done. Punish Quebec vs. work out the inevitable split and get on with it. After a brutal campaign, the Alberta-based Reform Party emerged victorious. It had campaigned on a mandate to be tough on Quebec, protect the integrity of the military, get the economy going once more and improve relations with the United States. The Liberals were soundly defeated, with the New Democratic Party forming the Official Opposition. All ridings west of Ontario except for two in Vancouver went Reform, along with most of the rural ridings of Ontario. The Atlantic provinces voted en masse for the Liberals as did metro Toronto. What was left of the country with the secession of Quebec was split. West vs. East, rural vs. urban.

The note was curt with a hand-drawn map. Meet me at this point on this road exactly two kilometers out of Drummondville going west. There is a turnoff into the woods. Trail is only four hundred meters long. Go to the end. Keep your lights off. 7 PM tomorrow.

"Marc, I have been discovered. I must leave. It is happening tonight. This meeting must be short. The driver has instructions to bring me to the airport and quickly. They know about you. We are sure of it. This is why I came to see you in person. Communications cannot be trusted. Get out while you can. And destroy all evidence of our relationship."

"Serge, there is no evidence anywhere of that. There is nothing to destroy. The only thing is the bank account. It's in Switzerland and in a different name. But I will not leave. I am on the verge of realizing my life's dream. If they expose me, so be it. It will be a rumor. What proof will they have? Leaving would only confirm it as truth."

"They may have pictures, Marc. One of our last meetings in Montreal. One of my guys has told me a couple of times he believes he was trailed to the cafe. It's why I never proposed it again."

"You never told me that."

"What happened, happened. I just never proposed we meet in Montreal again. It is always possible we are observed. Part of the business. I have stayed out of sight, but my time is up."

"So be it. I'll deal with it, if they have pictures. But I am not going to run."

"Goodbye, Marc. I must go. Congratulations on your accomplishment. I would like to think we helped."

"You did. Goodbye, Serge."

In the weeks following the election, the economy continued to deteriorate. Negotiations with Ottawa continued to be at a standstill. Everyday life in Quebec became fractious, tense and uncertain. Would deposits in banks be protected? Yes, it had soon been determined, but many people doubted it. Runs on banks led to restrictions on withdrawals. People could not get their money out. The European and American central banks, after supporting the Canadian dollar for weeks, lost patience with the uncertainly of the future of Canada and succumbed to pressure to reduce the support of the dollar. The dollar lost 5% of its value against the US greenback in one day of trading. People were unsure about other things, essential things. Where were employers to send their payroll deductions? To whom should people and businesses pay their taxes? Pension funds had lost over 50% of their value and the slide was continuing unabated. Would government pension and old age security checks keep coming? These questions and hundreds of others had not been resolved. Every passing day without resolution by Ottawa and Quebec plunged the newly declared republic-to-be further into disarray.

Students in Quebec universities and colleges took to the streets demanding the nationalization of the banks that were restricting credit and withdrawal of deposits. As orders dried up in key industries, workers were being laid off. The calls for nationalization quickly expanded to the forest products, aerospace and aluminum industries, all largely controlled by foreign interests. Quebec companies operating in the supply chains of major industries reducing or closing operations were caught in the downturn and laid off workers in large numbers. Unemployment in Quebec reached 30%, with the number growing week by week.

The uncertainty encompassed the military. What were Quebec-based military units to do? Follow orders and redeploy to Ontario and elsewhere or resign and join a new Quebec army? Some units resigned en masse, bringing their weapons with them. Military commanders were losing control of their Quebec contingents. Violence was barely avoided as frictions abounded on military bases.

In Parliament, the atmosphere was acrimonious. The need to close ranks and re-group the country for the future met with differing visions, primarily reflecting divisions between East and West. Ontario largely wanted to accommodate Quebec, ease the transition, and work things out whereas westerners were deeply against that. "Let Quebec go. They wanted it. They can have it." The new Reform government was hostile to ceding anything of substance to Quebec. Uncertainty concerning the future ran unabated.   Groups in Western Canada openly began to discuss alternate options for the Region, with the subject often turning to the potential benefits of becoming part of the United States. Commentators in Atlantic Canada, which was now cut off from direct access to the rest of the country, began to talk of the region forming its own country. Out of necessity. This had never been spoken of before. Further, the prospect of continuing to be governed by a right-wing government in Ottawa, at least in the short term, did not comfort anyone in Atlantic Canada. The region was used to a more social-democratic activist central government For Atlantic Canadians, relations with Quebec had to be productive with a minimum of friction to ensure passage of goods into and out of the region as well as a safe corridor for passage to the rest of the country. This was being jeopardized by an intransigent government in Ottawa. Maritimers, as they were often called, wondered about the continuing ability of Ontario to drive the prosperity and well-being of the country. They could see that hundreds of companies and businesses were closing their operations altogether, if not setting up south of the border. Many subsidiaries of American companies were pulling up stakes and moving operations and jobs back home or elsewhere. Employment in manufacturing in Ontario, the mainstay of the economy, had decreased by 40% over the previous two years to begin with, before the Quebec declaration of independence, with no end in sight. There were difficult and acrimonious discussions in virtually every corporate boardroom in the country. Do we stay or do we go? What operations do we continue with? Which ones and where? What people do we let go? Which ones do we keep? Do we honour our contracts or do we not? Board room divisions proliferated. There were the shareholder protection directors and there were the social responsibility directors, with others in between. The essential question in every corporate boardroom and management office was "what do we do?"

The West was different. The oil and gas industry continued to operate and grow, fueled by American demand. Sympathy for people in Ontario, whose leaders were viewed as the culprits in the demise of continental free trade, was running short in Western Canada. Attitudes were little different regarding Atlantic Canada and its dependence on the rest of Canada for the support of the region's government programs, infrastructure, and income levels. Atlantic Canadians in turn doubted the willingness of the prosperous West to accommodate visions of the future of the country from elsewhere. People in all parts of English Canada - west, central, east - increasingly expressed doubt about the ability of the country to continue to exist. For years, many had privately, if not publicly, felt that if Quebec wanted to leave, let them. What many had wished had happened and the results were not what they thought they would be.

Quebec had its own troubles brought on by the declaration. The questions of the exodus of businesses, capital flight, tax collection and division of assets, which were all serious, did not come close to the seriousness of what was happening in the north.

One morning a month after the Quebec declaration of independence, Crees, who had consistently stated their objection to having their territory considered as part of an independent Quebec, arrived in force at the installations of the James Bay La Grande hydroelectric complex. The complex supplied half of Quebec's power needs. The Crees declared that they, the rightful owners and lords of the land there, were henceforth in charge. The Quebec government was taken entirely by surprise. It had never thought that could happen. Relations had always been good with the Cree leadership over the years since the agreements on the use of the land twenty years before.

The Sureté du Quebec police contingent at each of the locations was overpowered and put under house arrest. The Cree leader, David Okanaway, stated to a radio reporter, "We told you we would not be part of the territory of the new country. You have not listened. You have not even come to us to talk about it. We still regard our land as part of the territory of our own nation, under the cooperation and legal jurisdiction of Canada."

The Crees threatened to cut off hydro transmission to the south unless their area was declared to remain within the boundaries of Canada. "Impossible for us to consider," stated Michel Perron. Instead, the Sureté du Quebec was ordered to retake the complex. The roads to the complex were blocked by Cree warriors and, taking cues from the warriors of Sioux Lookout, landing strips and runways attached to the relevant communities were blocked with debris. The Sureté could not get in. With the refusal of the government to consider their demands and with the sending of armed police, the Crees turned off the power generators, cutting supply to over half of the users in the province. Hydro Quebec scrambled to cover essential supply through other sources. Power was rationed. Supply of hydro to customers in New England was interrupted. Within days, the power authorities of the states of New York, Vermont and New Hampshire cancelled their contracts with Hydro Quebec. Blackouts occurred throughout New England. The Quebec government threatened to mobilize a force to retake the hydro complex. The Crees remained defiant. It would take three weeks before the Sureté du Quebec with a beefed-up invasion force managed to retake the installations without bloodshed. Cree warriors had sabotaged many parts of them. It would be a further four months before full power could be resumed. Power eventually flowed south, but the damage was done. Many businesses and industries reliant on hydro had scaled back production, some halting it altogether. The industrial base of Quebec had been essentially crippled.

The Crees retreated into the interior of their lands but remained defiant. Their leaders refused to acknowledge the authority of Quebec over their territory. The Sureté du Quebec tracked those who had fled and, using helicopters, attempted to land and make arrests. Shots were fired in the melee. Two Crees and one police officer were killed. The Sureté withdrew and did not return. On May 1, 1992, the Cree Nation formally declared its independence from Quebec. Power would continue to flow south, but only with the tacit realization that it could be cut again at any time. Quebec would have to be nice. While the James Bay occupation and its aftermath was going on, skirmishes occurred elsewhere across Quebec. Algonquins near Maniwaki north of Ottawa and beyond, Mohawks west and south of Montreal, Innu north and east of Sept-Iles all declared that their territories would not be part of the new Quebec. Many of the communities had already been in lockdown in support of the Mohawks since the incidents of the summer of 1990. Roadblocks that had been taken down went back up, barricades erected, and police cars torched. The independence declaration re-ignited the passions, driving the native movements to greater resolve to object to treatment and press more vociferously for a fundamental change in the way their issues were dealt with. Quebec was viewed as being broke, would only be more so going forward, and would have little ability to improve conditions for their people. The head of Quebec's native council announced that the aboriginal nations of Quebec were declaring their own independence and in the meantime, before that could be carried out, they would remain under the jurisdiction of Canada. "To hell with Quebec," one Mohawk leader told The Montreal Gazette.

While this was going on, provinces took steps to defend their interests. The legislatures of Saskatchewan and British Columbia voted to create their own law enforcement bodies, with timetables for the taking over of responsibilities from the RCMP. Alberta, Saskatchewan and Nova Scotia developed plans to collect their share of personal income taxes, replacing Revenue Canada in this regard. Across the country, hundreds of businesses closed shop while many others set up operations in the United States.

35

Ottawa, May 1992

Douglas Miller, the new Prime Minister, was with the Clerk of the Privy Council. "Gordon, you told me at our first meeting on national security you had evidence that Michel Perron's right-hand man on constitutional affairs had been on the payroll of the Russians for years. You told me my predecessor had decided to say nothing about it, ordering a ban on any mention of it. You suggested it would be wise for me to do the same. I agreed with you at the time." Miller paused for a moment, looked closely at the man in front of him, then continued. "Things have changed, Gordon. Quebec has declared its independence. Secession is underway. My concern is not with believability in Quebec. Quebec is leaving Canada; in fact, has left. My concern is Canada, bringing the country together and instilling confidence in our national security. I have changed my mind. The public must be told of all of this. I do not blame Caron for keeping it secret, but I can't keep it that way anymore. These Russian infiltrations happened under the watch of previous governments. The people should be aware of them, at least about this one. This is not about politics; it is about national security and solidarity. I want you and your officials to outline a scenario for me to inform the public. I assume you will suggest I call Perron to tell him. I can tell you right now that I will not. The hell with him. Do we know if he ever broached the subject with Dubé?"

"No, Sir, we don't. We are not aware of Perron broaching the subject with him or with anyone else for that matter. Perron would be at pains to alter that. Disclosing this to anyone would have disrupted his plans. Dubé is seen as a devoted public servant and even a hero in Quebec."

"Well, that may change now. Whatever, it must be told. Now, this other bit about the Russians and the native agitator. That will have to stay secret. I don't need things to get worse with those people. Who is aware of that, by the way? Can we contain it?"

"You, the Solicitor General, your Chief of Staff, maybe a half dozen people in CSIS including the head. The former Premier of Manitoba was told. There is of course Mr. Caron and, I believe, no more than three of his key people. I have spoken with the former Manitoba Premier about this. He assured me he has told no one else and does not intend to change that. Highly embarrassing for him if it ever got out, particularly concerning the relationship between the agitator and Ellison Ward, who is seen as a hero in Manitoba. I told him to invoke questions of national security if anybody ever asked him about it. We can probably get away with keeping it secret. I agree of course that we do not need any other provocations with our natives."

"Sir, please forgive me, but something important has just happened." Michel Perron's press secretary had come into the Premier's office without knocking. "Radio-Canada is reporting that the Solicitor General of Canada has announced in the House of Commons this afternoon that Monsieur Marc Dubé, Chief Constitutional Advisor to the Government of Quebec and Premier Michel Perron's right hand man and confidant, quote, unquote, is on the payroll of the Soviet KGB and has been for over twenty years. This just came out." The man continued, as the Premier remained silent and immobile behind his desk.

"The statement said this had been discovered over a year ago by the previous government and that you, sir, had been informed." Michel Perron remained immobile, looking at the young assistant with no expression. "Go on, Philippe. What else was said?"

"That Monsieur Dubé's activities had been monitored by CSIS and the RCMP up until the declaration of independence, but that it was up to the Government of Quebec to decide what to do regarding the matter. It stated that it would be inappropriate now for Canada to question or arrest M. Dubé, given that the police forces of the country no longer have jurisdiction in Quebec, but that the government had proof of collaboration of M. Dubé with the Russians.....Monsieur, is this true? That you were informed? That Monsieur Dubé has been working with the KGB?"

"Yes, Caron called me last year and told me that. It's ridiculous, Philippe. I told him he was playing games. His people were messing around. I did not even speak to Dubé about it then. It was beyond belief. Over the top. I dismissed it. A month ago, after our declaration, I was with Dubé in Montreal, just the two of us in our office there and I told him that Ottawa had called me months before, saying that he was working with the Russians. He said it was ridiculous, that Ottawa was undoubtedly trying everything at the time to disrupt our *option nationale*. I believed him. I did not think it could be true. Over twenty years and undetected, apparently. Not credible. Nothing ever came of it.... until today. You say they have proof. I will have to find out what it is. Philippe, we must be careful. We must deny everything. Everything. The press will be calling you. You must say that the charges are ridiculous and that I discounted totally what the federal government, M. Caron in particular, told me last year. But before we go too far in what we say, we must know what their proof is."

At that moment, the Premier's secretary announced over the telephone intercom that Marc Dubé was on the telephone and absolutely had to speak with him.

"Philippe, please. This discussion must be private. We will speak in a few minutes."

"Marc, we spoke about this a few weeks ago. You said it was not true. Is it? Is it, Marc? The damned KGB! On their payroll for twenty years. *Mon Dieu!*"

"I'm coming to see you. Be there in five minutes."

Dubé came in and shut the door behind him. "Yes, it's true. I lied to you, but I did it for us. They give me info. I gave them info."

"What did you tell them about us over the years, Marc? About our plans, what we wanted to do?"

"No, nothing about our true plans. I gave them bits and pieces, enough to satisfy them. They could pretty much see what we were doing. I gave them stuff on our dealings with Ottawa that they used to our benefit. Their intent was supporting us so we could disrupt Canada. That was their intent. The enemy for them is the United States, then Canada, not Quebec. They helped, gave me a lot of info on things happening in Ottawa, in Washington. I had inside info on constitutional affairs, on trade negotiations, on dealings with the aboriginals. It all fit into the development of my strategies, our strategies." Dubé came close to speaking about the financing of Gérard Rousseau and the Bloc National, but stopped.

"Well, we have a problem now. I have a problem. I am disgusted you had to do this with the Russians and that you kept it from everyone. Your motive may have been honorable, but still.

You must deny this. They say they have proof. We will have to see it. Depending on what it is, we will have to be good. Very good. We cannot have this jeopardize what we have achieved. Marc, are you still involved with them?"

"No, we ended it a while back. When the KGB changed to something else. No longer necessary."

"And the money? They gave you money, right? Must be a lot. Twenty plus years. Where is it? How much is it?"

"An account in Europe, but not much left. I spent a lot." He was lying.

"We will talk about that. In the meantime, we need to have a story. Work it out with Philippe and with Boucher at Justice. He will have to be our spokesperson on this. I want you here this evening. First draft of a response. We need to get it out, and quickly."

"Marc, what is this? Russian spy?" Hélène Beaulieu was on the phone with her husband.

"Hélène, I can't talk about this now. Come home. We will talk about it tonight."

"Not tonight. Now. What is this about? Everybody is calling me."

"Disappear. Do not answer the phone. Leave Montreal now. Come here. I will meet you at the apartment at 6."

"I did it for us. For our dream. Our country. They offered to help with this. And they did."

"With what, Marc?"

"With information. From Ottawa. From Washington."

"How long? Since when?" Hélène Beaulieu wondered whether to cry or to scream. Her husband a spy, paid by the Russians.

"1972. Chicago."

"All those years and you said nothing. All those years together! All those years. It's as if I never knew you. I can't feel anything."

"*Ma chérie*, we have our country. It was all about that. I could not tell anyone. Not even you. You would have had to live with the secret. I wanted to spare you that. But we have it now."

The couple paused as they looked at each other, Hélène holding back tears. Dubé broke the silence. "Nobody died because of this. If there was any betrayal, it was betrayal of Ottawa. It was not betrayal of us, our nation, our people, Hélène."

"I have no idea what to say. KGB. Russians.......did they pay you? They must have."

"Yes, they did."

"How much?"

"Over the years, a lot."

"Where is it?

"A bank in Switzerland. I didn't spend much if any of it, except in the early years. After we met, I did not touch any of it. A little over eight hundred thousand in an account in Zurich."

"What do you plan to do with it?"

"We'll see. Nobody else is aware of it. I told Perron I had spent mostly everything that I had received, just that I had a small amount in an account in Europe. I didn't want to tell him about the one in Zurich. I may need it; we may need it."

"Marc, on the radio while on the road, some supporters of ours claimed you were a hero, paid by the Russians, but 'so what', they said. '*Le Québec est maintenant aux Québécois.*' Other commentators were calling you a disgrace to the movement, that you had tarnished the victory; cheated the revolution. You had been a spy. Probably still are a spy. Brought disgrace to the independence of Quebec. How are you going to respond to that? What are you guys in the bunker on Grande Allée going to do about that?"

"We are denying it and calling Ottawa to show proof. They can't have very much. Documents that I received were destroyed soon after receiving them. I made sure to dispose of everything. Nothing stayed around. Everything I gave my contact was verbal. They will not have anything about the bank account. It is in a false name the Russians set up through an intermediary in Austria. What may be trouble could be photos, somehow taken when I met my contact, which was infrequent. We will get more on this tomorrow. I must leave. We have a meeting to deal with it."

"How could you have done this, Marc? Done this to us, to me? You are not who I thought you were." Hélène looked at her husband with tears in her eyes. "I am betrayed. Disgraced. Humiliated. There will be no more roles for me. Out of it. Forever. And people will come after us. You watch. You bastard, Marc!"

270

Hélène hesitated, while continuing to look at her husband, her eyes burning with rage. "I never thought I would say something like this to you, but you have ruined us!"

"We will deal with it, Hélène. It was for the cause. Your cause as well as mine."

"But not this way!"

"I have to leave. We will talk later."

As Marc Dubé left for the meeting to manage the exposé of his betrayal, Hélène Beaulieu crumpled into a chair and wept.

ARCHITECT OF SEPARATION A RUSSIAN SPY - headline in The Globe and Mail, Toronto

MARC DUBÉ - ESPION RUSSE - headline in Le Devoir, Montreal

The similar headlines betrayed very different storylines. In English Canada, newspaper editorials and comments showed a rage toward Quebec that went further than anything before. Commentators were incredulous that Quebec could defend so vociferously someone who had worked hand in hand with the Soviets to destroy Canada. In Quebec, the rage was towards Ottawa and the English media for insinuating that the independence of Quebec came from anything other than the patriotic expression of a nation to become its own country in a popular above-board plebiscite.

Premier Michel Perron and Marc Dubé, through the Minister of Justice of Quebec, denied that Dubé was ever an agent of Russian espionage. The federal 'proof' of a photo of Dubé with a man Ottawa claimed was a KGB operative was countered with the declaration that the man was Serge Colaros, a French student who Marc Dubé befriended in 1974. The two had remained in contact. Ottawa was at pains to explain that Serge Colaros was in fact a Russian and was a key Russian intelligence operative in the country for years. It was Ottawa's word vs. Quebec's word. The line in Ottawa's explanation of the treachery about the purposeful scuttling of the constitutional agreement of 1981 - the much-reviled Night of the Long Knives - could not be verified. The CIA claim about the Swiss bank account could not be used. The CIA was to be kept out of it. What was believable and accepted as truth in Ottawa was portrayed as lies and fabrications in Quebec. Nevertheless, Marc Dubé understood that his days were numbered. He had told Michel Perron that what Ottawa was claiming was all true. He had admitted it to his wife. He was a marked man. It was time to move on to another phase in life. Quebec had its country. He had done his job.

Later that day the phone rang in Marc Dubé's Quebec City apartment. Dubé had decided to not take phone calls that day, but was expecting a call from Perron, and answered, thinking it was the Premier. It was not. It was Gérard Rousseau.

"Marc, is this true? Working for the Russians? What is this?" asked the old friend.

Dubé had not expected a call from Rousseau. The deal he had made with him had been out of his mind for months. The deal that broke the back of Canada, that opened the floodgates of trouble. Rousseau must not be aware of the source of the money. "No, Gérard, it's not. Fabricated by Ottawa. They are desperate to save face in the rest of Canada. We have our own country now, and we did it by ourselves, with help from no one else."

"I'm coming over to see you, Marc. I will be there in a few minutes." Rousseau hung up the phone before Dubé could say anything.

"You are lying to me, Marc. The money didn't come from some French benevolent patriarch, but from the KGB. I should never have believed you. French rich person, no strings attached, nobody else in the party knowing about it. How naive I was. It came from the Russians, didn't it, Marc? You lied to me, didn't you?"

Marc Dubé looked at his old friend. He had used him. At that moment, he knew he could no longer keep the secret.

"Yes, I did, Gérard."

"You used me. Used me! You took advantage of my condition and our friendship. You sonofabitch."

"Gérard, we have our country. We can keep our secret as well. There are two people who know about it. You and I."

"And the Russians, Marc, for God's sake. They could use it at any time. They could blackmail me as they have probably already done to you."

"They haven't and they won't," replied Dubé. "They have what they wanted. The weakening of the alliance, trouble for America. It's done. They don't need us anymore."

"But how could you do this, Marc? Remember when we were growing up? We met one summer in Quebec, you were at Laval and I was studying in Montreal. Do you remember that?"

"Yes, I do. Political rally. Place d'Armes in front of the Chateau."

"We went to a café down the hill afterwards. We had a long discussion. I remember it very well. We were young, pure, full of ideas and ideals for our people, for a country. I liked you, I thought you were honest, dedicated, a true patriot, that I could trust you, as everybody did over the years. I always thought that way of you. This all came back to me this morning as I read the paper. What a travesty, Marc. You used me. You broke that trust. What the hell happened to you?!!"

"Gérard, Gérard, My God! We have our country. You were part of it. You needed help. I found it for you. Nobody else is aware of this."

"But at what cost? Being able to live with this. Used by the Russians, for God's sake." Gérard Rousseau looked at his old friend for a moment as they sat across from each other, then rose, came full circle around the table and sat down again.

"Do you not have any remorse of what you have done, Marc? Of what you have done to me?"

"I helped you out of a jam. It was ruining your life. I gave you an exit. I also gave you the chance to be a hero. You were that. You were the most popular person in Quebec when you left the government. You are respected and loved. This will not change."

"Bullshit, Marc. You betrayed me, took advantage of me. I will be looking over my shoulder the rest of my life."

Rousseau continued. "Remember when Trudel threw just about all of us in jail in 1970? You and I did not get rounded up, but nearly all our friends did. We had a discussion at the St-Denis one night. We said we would never do what Trudel did, never betray our people, compromise our commitment to justice. *Les Anglais! Le pouvoir!* Never violate justice, principle, rights and freedoms. You've done that and you dragged me along."

"What do you want me to do, Gérard? I go back to what I said. We have our country now. We are surrounded by three hundred million people who do not speak our language and don't care about us. We needed to use all the resources that were out there to release us from the bondage, from the humiliation. Remember the song from Vigneault, "Gens du pays, c'est à ton tour..." It's our turn. We are free from that bondage."

"I'm still betrayed, Marc. You fucked me. You stained everything."

"This will remain between us, Gérard. Nobody else knows."

"Except the Russians." Rousseau rose, grabbed his coat, went to the door, then turned before opening it. "You won't admit it, will you? That you were used? The ideal consumed you, ate you alive. It's all stained. Stained! Bloodied! You sonofabitch..... Goodbye, Marc. I'm out of your life. Now you stay out of mine."

"I'm sorry, Gérard....." Dubé could not finish what he wanted to say before Rousseau closed the door and walked away.

Two days after the announcement in Ottawa and the denials from Quebec, a journalist from the La Presse newspaper managed to reach Jacques Caron, the former Prime Minister, and requested an interview. Caron knew the journalist and agreed to meet him. The first question he was asked was "Is it true about Marc Dubé? Were you informed by the RCMP or CSIS that Marc Dubé was most likely a Soviet spy?"

The former Prime Minister knew that question would be coming and was prepared. "Yes, I was informed of that. But I avoided telling people about it because I did not think anyone would believe it. I thought it would only exacerbate the poisonous relationship with Quebec. I ordered people to say nothing. I only told Monsieur Perron. He was very upset with me. I do not believe he told anyone else of our discussion. Nothing showed that he had. But it is true, I'm afraid. Marc Dubé has worked with the Russians since the early 70's. The concrete proof of it may seem elusive, but it is there. I cannot tell you much more than that. Questions of national security. We can talk about other things, but not much more about Marc Dubé and espionage."

After the announcement in the House of Commons and the publication of the interview with the former prime minister, public opinion in Quebec turned against Dubé and Perron. The declarations from Ottawa and the words of Jacques Caron had their effect. People began to believe that Perron and Dubé were lying. As well, more and more people voiced their discontent with what independence was bringing - hardship, demonstrations, acrimony and anger. The assurances by the government prior to the referendum and the declaration of independence, that transition to independence would involve minimal hardship, were cited as lies and messages of manipulation. A movement emerged with the aim of asking Ottawa to accept Quebec back. Students quickly reacted to the news of this, with a group occupying the National Assembly for a day, demanding that the government silence the movement. Two days later, La Presse published an extensive report on the exodus of companies from Quebec. Demonstrations were held in Montreal with people blaming big business for leaving and scuttling their assets, leaving tens of thousands without jobs. A week later, La Presse published a front page story on the evolving crisis in the health care sector as many doctors over the preceding year had left the province with others indicating they were intending to do the same. Soon after, the Montreal Gazette reported that McGill

University had leased several buildings in Toronto and would be offering undergraduate courses there the following year. The undergraduate programs offered at the Montreal campus in commerce, engineering and the arts would be phased out over the following two years. The McGill chancellor admitted in an interview that the university would be gradually shifting most of its programs outside of Quebec. "Professors are leaving, going to other universities. Students are doing the same. Out of province enrollment is down 90% this year. And the students we would usually get from Quebec are looking elsewhere, with many of their families moving away. We must deal with that. McGill must and will continue to be a leading world class university. It will always have an attachment to Montreal, but events have forced the institution to adjust."

36

Frank Russo and Bill Wilson were at CSIS headquarters in Ottawa. "Bill, we don't look good in any of this. Dubé under our nose for twenty years, Cromwell for a good many years as well, and now what we have learned about Andrew Brown. I don't think I told you we spoke to his wife after his death. Anything about that has been kept under wraps. The lady still has a career, even in this government chaos, and was not aware of what Brown was doing. He kept everything from her."

"What was he doing? The chief editorialist of the biggest daily newspaper in Canada. Working with the Russians. Can you fill me in, Frank? I've been involved with these guys for a long time. I'm not surprised, but tell me."

"The boss wants this one under wraps, but here is the essence of it."

"We had followed him for a time. We realized he had been meeting with an attaché at the Russian Embassy. We asked his wife what she knew. We had to find out if there was a possible leak of stuff from there. She broke down and told us. The guy had been gathering info from the Russians for fifteen years, had been recruited by them at Cambridge in 1975......." Russo continued with his description of what the force had discovered about the Russian connection with Andrew Brown.

"What does the boss say about keeping all this under wraps?" asked Wilson.

"He wants it buried, just like the stuff about Cromwell, his role in the uprisings as well as the stuff in Manitoba concerning the Meech Lake Accord. Says the Canadian people will lose confidence in our capacity to defend the country if any of this gets out. The only part of all this that is known is the Dubé affair. That is enough to be out there about the intrusion, the Russian intrusion, I suppose one could call it."

"Where is Cromwell?"

"CIA tracked him down in Peru. Has a nice little pension from the Russians. They brought him to Moscow, but he did not fit in very well. They did a deal, apparently. He was to keep his mouth shut, stay away from Canada, and they would leave him alone. They gave him a Costa Rican passport as well as enough money to live on for a good while. We have an extradition arrangement with Peru, but the government does not want to exercise it. They want to leave him there. They don't want anyone to know about him."

37

Quebec seethed with anger at economic hardship, power outages and rationing, at the story of a key government architect of independence being in the employ of the Soviet Union, and at a movement preparing to ask for re-integration into Canada. Meanwhile, what remained of Canada was not spared from acrimony and disruption.

Negotiations over the corridor through Quebec to the Atlantic Provinces were at an impasse. Ottawa blamed Quebec for asking too much money for it. Quebec blamed Ottawa and the obstinacy of New Brunswick and Nova Scotia to have a wide corridor through private farmland but not pay the cost of it. It was becoming clear there would be no direct land corridor between Atlantic Canada and the rest of the country. The idea of forming a country gained in public opinion in Atlantic Canada. Oil and gas discoveries fueled mounting confidence in its viability of in the minds of many, including influential commentators and community leaders. The premiers of the four Atlantic Provinces convened a conference in Charlottetown to consider forming their own federation. There, the path to agreement became rockier than had been anticipated. The Premier of Newfoundland and Labrador deplored the insinuation that the province would have to share its oil royalties with the other provinces. Nova Scotia, on the other hand, pledged to pool its own oil and gas royalties and encouraged Newfoundland and Labrador to do the same. Bickering on this and other issues were preventing an agreement on union. Uncertainty in Atlantic Canada continued to reign.

More worrisome still for Canada, however, was the resource rich province of Alberta holding a plebiscite on annexation by the United States, despite Alberta having one of theirs as Prime Minister in Ottawa. The plebiscite passed. The government in Ottawa objected strongly, advising Alberta that it could not decide so easily to separate from Canada and join the United States. "It will be the end of Canada if you do it," said the Prime Minister to his home province. "Canada is not Canada anymore already. We must look after ourselves. The hell with the East. We can't support you anymore," replied the Alberta Premier. He announced that a delegation would be sent to Washington to open talks on joining the United States.

Pressure built in British Columbia to do the same. The prospect of being on its own led the B.C government to hold its own referendum. The leading columnist in a front-page piece of the Vancouver Province reflected the mood of a large percentage of the population. "Our strategic interests are more North-South than East-West. This has always been the case. Being cut off from the rest of Canada if Alberta goes will leave us little option but to further develop the North-South ties we have with Washington, Oregon, California and Alaska. The failure of securing free trade led to this. Our industries are dying a slow death without it. Canada has been going downhill since and nothing is on the horizon to change that. The elites of Central Canada put a horse collar on the country. Quebec is gone. It was destined to happen. We must go forward. Our standard of living and prosperity depend on our relationship with the United States."

Alberta and British Columbia had taken the big step. Within a few weeks, Saskatchewan had done the same. In early 1993, the three provinces entered formal discussions with the United States government. Concurrent with this, the four Atlantic provinces commissioned a high-level study group to come up with draft terms of union for their own country, despite the acrimony over the failure of previous discussions. The exodus of companies from the industrial heartland of Ontario continued. Large numbers of people were either leaving Canada and moving to the United States, requesting special resident status, or making plans to do so. In February 1993, the U.S. Administration was petitioned by several northern states to ease the requirements for Canadians to be accepted as residents.

Many of the native occupations of roads and infrastructure continued across the country. Conditions on reserves were deteriorating as funding from Ottawa was jeopardized by the reductions in government revenues and the ability to pay. This was compounded by the turned opinion of a population exasperated with native uprisings. Over two years of troubles had taken their toll.

The St. Lawrence Seaway had reopened in early 1991, but only with the takeover of the Welland Canal by the army. The U.S. Administration had threatened to have its own armed forces take over the Seaway if Canada failed in reopening the Seaway to safe and unimpeded traffic. As conditions on reserves remained in chaos on the Canadian side, Six Nations warriors were threatening to shut the Seaway again. Several military units with Quebec components experienced internal troubles, resulting in the break-up of two special forces units and an infantry regiment. It had started with French-speaking soldiers refusing to participate in the retaking of the Welland Canal, quickly followed by paratroopers refusing to participate in the retaking of the Sioux Lookout airport. Other army units experienced scuffles between English and French speaking soldiers. When the declaration of independence came, it unleashed internal dissent, with whole sections of the forces resigning and offering to join a Quebec army. In January, the Quebec

282

Government passed a resolution creating the Armed Forces of Quebec, with provisions for an army, a navy, and an air force. There would be no navy or air force for a while. There were no ships to sail or planes to fly. Only the senior officers from those services were asked to remain and participate in the formation of their respective services.

The banking and financial services industry had its own troubles. The Canadian chartered banks continued to operate in Quebec, honour deposits and continue with business under the difficult economic conditions. This happened only under a new set of banking regulations that had been adopted by the Quebec legislature. The earlier run on deposits had largely abated, but the Toronto-based banks were obliged to operate in Quebec under a different regime if they wanted to continue to do business there. A faction of the Parti National continued to call for nationalization of the Quebec operations of these banks. In this turmoil, the finances of the government, of businesses and of large swathes of the population were in disarray, with interest rates at 18% and rising. Quebec government debt was being given junk bond status, effectively limiting the new country's ability to borrow money. In this environment, the Canadian banks began scaling back their Quebec operations, closing branches, laying off employees and in the process, creating a financial services vacuum. Virtually all economic activity was disrupted in one way or the other. Many export-oriented Quebec companies began to divert funds to expand or set up operations in the United States.

The Reform government in Ottawa of Douglas Martin was being vilified in the national press and had essentially lost its moral authority in what remained of Canada. In February, it resigned, declaring it did not have the confidence of the country. Following the resignation, the Governor General asked the opposition to form a caretaker government. At the same time, he called for the convening of a constitutional conference to discuss a new Canada.

The provinces of British Columbia, Alberta, Saskatchewan, New Brunswick, Prince Edward Island, Newfoundland and Labrador, and Nova Scotia, declined to participate. They were on their way out. Ontario took the lead and asked Manitoba, the Yukon and the Northwest Territories to join the province in the formation of the new Canada. The Manitoba legislature in a special vote elected to do so, quickly followed by the legislatures of the two territories. Despite the declared intent to remain within Canada, the territories clearly looked with skepticism at how they could support their communities and related costs with the drastic reduction in the size and wealth of the country. In time, many communities in the North would lose large portions of their populations. Many resource companies in the North had already put their expansion projects on hold, and in some cases had ceased operations altogether.

While this was going on, the American government contemplated the consequences of a fractured Canada. Attention was diverted away from Europe and elsewhere. Questions of defense of the continent took priority, followed quickly by those concerning the protection of American economic interests. The Pentagon drew up plans for the occupation of the Arctic. This was to thwart a Russian takeover of the area around the North Pole. Plans were also drawn up for the occupation of radar sites in the north that were part of the continental defense system. Special tax measures were introduced in Congress to facilitate American companies' withdrawal from Canada and their relocation and re-investment south of the border. The formal discussion of acceptance of British Columbia, Alberta and Saskatchewan as states of the United States began in Congress, with committee hearings in both the House and the Senate. In April 1993 the U.S. Administration tasked the Department of Justice to come up with draft terms of acceptance of the three provinces as the 51st, 52nd and 53rd states of the United States. American commentators lauded the initiative. Resources would come with the new territory along with a direct link to Alaska. America would have greater control of the northern access to its heartland.

March 1993..

Riots and demonstrations led by blue-collar workers and union leaders erupted in Montreal and other Quebec cities. They were over unemployment, interest rates and increased taxes that were announced in the budget announced by the Finance Minister. Michel Perron and Marc Dubé were vilified by leftists in academia and the media, accused of having betrayed the independence movement. The Premier's carefully laid plans for economic survival and growth for Quebec were in tatters. Calls continued for nationalization of all key industries in resources and manufacturing, banks and insurance companies to protect employment and prevent further flights of capital. Michel Perron defiantly announced he would continue on the path he had set out for the economic management of Quebec - shoring up public finances, providing essential services and working with major industries to restructure and retain operations in Quebec. The radical wing of the Parti National would have none of it. On March 15, 1993, Michel Perron was found on the floor of his office, dead of an apparent heart attack.

The new country was in shock. Michel Perron, hailed by many as a courageous visionary and respected throughout his long career, had become derided as a dreamer who had taken Quebec into an abyss of chaos. It was said by an editorialist of Le Devoir that Perron "had become a disappointed, downtrodden man, beaten down by the condition of Quebec in its throes of independence. Beaten by the anger of its people, the knowledge of worsening economic conditions of the working man and woman, by the internal conflicts in the party, and the effective takeover of the party by the far left. His inability to bring the natives of Quebec to his side, the occupation of the James Bay hydro complexes, his inability to have an orderly transition and sharing of assets with Canada which he should have known would be problematic, took a toll on the man and led to his untimely death."

After Perron's passing, the new Premier called for an election five weeks later. The campaign was one of acrimony, of high emotions that saw a split in the ranks of the governing Parti National between the radical and moderate factions. Many voters had had enough of independence and voted the Liberals back into power in a minority government supported by the dozen elected members of a new provincial Conservative party. The Liberal leader had campaigned on a promise of negotiating the re-entry of Quebec into Canada and promised in his victory night speech to begin the process the next day. The Conservatives had pledged the same. The same evening, student demonstrations erupted in Montreal, Quebec City and Sherbrooke with extensive damage to police cars and store windows. The troubles lasted well into the night. A large group of students occupied the National Assembly in Quebec City to protest the result of the vote and what it could mean for independence. They overran the security contingent and entered the building before units of the Sureté du Québec could act. The standoff at the National Assembly lasted for 48 hours before the police managed to retake the building. Eight students were hospitalized with injuries received in the melée. Three police officers were hospitalized with cuts and bruises from flying bottles, chairs and other objects.

Three weeks after taking power and the occupation of the National Assembly, despite ongoing protests in the streets from student and radical factions, the newly elected government decided to put the question of re-entry into Canada to a referendum. It would be the third in Quebec in two years. The question was "Do you want Quebec to re-become part of a renewed Canada or do you want it to remain an independent country?" Surprisingly, 'the remain an independent country' vote narrowly carried the final result - 50.5% to 49.5%. Several factors combined to influence the vote. First, it was not clear to Quebecers that the rest of the country wanted Quebec back. In many communities in Ontario and Manitoba, citizens declared that Quebec should not be accepted back, that the new Canada would be better off without 'Quebec, bilingualism and all that came with it.' Second, many of the people who would have voted to have the former province re-enter Canada had already left, with thousands having moved to Ontario and points south and west. Many immigrants who had settled in Quebec over the previous decade and had no interest in being part of a new country, had moved out, with the exodus accelerating in the months preceding the vote. Third, students, who often neglected to cast ballots in general elections, voted en masse for continued independence. The die-hard *indépendantistes*, the radicals and a large portion of the youth of the province managed to halt the re-entry of Quebec into Canada. The result compounded Quebec's festering economic uncertainty and slide into hardship that was seeing no end.

In this turmoil and under a cloud of accusations of treachery to the true independence of Quebec, Marc Dubé stayed out of the public eye. He would only take occasional walks in his Old Quebec neighborhood late at night. One rainy evening he went for a walk to get some cigars at his preferred tobacco shop. A group of young men emerged from a pub on the corner, recognized Dubé and proceeded to rough him up. He was rescued by two policemen going by in a patrol car before he could be seriously injured and taken to hospital as a precaution.

Ten days later, Marc Dubé and Hélène Beaulieu were in a small chartered plane, landing in Portland, Maine. They continued to Boston on a regular commercial flight under assumed names, using forged Belgian passports that Serge the Russian had given Dubé three years before. They proceeded to Zurich and then beyond, after a stopover at a bank. In Zurich, Dubé emptied his bank account and with his wife and eight hundred thousand US dollars, flew to Panama City.

"Frank, my contact at the Sureté called me." Bill Wilson was in Frank Russo's office in Ottawa. "The guy said that Marc Dubé had apparently disappeared, along with his wife. Also that a real estate agent was looking after the sale of their apartments in Montreal and Quebec City. He told me in a sarcastic tone that Dubé was probably in Moscow by now. I asked him why they never arrested Dubé. He said they would not have dared. Dubé was considered a hero, at least up until recently. He also mentioned that Perron protected him; told the boss of the Sureté to do nothing. The word was that the Russian thing was a fabrication. I asked him if he believed that. He responded that he didn't really care. Said it all happened on our watch."

38

Marc Dubé and his wife were in their hotel the night of their arrival in Panama. "What are we doing here?" blurted out an exhausted and angry Hélène Beaulieu, who had hardly spoken since leaving Quebec.

"What do you mean, what are we doing here?"

"I mean, what in the world are we doing, Marc? We are fleeing our dream. Quebec is a country now. You wanted it all your life. Running from it now. This is crazy. Your damned relations with the Russians. You did not need to do it. I don't know why I came here with you. This is crazy."

"Yes, I did it. How many times have we talked about this? I'm sorry for you, Hélène. Maybe I didn't need to do it, but that was not so clear twenty-five years ago. It was such an uphill, impossible road then. I never thought we could do it by ourselves. It seemed impossible. So I accepted some help, an ally."

"An ally? They used you, Marc. They played you. You are the fool in all of this. Why couldn't you drop it? You could have dropped them. What could they have done to you?"

"They could have killed me. They don't let people out. I realized that years ago. When you're in, you can't get out. They don't let you. And I believed it was all worth it."

"You've ruined my life. As an actress it is over. My country back home is going forward, and I am not there. All my friends who I cherish and love, are viewing me as the concubine of the traitor to the cause. You didn't have to run. We didn't have to run. I can't believe I came with you. This is all wrong. And so stupid."

"It's not what I wanted. I didn't want chaos. I thought people would look up to me, see me as a patriot, as one of the fathers of the country. They did not. My colleagues, they despise me now. My friends, they can't believe I worked with the Russians. They didn't use me. I used them. It was a means to an end. An honorable end. But, leaving....I had to, we had to.....Life in Montreal and Quebec was becoming unlivable. I would not be able to go anywhere. It was that way already. I got attacked. This is about my life, your life as well. I'm sorry, my dear. It's not what I wanted."

"I understand now why you never wanted to have children. I wanted them; I was still young enough, but you said no. I realize why now. You knew this would get out. You knew it would be difficult. Spare any children, but not your wife! Tell me!"

"That was part of it. Yes, all of this could come out some day. I'm sorry."

"You're sorry. Sorry! I can't go forward with this, Marc. On the run. In Panama. You and some Russians. *Merde*! What are we to do here?" Hélène pounded the bed with both fists, turned off the lamp, turned her back to her husband, and drew up the sheet.

Back in Montreal and Quebec City, the people who could not leave and others who were committed to the new country made the best of the situation. The country that had lost a part of its population, much of its most entrepreneurial elements and was in throws with its indigenous peoples who demanded their own independence, staggered along.

By the end of 1993, the Canada that everyone had known was no more. In early 1994, the United States would have three new states in the union. Soon after, Atlantica would be born out of what had been Canada's eastern provinces.

After a month in the hotel in Panama City, Marc Dubé found a small house on a cliff looking out over the Pacific Ocean and bought it. Hélène had not participated in the choice of the property or its purchase. She had left Panama a few days after arriving and had returned to Montreal. The divorce a few weeks later was quick. She received title to the apartment in Montreal and the proceeds from the sale of the one in Quebec City. No mention was made of any money in Panama or anywhere else. She never saw her husband again. Six months after Hélène left, Dubé died in a car accident. He missed a curve on a winding road, ramming his car into a tree. He was 49 years old.

"Such a fragile country. But America could be stronger with all those resources. We may have overdone it." The two old spies looked at each other, rose, put on their coats, and walked out into the cold Moscow night.

Tom Creary

www.tomcreary.com